Mixed Signals

Books by Jane Tesh

The Madeline Maclin Mysteries
A Case of Imagination
A Hard Bargain
A Little Learning

The Grace Street Mysteries
Stolen Hearts
Mixed Signals

Mixed Signals

A Grace Street Mystery

Jane Tesh

Poisoned Pen Press

Copyright © 2012 by Jane Tesh

First Edition 2012

10 9 8 7 6 5 4 3 2 1

Library of Congress Catalog Card Number: 2012936478

ISBN: 9781464200618   Hardcover
       9781464200632   Trade Paperback

Chapter titles are from "Messiah" by George Frideric Handel,
1741

Poisoned Pen Press
6962 E. First Ave., Ste. 103
Scottsdale, AZ 85251
www.poisonedpenpress.com
info@poisonedpenpress.com

Printed in the United States of America

This book is dedicated in memory of
Sandy Beam and Benny Younger,
now playing and singing "Messiah"
in a much better place and making sure
the angel choir gets every note exactly right.

Acknowledgments

Thanks to my family and friends and everyone at Poisoned Pen Press for their continued support. And thanks to the readers who have come back to Grace Street.

Chapter One

"Behold, I Tell You a Mystery"

It's a good thing Handel's already dead, because if he weren't, I'd have to kill him. I'd heard Camden practice singing "Every Valley Shall Be Exalted," his solo for the Parkland City Chorale's Christmas concert of "Messiah," until I thought I might have to kill him, too. He sings really well, but talk about monotonous! Handel must have enjoyed seeing how much he could cram into a song. Maybe he was paid by the note.

So I was relieved that evening when Camden stopped singing. He paused at my office door, toolbox in hand, and asked me if I'd take him by his friend Jared's house.

"Thought you'd finished those cabinets."

"I have one more door to put on. It won't take me five minutes. You can wait, or Jared can bring me home."

"I'll wait."

I obligingly turned my '67 Fury toward Jared Hunter's neighborhood. When I pulled up in front of the small brick house, Camden frowned at the dark windows.

"Is he home?" I asked.

"There's a light on in the garage."

He got out of the car and went toward the open garage where Jared kept a fine 1959 blue and white Marlin. I yawned and then drummed my fingers on the steering wheel, annoyed to find I still had the tune and rhythm of "Every Valley" in my head. I was considering which of my many New Black Eagle Jazz Band CDs to play when the music abruptly slid into a strange minor key, horns blaring, violins shrieking. I felt a sensation of panic from somewhere in my brain, panic that wasn't coming from me. I was already running for the garage when I heard Camden's voice full of horror.

"Oh, my God. Randall! Randall, come here."

I ran to the garage and stopped. Jared Hunter lay in a pool of blood in front of his washer and dryer, a pile of laundry scattered across the floor. It looked as if he'd been stabbed several times. For a few moments, I couldn't move, my brain trying to process what I was seeing. I've seen some bad things in my time, but the crumpled body and the stark red blood splattered against the white floor and colorful towels was so horrible I had to take a few quick panic breaths to keep myself upright. There didn't seem to be a chance in hell the man was still alive, but I leaned down and carefully checked for a pulse in his wrist.

"I'm sorry, Camden."

He was holding onto the car, his face chalk white and his eyes glazed over. I couldn't begin to imagine what visions he was seeing. "No," he said, shaking. "No."

As I punched nine-one-one on my cell phone, I heard a thump from somewhere in the house, and a noise that sounded like a door slamming shut. I ran out of the garage and around to the front of the house, my angry private detective self wanting to catch the murderer and my sensible self screaming that a killer with a knife could be planning to attack again. But I couldn't see anything. For the moment, both Camden and I were completely in the dark.

Well, this was going to be one hell of a Christmas.

If the killer had been hiding in the house, by the time the police came and searched the area, he or she was gone. Officer Jordan Finley was one of the first to arrive. He usually warns me away from crime scenes, but when he realized Jared Hunter was a friend of Camden's, he agreed to let us stay.

"Don't touch anything," he said to me, as if I didn't know this.

The coroner finished his examination and the EMS team took Jared's body to the ambulance. I had managed to calm my breathing, but Camden sat on the ground, trying to control the tremors that still shook him. I told him several times I'd take him home, but he said no. After a while he got up and slowly crossed the garage to the dryer. One of Jordan's colleagues started to stop him, but Jordan said, "It's all right."

Camden put his hands on the dryer as if to steady himself. He was trembling, and his blue eyes were an odd murky color. "If I can get past the blood—"

"Try the car," I said.

The blue and white Marlin sat gleaming the in the half-light. Despite the lingering smell of blood, I smelled car polish and something sweet, like auto air freshener. Camden moved over to the Marlin and put his hands on the hood.

"Anything?"

"It's not the car. Someone came by."

"What did they want?"

"They're angry, frustrated." He shuddered. "I want to look in the house."

I glanced at Jordan, and he nodded. Even though he can't officially use psychic evidence, Jordan's found Camden's talent useful in the past.

Inside Jared's house, the furniture was unremarkable, the curtains plain beige, the carpet a dreary gray. The bedroom and bathroom were also very plain, with nothing out of place. In the living room, an entertainment center took up one wall. A few framed photographs hung on the opposite wall. One picture showed Jared with a tall black woman. She stood with one arm draped around his shoulders.

"Who's this?" I asked.

"Alycia Ward, a friend of Jared's," Camden said.

Alycia was wearing an elaborate charm bracelet, large gold earrings, and a nose ring. "Looks like an expensive gal."

"Jared was always buying her jewelry."

"Are they engaged? Maybe they had a quarrel."

"No, they're just friends."

In my experience there's often more to "just friends." "And these guys?" A row of grinning men stood in front of the Marlin and a 67 Mustang.

"The guys at Jared's auto club."

There was a photograph of Jared, Alycia, and somebody dressed in a green monster costume. "Halloween?"

Camden took a closer look. "Comic convention."

"What's this guy supposed to be, the Incredible Hulk? Who is he, do you know?"

"It's probably Boyd Taylor. He went to a couple of conventions with us."

Jordan had been taking notes. "Alycia Ward, Boyd Taylor. Anyone else?"

Abruptly, Camden sat down on the sofa and put his head in his hands. "Oh, my God. Terracon's next week. Jared wanted to go. I forgot to tell him."

Jordan gave me an anxious look. "It's okay, Cam."

He pushed his pale hair out of his eyes. "I can't think right now. I came over to fix his cabinets. He'd been wanting cabinets in the garage. I was almost through—"

"Cam, you need to go home. We'll take care of this."

"The blood—I wish I could see something useful! I have no idea who'd want to kill Jared."

"I'll keep you posted on how the investigation is going." Jordan pointed his pencil at me. "You, however, are going to keep out of this."

"Somebody kills one of Camden's friends, and you want me to back off? I don't think so."

"Both of you are way too close to this. Let me handle it."

I started to argue and then reconsidered. I already had two starting places: Alycia Ward and Boyd Taylor, plus whatever else

Camden could tell me about Jared and his activities. With or without Jordan's approval, I was going to work this case.

I took Camden home. 302 Grace Street is Camden's old three story boarding house in what used to be Parkland's wealthiest neighborhood. Tenants come and go, but for now, 302 Grace was home to a huge bawdy couple named Rufus Jackson and Angie Dawson, Fred Mullins, World's Grumpiest Old Man, and Kary Ingram, my soul mate, if I can ever convince her of that. Since October, the house, to my surprise, had become my home as well, and the office for my detective agency.

Rufus and Angie had gone to her sister's for the holidays, Fred was already in bed, and Kary was playing piano for a Christmas party, so the house was quiet. Before beginning my investigation, I parked Camden in the living room. We call the sitting area in the middle of the room "the island" because it's filled with mismatched but comfortable cushions and chairs from many lands and many time periods, including my favorite, a big faded blue arm chair that had been a recliner in a past life. Kary likes a little rocking chair with red cushions and keeps a basket filled with yarn next to the coffee table, which is piled with magazines and coupons held in place by a pear-shaped paperweight. Camden's usual place is on the green corduroy sofa. I settled him with a big glass of sweet tea and a couple of brown sugar Pop-Tarts, and then I went across the foyer to my office, which is located in what used to be a parlor.

I sat down behind my desk and clicked open my search program. My mind was still whirring, and I felt as if I'd run a marathon. I had to do something, anything to block out the picture of Jared. I put in "Alycia Ward" and hit "Search." A long list came up. I waded through this for a while, and then got up for a drink.

After the nightmare in the garage, it was jarring to see the Christmas tree beaming by one of the front windows. I replaced an ornament that Cindy, our gray cat, had dislodged and then walked around the island past Kary's old upright piano in the corner and the bookshelves flanked by large potted plants. In the back bay window across from the dining room table and chairs Cindy sat watching moths bounce off the outside light. Camden was in the kitchen washing dishes, which is his fallback plan whenever he needs some down time. I took one of the stools at the counter that separated the kitchen from the dining room. "Anything else you can tell me about Alycia or Boyd?"

"They didn't do it."

"Are you sure?"

"As sure as I can be. I'm trying not to think of anything right now."

"Did you call Ellin?"

Ellin Belton is the woman Camden says he loves, which makes me question his sanity. She doesn't have a scrap of psychic ability, but Camden says holding her hand helps him erase the worst visions.

"No. There's no need to bother her with this."

I glanced at the cow-shaped clock above the sink. "It's almost ten thirty. Why don't you call it a day?"

"I'm afraid of what I'll dream."

I knew what he meant. In the past, there had been some nights I forced myself to stay awake. Fortunately, the nightmares of the car crash and my futile attempts to find my little daughter were fading, thanks to one particularly good dream of her he'd helped me see.

He wiped his hands on a dish towel. His hands were still shaking. "This is going to be nice and cheery for your mom's visit."

I usually make the trip to Florida for Christmas. This year, Mom decided to spend the holiday with us. I'd told her a little bit about my new situation. I knew she was curious to see for herself. "Too late to cancel those plans. She'll understand. Hand me a Coke, will you? Maybe there's something mindless on TV tonight."

We went back to the island and channel surfed until we found "The Beast of Yucca Flats."

"Perfect," I said. "That'll put you to sleep."

But neither one of us could sleep. We stayed up, willing ourselves to watch so we wouldn't have to think. Finally Camden dropped off from sheer exhaustion. I dozed in the arm chair until after two and then went up to my room. The shock was wearing off, replaced by anger. Jordan had better hope he found Jared's killer before I did.

The next morning, I got up later than I planned. Camden said he was all right, so I took him to Tamara's Boutique in Friendly Shopping Center where he works part time as a sales clerk. It's not a stressful job, which he says is perfect. He definitely didn't need any more stress.

I parked the Fury in front of Tamara's. In the window, large gold and silver ornaments rotated slowly around mannequins in what I'm sure were very stylish Christmas colors of neon pink and green. "I missed seeing Kary this morning. Did you tell her what happened?"

"I told her Jared had been killed. I didn't go into any details."

"Anyone or anything else you can think of? Any helpful insights into what Jared had that the killer wanted?"

"No." His eyes were back to their normal blue. "This is a stupid, useless talent."

Ordinarily I would say something like, "I think you should brood today and mope around the store," but I cut him some slack. "Give me a call if you want to go home."

"Thanks." He was also thanking me for holding back on the snide comments.

"You said Jared was always buying Alycia jewelry. Wal-Mart specials, or did he spring for the good stuff?" My search program had found plenty of Alycia, Alicia, Aleeshia, and Aleisha Wards in town, but none fit the description of the woman in the photograph.

"The good stuff, usually."

I drove downtown to Royalle's Fine Jewelry in Old Parkland, the historic section of Parkland, to talk to my friend, Petey Royalle. If I was really lucky, Jared did his shopping at Royalle's.

Things did not look very lucky at the jewelry store. A police car was parked out front. I greeted the officer as he came out of the store, and met Petey at the door.

"What's going on?"

"Somebody helping themselves to an early Christmas." Petey Royalle was glum. He's a trim man in his thirties with a shiny round bald head and brown eyes behind thick glasses. "We had a break in last night. The thief took several expensive bracelets and a tray of emerald and sapphire rings."

"What about your alarm system?"

"Disconnected. I don't know how the hell the thief knew where it was."

All of the buildings in Old Parkland are at least seventy-five years old. Royalle's Fine Jewelry is in a large three-story building, and Petey explained that the older wiring system made it difficult to install a regular alarm, so he'd kept the original one. He took me down a hallway to the back of the store and showed me the control box, hidden behind a secret panel.

"I'm the only one who knows this. Now that you know, I'll have to kill you. See where the wire's been cut? Somebody knew exactly what to do."

"You've never shown it to an employee, an insurance man, a repair man?"

"No one."

"Who installed it?"

"As I said, it's been here for years, and it works, so I never had to call anyone. The few times it's broken, I've been able to repair it."

I looked on the box. "Winthrop, Incorporated" was imprinted in black letters. "Quality Merchandise." "Maybe somebody at Winthrop decided to come in and look around."

"Maybe. I don't think the company's in business anymore."

"I'll find out. What did the police say?"

"I told them the same thing. They seem to think it's a simple burglary, but I don't know. The fact the thief knew about the alarm box worries me. Seems a little—I don't know—spooky. Will you take this case?"

"Of course. I specialize in spooky cases. But let me suggest a trade. Last night, someone killed one of Camden's friends, a man named Jared Hunter. Jared liked to buy his girlfriend Alycia jewelry. Do you remember a customer by that name?"

"I'll be glad to check my records."

"And if you'd check with some of the other jewelry shops, I'd appreciate it. I'm trying to find the girlfriend, Alycia Ward, and I don't have a lot of leads."

"Sure. I'm really hoping this thief isn't one of my employees, Randall."

"Anybody got it in for you? Bill collector? Dissatisfied customer?"

"As far as I know, everyone's happy. I pay my bills, and we have an unconditional money-back guarantee on all merchandise. I inherited the store from my father, and he inherited it from his father, and so on, back at least seventy years. We have a great reputation."

I looked around the carved mahogany walls and up at the elaborate ceiling with its old fashioned light fixtures and the glass display cases filled with rings, bracelets, watches, and necklaces, surrounded by twinkling Christmas lights and artificial poinsettias. "I'd like to talk to your employees."

"Any time. Like I said, I hate to think any one of them is responsible. Gert Fagan's been with me for years, and my two part-time kids are great. J.C. Chapman and Sim Johnson help me out every Christmas. They're great kids, lots of fun. At first, I thought the call about the robbery was one of their jokes."

He was plainly upset at the thought of his staff betraying him. "Maybe it was just a burglar who got lucky."

"Or a burglar who knows the architectural history of Parkland."

Most burglars don't go to that much trouble. As much as Petey Royalle hated it, this did indeed look like an inside job.

"Can you think of anyone who might have a grudge against the store? Anyone suspicious who might have been in, looking around?"

He pointed to another monitor. "We have a security camera, but it was also disabled that night. I reviewed the tapes for the past week, and I didn't see anyone but normal customers. Of course, this close to Christmas, we've been busier than usual. There's a good chance I may have missed something."

"Do you still have the tapes?"

"The police took them. They're really boring. The only thing we caught was Gert adjusting her panty hose."

He was trying to make light of the situation, but I could tell he was still upset. "Any idea why the burglar took those particular items?"

"Now that's really got me stumped. The guy takes a box of rings and a few jeweled bracelets. In the same case, you've got piles of gold necklaces and some very expensive sterling silver charms. He could've easily scooped those up. I'm glad he didn't, but it wouldn't have taken a second."

"Maybe someone or something surprised him."

"Maybe it was the Avenger."

"The what?"

"You haven't heard about the Parkland Avenger? Some goof-ball in a cape and tights has been running around the city at night. He's supposed to be a crime fighter, but he's getting in the way."

"I've missed that news item. Sure he's not using his secret disguise to rob stores?"

"The police would like to ask him that same question."

I looked around the small, elegantly paneled office. "Is there a back door?"

"Down that hall to your left."

"So anyone who comes in the back passes by your office?"

"That's correct. In fact, the kids make a joke about sneaking in. They may pull a few pranks now and then, but they're never late. You couldn't find better employees. There has to be an answer to this."

I was sure there was, but it might not be what he wanted to hear. "I'll do my best to find one, Pete. I'll talk to your employees when I can. Right now, I'm going to see another of Jared's friends."

I had an address for Boyd Taylor. I was on my way to his house when my cell phone rang. It was Tamara Eldridge, Camden's boss. Like most of the women I know, including my mom, she called me by my first name.

"David, I need your help. Cam's having a problem. He keeps seeing a murder, and I don't know what to do."

"I'll be right there."

Chapter Two

"Since by Man Came Death"

I drove back to the shopping center and found a parking place near Tamara's Boutique. Inside, I found Tamara and Camden in her office. She was sitting next to Camden, patting him on the back. He had his head in his hands, and he was shivering.

Tamara looked up. "I'm so glad you came, David. He's been like this for almost thirty minutes now."

She got up and I took her place. "Come on, Camden. I'll take you home."

He shuddered. "Oh, God. So much blood. I can't see."

"It's all right. It's over. Look at me."

He raised his head, his hair in its usual disarray. His eyes refocused, clearing from that eerie gray to their regular blue. "Randall."

"Let's go home."

He took a few deep breaths. "I'm okay."

"I don't think so," Tamara said. "You go get some rest."

He tried to protest, but we weren't having any of it. I took him out to the car. He didn't say anything on the ride home. When he sat down on the sofa, he began to shake again.

I knew what would help. "Where's Ellin?"

"I don't know."

"Yes, you do. Concentrate."

He shut his eyes for a moment. "A broadcasting conference."

"What's her cell phone number?"

He held his arms, trying to stop the tremors. "Don't call her."

"If she cares about you, she'll come."

"I'm all right."

"I don't think having nightmares during the day can technically be called all right."

I put some ice in a large plastic cup and filled it with tea. I stirred in a pound of sugar, took the tea to Camden, and punched in Ellin's cell phone number. Even over the phone, Ellin's snarl came in clearly.

"Who gave you this number, Randall?"

I came right to the point. "Last night, one of Camden's friends was murdered. He found the body, and now he's having flashbacks. When can you get here?"

I heard her intake of breath. "As soon as I can."

I hung up and turned to Camden. "Ellin's on her way."

He took another drink, tea slopping over the rim of the cup. "I keep seeing—" He stopped and swallowed hard.

"Yeah, it was pretty awful. You're empathizing a little too much. In fact, I'm even picking up on some of it, so try to think of something else."

"Randall, Jared was a good friend, but what if this had happened to you, or Ellie, or Kary? I'd go insane."

"This was too gross. You'll get over it."

"It hits me like a wave. It's like I'm Jared and his killer all at once. I see and hear everything."

"Ellin will be here soon. That'll help."

He was still shaking. "I can't take much more of these reruns. And you know what the worst part is? I couldn't help him then, and I can't help him now."

"What do you think you could've done? The murderer surprised him at home. There was no way you could've stopped it from happening."

Camden's eyes headed toward gray again. "That's what I hate about this stupid talent. Why didn't it let me know Jared was in danger? Why didn't it show me he was going to be killed, instead of showing me now, when there's nothing I can do? And why the hell won't it go away?" He stopped his rant and took a steadying breath. "Times like this almost make me want to tell you to go ahead and find my father so I can kick his ass."

Camden's father abandoned him and his mother when Camden was a few days old, and his mother then left the baby at the Green Valley Home for Boys. I'd found his birth mother. She was glad to hear he was alive and well, but she didn't want to see him. His father, however, was still out there, and Camden has decided since his mom is normal, Dad must be the source of his psychic powers. Alien psychic powers.

"Say the word, and I'll beam you up."

"No, thanks. He didn't care about me then. He sure as hell wouldn't care about me now."

"You don't know that."

"Well, apparently, I don't know anything." He took another drink and sat back on the sofa. "What did Ellie say?"

"She said she'll be here as soon as she can."

"Nothing about how important the conference is, or wait until after this program, or how can I use this in a show?"

"Nope."

He stopped shaking. He looked at me, his expression skeptical. "Did you tell her I was dying?"

"Did you want me to?"

"Sometimes I think that's what it takes." He set his cup aside. "That's what's so frustrating. I'm still wild about her. I want her so much, it scares me."

"Scares me, too, pal. The question is, does it scare her?"

"Oh." He thought a moment. "You think she's afraid of a deeper relationship?"

"Trust me. I know where she's coming from. It's the big 'C.'"

He must have still been shaky, because he didn't get it. "Christmas?"

"Commitment."

"How can she be afraid of commitment? She's a woman. Isn't that what they want?"

"It's my theory. Take it or leave it."

"I'm leaving it right now."

I went to my office and called Boyd Taylor, but either he wasn't home or he wasn't answering his phone. I checked my search programs in case the Alycia Ward I was looking for had shown up. She hadn't.

Camden and I decided we needed a snack and some educational program viewing. We were both startled by Ellin's entrance.

It might have played better if Camden had been unconscious and/or bleeding, but he was stretched out comfortably on the sofa with a big bowl of ice cream in his lap, a giant cup of Coke on the coffee table, and "Monster Battle" on the TV. Ellin dashed in, breathless. They stared at each other for a long charged moment before he realized he'd better sit up and say something.

"Hi."

She caught her breath, gave me a look that had me checking for scorch marks, and tossed her pocketbook and briefcase onto another chair. "I thought—Randall said—are you all right?"

"I'm okay now."

"Obviously." She pulled off her coat. She had on one of the midnight-blue power suits that hugs her great figure and makes her golden curls shine. "I drove over an hour in less than perfect weather because I thought—"

She paused as if unsure of what to say. "I'm sorry, Ellie," Camden said. "I told him not to call."

She sat down beside him and took his hand. "Whose murder are you seeing? I didn't know you had flashbacks like this."

"Neither did I. My friend Jared was stabbed to death last night. I guess the shock of finding him caused this reaction." He took a deep breath. "Whew, I wish you'd been with me a few hours ago."

"Did you see who killed him?"

"No, nothing useful."

I went into the kitchen. These two drive me crazy. Here is the woman Camden says he loves beyond all normal reasoning. Why doesn't he grab her and go to it? And Ellin supposedly cares for him—after all, she left her conference, a huge sacrifice, knowing how much her career means to her. They should be terminally lip-locked, and here they sit like it's teatime at the Plaza and they have a burning desire to discuss the stock market.

"Are you better now?" she asked.

"Yes, thanks."

"Well, if you're all right, I think I'll go over to the network and check on things."

"What about your conference?"

"I made some good contacts, some possible sponsors for the PSN."

"I mean, is it too late to go back?"

"There were only two more sessions to go, and I know enough about scheduling and broadening the audience base. Our audience is only going to get so broad, you know. What we need are some new and exciting features."

I knew what she was leading up to, so I wasn't surprised by her next proposal. I doubted Camden was, either.

"Cam, this flashback thing—do you suppose you'll eventually be able to control it?"

"I want it to go away. If I could control it, I wouldn't be so staggered every time it hits. And no, I'm not coming on your show."

I heard her gathering up her things. "Just think about it."

"I don't want to think about it. That's the whole problem."

"We can discuss this later."

"No, we won't." He tried to change the subject. "Randall's mother will be here tomorrow. I want you to come to dinner and meet her."

"I'm sure Randall's mother is every bit as charming as Randall," she said. "We'll see."

As soon as she left, I came back to the island. "What the hell was all that?"

Camden knew what I meant, but he didn't want to talk about it. He got up. "I'm going to check on the guest room."

I went out the front door to see Ellin off. "I'm so bowled over by your passion I can hardly walk."

She was searching for something in her briefcase and paused to give me a dagger stare. "Don't ever call me on my cell phone again."

"He was flipping out. I thought you could help."

"I came and I helped, didn't I? He looks fine to me. Don't lecture me about my relationship with Cam."

"What relationship? You might as well be his maiden aunt."

She closed the briefcase and opened her car door. "I'm not going to listen to any more of this."

"Wait, wait, before you go, let me get this straight. The next time he's a shuddering wreck stuck in a nightmare vision from some psycho's personal hell, you'd rather not be involved?"

"That's not what I said. And why do you think this is any of your business?"

"I guess it isn't. Sorry. Have a nice day."

She growled something under her breath, got into her car, and drove off. About the time she left, I heard the familiar chugging sound of Kary's '89 Festiva as it rounded the corner of Grace Street bringing her home from Parkland Community College where she was working on a teaching degree. Because the Festiva is an unusually bright shade of green, we've nicknamed it the Nuclear Pea. Kary parked the Pea alongside the Fury and got out. With her long silky blond hair tucked under a green hat, her long green coat, and red and green muffler, she looked like a Christmas angel.

Most blondes have blue eyes, but Kary's are a warm brown and very expressive. "Is Cam home? Is he all right?"

"He's okay. He's getting Mom's room ready."

Kary took off her hat, shaking that gorgeous waterfall of hair. She hung her coat and muffler on the hall tree and tucked the hat in the coat pocket. "He and Jared were just getting to know each other, and right before Christmas it's even more upsetting. Did you tell your mother about this? I hope she's still coming."

"Yes, she'll be here tomorrow."

"Maybe she can keep an eye on Cam while we're on the case."

"Whoa," I said. "Hold on. 'We'? I'm not even officially on the case."

"But you're going to find the killer."

"Yes, but—"

"And I'm going to help you. No arguments."

For a scary moment, she looked as fierce as Ellin. I was searching for a way to discourage her when Camden came back down the stairs, and Kary immediately focused on him.

"Are you okay? You still look a little pale."

Since Camden is always a little pale, I'm not sure how she could tell.

"Better," he said. "Thanks."

"Any more women I can call for you?" I asked.

Camden's go to hell looks are famous for their intensity. This one made the Christmas ornaments tremble. "No. Thank you. I'm going to check on the lights out back."

"Good," Kary said when he'd gone. "Now we can plan."

"Kary."

"Do we have any more diet sodas?"

She had me so addled I'd almost forgotten my daily mission. She sat down at the kitchen counter and took one of the many notebooks from a stack next to the ceramic frog we use as a dish for spare change. "I'll start a list."

I brought her drink and sat down across from her, wishing I had something stronger than Coke. "I think you should leave this to me. Jordan's already warned me off."

"Jordan always warns you off, and you always ignore him. Didn't I help you solve your last case?"

"Yes, but that involved doing research." Research that kept her safely away from any danger. "Whoever killed Jared slashed him repeatedly with a knife. You're not getting anywhere near this case."

She'd been numbering a list and now looked up. "Cam is the closest thing I have to a brother. I'm going to do whatever I can to help him."

Since Camden is the closest thing I have to a brother, too, I couldn't argue this point. "Just don't do anything crazy."

"David." I got the full teacher look. "I'm not going to sneak down dark alleyways or meet strangers in parking garages. Now, are there any suspects?"

I resigned myself to the fact that she was not going to let this go. "Boyd Taylor and Alycia Ward."

She wrote down the names. "I don't see any reason why I couldn't look them up. I might find something useful. Anyone else?"

If this kept her at the computer, then that was fine with me. In fact, I made up a few more names to keep her busy. "Susan Carlyle and Morris Otto. All friends of Jared's. Oh, and the guys at his auto club. I'll get their names, too." There was a chinking sound from the island. I was glad for the distraction. "I think Cindy's in the tree again."

Kary got up to check on the Christmas tree. Sure enough, Cindy's little gray cat face was poking out from the branches.

"Cindy, this is not your personal playground." Kary pulled her out and set her down.

I found the fallen ornament and put it back on the tree. "No harm done."

Kary inspected the pile of presents. "Did you get that UFO book for Cam?"

"Yes, and I wrapped it." Not that wrapping his presents ever did much good.

"I bought a scarf for your mother."

"She'll love it."

She straightened one of the angels Cindy had dislodged. "I hope Fred likes the space calendar Cam and I found. He hasn't been in a very good mood lately."

Fred, Camden's oldest and moldiest tenant, was born in a bad mood. "I don't think Christmas is his favorite holiday."

Ever since we brought in the tree, Fred had been sniffing and grumping about the foolish waste of time and money. Despite Fred, we'd put a wreath on the door, a row of wooden angels across the mantel, and Christmas cards on top of the piano. Camden spent one whole day stringing lights along the porch roof and sticking giant plastic candy canes along the walk. Because they missed a lot of Christmases, the holiday's a big event for Camden and Kary, so every time Fred tunes up, I tell him to shut up. I can tell by his squinty gaze there won't be a package signed, "All best holiday wishes, Fred," under the tree for me, either. But Kary, as usual, was her understanding self.

"I know how he feels. For a long time, Christmas wasn't my favorite holiday, either. I kept remembering all the happy Christmas times I had when I was little and wondering if they'd ever be like that again."

Christmas didn't mean the same to me, either

Her hand lingered on the angel. "But now I have new Christmas memories that are even better."

"I'm glad to hear that."

Here we were, standing beside the tree, a perfect time and place for me to declare myself, but I held back, anxious not to make another mistake. Our relationship was in two different places. Kary was focused on finishing her degree and getting a job. I was still floundering after divorce number two. Although we had a great deal in common, we had a long way to go to even meet in the middle. Still, our friendship was solid and that meant more to me than I cared to admit.

Kary stooped to rearrange the presents and then straightened. "I'm really looking forward to meeting your mother."

I was glad she was looking forward to meeting Mom, but I was concerned about Mom meeting Kary.

Because I knew exactly what my mother would say.

Chapter Three

"Why Do the People Imagine a Vain Thing?"

Since Kary was home in case Camden had another bad spell, I went to Boyd Taylor's neighborhood and found his house. I also found a squad car parked out front and a grim-faced Jordan standing by the door. "Don't even think about it," he said.

Before I could reply, he came around to block my way.

"I warned you. You will not interfere in this investigation."

"I just stopped by to see how Taylor was getting along."

"Boyd Taylor is our prime suspect. We have witnesses who can put him at the scene. And we have a report of an argument he had with Jared Hunter yesterday. As far as I'm concerned, he's our man."

"Camden says he didn't do it."

Jordan paused for a moment. "I saw how Cam was. Do you really believe he was thinking clearly? Besides, I can't use any psychic information. I need solid proof. And that's what I've got."

"What about the murder weapon? What about a motive? They could've been arguing about anything. That doesn't mean Taylor killed him."

"Why are you defending this guy? You want Jared's killer found as much as I do."

"But I want to find the right guy. If whoever stabbed Jared is still running loose, then locking Taylor up isn't going to help."

"If you don't leave this alone, I swear I'll have your license. Back off."

Jordan gets mad, but not this mad. He must have doubts about Taylor's guilt. That was the only reason I could think of. And could Camden be sure of anything as disconcerted as he was?

Jordan folded his arms and glowered. "Why are you still here?"

He was as immovable as a tank. But there were ways around this tank, and I was determined to find one.

That night, Camden wanted to go to chorale practice, so I drove him to the First Baptist Church for rehearsal. The Parkland City Chorale has its share of divas, male and female, temper tantrums and power struggles, but Camden says he likes learning new and difficult pieces of music. I say, if you've heard one requiem, you've heard them all. So while the singers were going over their interminable runs and trills, I stepped outside to call Petey to see if he had any news for me.

I had my cell phone ready when a strange jangly version of the "Hallelujah Chorus" sounded from the park across the street. I walked over to investigate and saw Camden's huge friend, Buddy, and Evelene Fiddler pounding away on banjo and hammered dulcimer for a small audience. This unexpected spin on the music completely changed its somber mood. A few people walking by had their noses in the air, but most of the crowd loved it. Some people hooked arms and danced around. Tonight Only: Barn Dance at Handel's.

After the last hallelujah rang out, Buddy gave me a big wave and turned to spit a stream of tobacco juice into the grass. "Merry Christmas, Randall!"

"Merry Christmas. What's going on here?"

He jerked a thumb at his teenaged partner. "All Evelene's idea."

Evelene had joined Buddy's group for the Falling Leaves Festival in October. With her spiky pink hair and nose ring, she looked like a punk rock princess, but apparently bluegrass was in her soul.

"I call it the 'Alternative Messiah,'" she said. She pointed toward the church with one of the dulcimer hammers. "Not like that stiff stuff over there. We're going to be playing here most every evening. Give people a choice, you know?"

"Not a bad idea. What are you calling yourselves these days?"

Frog Hollow Boys and Goose Creek Fever had been top contenders for the group's name. Buddy scratched his unshaven chin and readjusted his ever-present baseball cap. This one said, "Beer Me." "Well, Evelene's thought up a few."

"I like Zombie Strings," she said. "Only Buddy and the others don't want to dress up like zombies. I told them they wouldn't have to go full zombie. I could do that. Or Shock in the Grass, you know, for bluegrass, because we're shocking people with our song choices. Bet nobody's ever thought of doing the 'Messiah' like this before. And it sounds like snake in the grass. Kinda edgy."

Buddy gave me a look and a grin. "That's us. Edgy."

Evelene raised her little hammers. "Wait till you hear what we do with 'For Unto Us a Child is Born.'"

I listened for a while until it ran together and sounded like every other bluegrass tune. I tossed a few dollars into Buddy's banjo case and went back across the street to call Petey. He apologized for his lack of information.

"I've talked to Main Street Jewelers, Silver Palace, and the new little shop called Charming. They're going to check their records, too, but so far, no Jared Hunter. We'll keep looking."

I thanked him and went back inside. Someone had left a *Parkland Herald* on a back pew. I read the newspaper account of the burglary at Royalle's, which didn't tell me anything I didn't already know. There was also a story in the *Herald* about the Parkland Avenger. As Petey had said, a would-be superhero was attempting to foil crimes and getting in the way of legitimate police business.

The by-line for the Avenger article said "Brooke Verner." I grimaced. I'd met Brooke Verner a few times, and she impressed me as a woman, somewhat like Ellin, who was determined to get her way, even if it meant annoying and alienating everyone in the city. Plus Brooke seemed to think I'd be attracted to her. Well, ordinarily, I might be, but once I met Kary, my hound dog ways were over.

Back to business. I read the Avenger article. "'Last night, two armed men broke into the Fidelity Trust Bank on Creek Street, escaping with an estimated fifty thousand dollars. Witnesses say the thieves would have been apprehended, but police efforts were hampered by a man calling himself the Parkland Avenger, who tried to block the getaway car and instead blocked the police car. The robbers, two white men of medium build wearing black clothes, got away in a gray van. The Avenger, who also escaped, is described as a white man in his thirties wearing a red costume, a mask, yellow tights, and a red cape. Anyone with information is asked to call Crimestoppers or the *Herald*.'"

Creek Street was one street over from the Old Parkland district. If this inept Avenger had been around last night when Petey's was robbed, and if he wasn't the robber, he might have seen the real thief. I didn't want to ask Brooke Verner about it. There were other people at the *Herald* I could talk to.

So what else was in the paper? A waste of paper and ink called "Your Turn."

"Your Turn" was a fairly new feature in the *Herald* and had caught on like a particularly sticky disease. Readers were encouraged to call a special phone number and record their opinions on whatever's pissing them off at the time. Unlike letters to the editor, no one had to reveal a name or address. The rambling, grammatically challenged musings were printed the next day, so all the world could see the subterranean workings of the average Parkland citizen's mind. Hate your job? Hate your boss? Think your wife's running around? Careless teens peeling rubber in the church parking lot? Neighbor's dog peeing on your rose bushes? A simple phone call and slam, bang, into the *Herald*.

Camden started his solo, and I noticed with amusement how all the women in the chorale turned rapt expressions toward him. Camden's singing voice doesn't wobble or squeak like some tenors. It's a very nice clear sound, and, as I've jokingly told him, the chicks dig it. The women were giving him their full attention. Tons of attractive, willing women—and he wants Ellin.

Camden finally got that valley exalted and sat down. The chorus started in on another pile of notes. The director led the group through two more numbers, and then they were dismissed.

"Sounded good," I told Camden as we walked up the aisle.

"Thanks," he said. "Singing helps."

"Pizza would probably help, too."

◇◇◇

Before stopping by Pokey's Pizza to pick up a large pepperoni, we walked across the street where Buddy and Evelene were still plunking away on their "Hillbilly Handel." Camden tried to sing along, but they were going way too fast, and everyone had to stop because we were laughing too much. Our plans for food and a bad science-fiction movie were put on hold when we found Jordan waiting at the door of 302 Grace Street.

I was a bit surprised that he'd come calling. I offered him the pizza box, but he waved it away.

"Cam, when's the last time you saw Alycia Ward?"

"Not since the last comic convention."

"How well do you know her?"

We went into the house and stopped in the foyer to hang up our coats. Camden unwound his muffler and hooked it onto the hall tree. "About a week ago, she and Jared went to a party, and she stopped by here afterwards. She was more Jared's friend than mine."

Camden's friends add whole new dimensions to life in Parkland. You could find any one of them in the Guinness Book: World's Weirdest; World's Stupidest; World's Most Likely to Cause Grief and Death—and we'd have to include me, World's Most Promising Yet Struggling Detective.

Jordan followed us around to the island. "You got a number?"

"No, sorry. Come have some pizza."

Camden switched on the lamps and moved piles of magazines, coupons, and other debris off the coffee table. He sat down on one end of the green corduroy sofa. Jordan took the other end. They made quite a study in contrast: the cop, big and block-shaped with his short black hair standing at attention and his shrewd little eyes narrowed as if the world was one big suspect; Camden, small and slight, with all that pale uncooperative hair and large blue eyes seeing right through time.

"She didn't kill Jared if that's what you want to know."

I put the pizza box on the coffee table and took my usual seat in the faded blue armchair. "Maybe she's the Parkland Avenger and she's meeting with the Justice League."

Another glare from Jordan. "This isn't a joke, Randall. This Parkland Avenger clown is interfering with police business, plus now he's got the press behind him. That Verner woman is chewing up our asses."

"Don't mention Brooke Verner."

Jordan's glare turned into a grin. "Oh, that's right. She's in love with you, isn't she? How about telling your girlfriend to back off?"

"She's not my girlfriend. She just thinks she is."

"And Mister Lothario doesn't want her?"

I paused, a piece of pizza halfway out of the box.

"What's the matter?" Jordan said. "Amazed by my insight?"

"No, I'm amazed you can use 'Lothario' correctly in a sentence."

"She's not bad looking. What's the problem?"

"She's not my type."

"She's breathing, isn't she?"

I pointed my piece of crust at Jordan. "You have this Avenger running around the city and no clues as to who he is. You do have me, however. I'm very good at finding things. Hire me. I'll crack this case, and you can return to your Fortress of Solitude."

"Believe me, you'd be my last resort."

"I'm everyone's last resort."

"It's only a matter of time until we catch this clown. Then Ms. Verner and everybody else at the *Herald* can find someone besides the police to gnaw on."

Camden peeled a piece of pizza from the box. "I thought the paper cooperated with you guys."

"When it's to their advantage. But apparently making us look foolish sells more newspapers. Ralph Galvin is having the time of his life. Of course, we were on his shit list long before this."

"How come?" I asked.

"He thinks we botched an investigation involving his family. That's why all this Avenger crap suits him just fine. Makes us look like idiots."

"What about his family?"

"Galvin thinks we ruined his son's reputation." He glanced at Camden. "Jared had a record. Did you know that?"

"He mentioned once he'd done something stupid he regretted, but he didn't tell me the details, and I didn't ask."

"About a year ago, he was caught breaking into the history museum. The arresting officer was certain Galvin's son Bert was there, too, but he got away. Ralph Galvin was on the museum board at that time, and he was livid that his son was accused."

Breaking into the history museum didn't sound like big time crime to me. "Didn't Jared rat him out?"

"Nope. He took the fall. He said somebody had dared him, that it was just a prank, and Ralph Galvin, for some reason, convinced the museum not to press burglary charges. The museum couldn't determine that anything had been stolen, so Hunter was charged with trespassing."

"Did he serve time?"

"It was a first offense. He was fined, put on probation, and did community service."

I got myself a beer from the fridge and a Coke for Camden. "So this Avenger stuff is personal. Ralph Galvin's editor of the *Herald*, isn't he? Could he be making it all up?"

"No, there really is a nut out there, and he's really getting in the way. But we'll catch him, and we'll catch whoever killed Jared Hunter."

Now I knew why he was here. There hadn't been enough evidence to hold Boyd Taylor, and Jordan was sniffing around for more clues. "You had to let Taylor go, didn't you?"

He glared. "For now."

Camden set his Coke on the table. "Boyd Taylor didn't kill Jared, either."

"Yeah, so I've heard. How about telling me who did?"

"I wish I could."

Nobody said anything for a few moments.

Jordan got up. "Doesn't matter. I'd still have to have real proof. And you could be wrong about Alycia Ward and Taylor. But I don't want you to be dead wrong. So stay out of it."

I saw Jordan to the door and out onto the porch. "Camden zoned out again today. He keeps seeing Jared Hunter's murder. I'm thinking he might be picking up bad vibes from the killer. He's done that kind of thing before."

Jordan reached into his pocket for his cigarettes "Must be hell having all that going on in your head. Why doesn't Ellin come by and take his mind off things like that?"

"She did, but she didn't stick around."

"I thought they were an item."

"It's a bit one-sided right now."

"Too bad."

It would be better for everyone if Camden could find a new girlfriend, but what do I know?

Jordan took out a cigarette and his lighter. "Couple a months ago, Cam was channeling some dead guy. You saying he's sharing a brain with this killer?"

"Who knows?"

"Is Cam going to go through this every time somebody gets killed?"

"I think he's connected because he and Jared were at Green Valley at the same time."

"Green Valley. That's the orphanage he lived in, right?"

"Jared was several years older, but they had the same stories. I guess Camden thought of him as an older brother, or at least a veteran of the same war."

"We'll be questioning all of Hunter's friends and co-workers. And as I said, I'd better not see you anywhere around."

Oh, he wouldn't see me. "Then why did you come to the house? I know it wasn't for pizza."

"Maybe I wanted to check on how Cam was doing."

"Maybe for once you were getting into my territory."

"What, Visionland? You're welcome to it." He lit his cigarette and blew a long stream of smoke. "Do me a favor—a big Christmas favor—and back off like I said."

Not if Alycia Ward could help Camden clear his brain. I was going to talk to Boyd Taylor, too, and anyone else who might have useful information.

Jordan smoked for a while and regarded me with narrow eyes. "You'll let me know if Cam has any contact with Alycia Ward?"

"Heck, yes."

"All right, then. We'll see how it goes."

As he went down the porch steps, I gave him a wave and a "Merry Christmas." He gave me a hand signal of his own.

Chapter Four

"Every Valley Shall Be Exalted"

I was tired of not finding Alycia Ward, so I did a search for Bert Galvin and was soon tired of not finding him, either. Wednesday morning, neither of them showed up, but Brooke Verner did. She ambushed me on the porch as I stepped out to get the paper.

"Good morning, David."

I had on my sleeping attire, t-shirt and boxers, my hair leaning north and a good crop of stubble. "I hope you've got your camera ready."

"No pictures today. I need info."

"Forget it."

"Why was Jordan Finley over here last night? Does he think you have something to do with the Parkland Avenger? Does he think Cam can tune into the true identity?"

"He came over for pizza. Go away."

She gave me what I'm sure she thought was a charming smile. "Now you know you don't mean that."

Brooke Verner looks like she should be hosting bridge parties at the country club. She's a tall, leggy woman with hard blue eyes, streaked blonde hair, and a fairly attractive smile, but none of this is worth a damn when you realize all she cares about is getting a story.

"Hell, yes, I mean it. Why aren't you out looking for Elvis?"

Her eyes sparkled. "Don't be cruel. I know Cam has helped the police department before. What did Finley want?"

"Extra pepperoni. Beat it."

She plopped down in the porch swing. "I'll wait and talk to Cam."

"Fine by me."

"I'd much rather talk to you."

"Sorry, I'm busy."

I didn't invite her in. Camden had staggered down to the kitchen looking like me, his hair in all directions.

"Don't go on the porch unless you want to be ambushed by Brooke Verner."

"What does she want?"

"Juicy news. Why don't you go into a trance and give her some spooky predictions? Then maybe she'll leave us alone."

"I thought she was after you."

"She's after a story. Make up one."

Camden stared in the direction of the porch. "That's not what she wants."

"What, then?"

Another long stare. "You're not going to like this."

I was trying to pour coffee and not spill any. "Tell me later."

He went out to talk with Brooke and came back looking thoughtful.

"Is she still out there?" I asked.

"No, she had to get back to the paper."

"Probably got a call about a two-headed baby. What did she want, really?"

"A place to stay for a few days."

"Here? Oh, that'll be fun. She wants in on this case, that's all. I hope you told her no."

He took the box of brown sugar Pop-Tarts out of the cabinet. "I told her I'd let her know."

"Thank you."

"When do we need to leave for the airport?"

I checked my watch. "Not till eleven. I'm going to talk to some of Petey's employees this morning. Are you going to Tamara's?"

He put two Pop-Tarts in the toaster. "Not today. She told me to take it easy."

"I could drop you off at the Psychic Service Network."

His dark look could've easily toasted the Pop-Tarts. "No, thanks."

Kary came into the kitchen already dressed for school in jeans and another attractive sweater. This sweater was red with little green holly leaves. Her golden hair was held back with a red ribbon. "Good morning, guys. When will your mother be here, David?"

"Her plane arrives at noon."

"I wish I could go with you, but I have a test today and a lot of research to do." She gave me a meaningful look. "How are you feeling this morning, Cam?"

"Better, thanks."

"Pass me a Pop-Tart, please. I'm going to have to eat on the run."

He handed her one of the silver packages.

"Thanks. Did I leave my books on the table? There they are." She gathered up the stack of textbooks. "See you later."

She hurried out, but not before I'd seen the book on top of the stack. *Adoption: Is It Right For You?* the title read in big black letters. I'd been thinking about breakfast, but my appetite was gone. Did I mention that Kary and I were in two different places? Well, adoption is the huge chunk of rock that always slams down in the middle of the highway to happiness. Kary is determined to have a child, and I'm just as determined not to have one. I had no idea how we were ever going to solve this problem—provided she ever accepted one of my many marriage proposals.

Camden brought his toasted Pop-Tarts and Coke and sat down across from me at the counter. I didn't want to ask him about my future with Kary. I was afraid to know. So I didn't come near the subject.

"What can you tell me about Boyd Taylor?"

"I've met him. He and Jared weren't close friends. They were acquaintances, co-workers at Ben's Garage. I know Boyd wanted to buy Jared's car."

"If Boyd was in the house when we got there, why didn't he come out? Or call for help? He must have been afraid he'd be accused of the murder, which is exactly what happened anyway."

"Jared had been through some rough times, but he was getting his life back together." He picked up a piece of Pop-Tart and then put it down. "I still don't understand why I had such a violent reaction."

"Maybe Boyd has killed a lot of people."

"Maybe I'm going crazy."

"Well, wait till after Christmas, okay? The asylum gets crowded during the holidays."

Camden took a deep breath. "I want to go back to the house."

This came out of nowhere. "What?"

Most of the time, Camden looks like you could push him over with one finger, but occasionally, he'll get fed up and go all steely. "I want to go back to Jared's house. There has to be something there that will tell me who killed him. If I'm going to be a wreck, I might as well be a useful one. I'm not going to sit around here all day waiting for another attack."

"You want Ellin to come along this time?"

"She'll probably want to bring a camera crew."

"I dare you to ask her."

"You want to bet money on the outcome?"

Typically, Ellin was busy with something at the studio. She has the kind of voice that carries, even through concrete, so I could hear her over the phone.

"Cam, I'm kind of busy right now. I thought you didn't want to go back over there."

"Maybe I'll see something that solves the murder."

There was a pause. I could hear wheels turning. "If you can wait till three, I'd like to bring my cameraman along."

Camden punched my arm. "What did I tell you?"

I punched him back. "Okay, you win."

He spoke into the phone. "Ellie, you are not going to film me flipping out."

"But if you tune in on something that solves the crime, it would be terrific for the show."

"No, forget it."

"Cam—"

"I'm hanging up now." He ran his hand through his hair, making it even more disheveled. "If I weren't already crazy, she would drive me right over the edge."

"So you want to attempt this without Ellin the Eraser?"

"I can't sit here all day waiting to fall down."

"Finish your Pop-Tart and let's go."

◇◇◇

As Camden slowly walked around the garage, we both tried not to look at the stains on the floor. He carefully touched the car, the garbage can, the washer and dryer, and the few tools hanging on the walls. He faltered for a few minutes at the pile of old sneakers and boots and then put his hands gently on the shoes. He shook his head.

We went into the house and looked through Jared's meager possessions. Besides clothes, Jared had a few books, a basketball, a baseball, bat and glove, and some video games. Aside from the photos on the wall, there weren't any other pictures until we found a cardboard box in the closet with a small album.

Camden turned the pages. Instead of photographs, Jared had cut out pictures from magazines and pasted them in. Here was a picture of a family around the dinner table. Here was a picture of a father throwing ball to his son. Here was a picture of a grandfather taking his children fishing. From the age of the album and the style of the pictures, I could tell Jared had created his family dream a long time ago.

I felt my throat close. I'd had the perfect little family dream, too, only mine had been real for eight precious years.

The album was full, but Camden looked at only a few more pages before closing the book. "Jared was never adopted. He stayed at Green Valley until he was eighteen."

"So he never had a family of his own."

"No." He put the album back in the box and looked around the dreary room. "This is what my life might have been if I hadn't found the house on Grace Street."

"Maybe that's why you have such strong feelings about this."

Camden checked all the rooms. He didn't have a vision, but he didn't fall down, either, so we figured either the vibes had cooled, or something was blocking them. Before we left, Camden decided he wanted the album. I wasn't sure if he needed a memento of his friend or a reminder of how his life had changed. He held the book in his lap all the way back to 302 Grace. It seemed to help.

After I took Camden home, I drove to Royalle's. I decided to have a word with the next person on the list Petey had given me, Gert Fagan. With a tough name like that, I expected a heavyset woman with a grim look and a snake tattoo, but Gert Fagan was elegant and pleasant, her silvery hair cut in a fashionable style, her voice soft, her manner helpful—in short, the perfect employee for an upscale jewelry store. She had on a forest green suit and an expensive-looking emerald brooch shaped like a wreath sparkling with little rubies.

"One moment, please, Mister Randall." She went to assist a customer and then returned, smiling. "Mister Royalle said you'd be by to talk to us. I'm not sure how much help I can be, but please, ask me anything."

"If you could tell me what happened the day of the robbery. Did anything happen you might consider out of the ordinary? Any strange customers, people loitering, any distractions?"

"As you can imagine, we've been quite busy. A lot of people have been in the store buying Christmas presents. I've had my hands full."

I checked my list. "What can you tell me about J.C. and Sim?"

"They are very nice young people, so much fun to have around. I've worked with them several holidays now, and I have nothing but good things to say about them. They're always on time, they don't take long breaks, and they are very polite to the customers."

"And Mister Royalle never told any of you about the alarm system?"

"All I know is it's an old system somewhere in the back of the store." She lowered her voice. "Mister Randall, I know this looks bad for the employees, but we're paid very well, we get excellent discounts on all merchandise, and we're all loyal to Petey. It can't be one of us."

"I hope it isn't."

Another customer asked for help, and Gert Fagan left me to assist them. I watched as she took a tray of rings from the glass cabinet and helped the young man choose the right one for his girlfriend. She obviously enjoyed her work. Would she jeopardize her job for a couple of bracelets, bracelets she could probably afford?

Inside one cabinet was a large gold pocket watch that looked exactly like the one my dad used to have. After Gert rang up the young man's purchase, she came back to me.

I pointed to the watch. "Could I have a look at that, please?"

"Certainly." She slid the case door over and reached in.

"Ms. Fagan, does Mister Royalle have any enemies, rival jewelry dealers, angry ex-wives?"

"No. Mister Royalle is a bachelor, and as far as I know, has no enemies. Besides, wouldn't an enemy take more things, smash the cases, and make as big a mess as possible? We lost some bracelets and a tray of rings. It could've been much worse."

"Do you know if his father used the alarm system, too?"

"Yes, and a large Doberman he used to leave in the store at night. I told Mister Royalle he might like to get another dog, but he's allergic to them, so that wouldn't work." She wound the watch, listened to it, and then nodded, satisfied. She handed it to me. "You don't see watches like this every day."

I admired the smooth gold cover with the delicate tracings. When I opened the watch, it played a tinkly tune. "My dad had one like this. I don't know what happened to it."

"If you find it, bring it in. I'll fix it and clean it. You don't see workmanship like this anymore. Recognize the tune?"

"'Grandpa's Spells.'"

She looked surprised. "That's right."

"I'm a fan of traditional jazz."

She beamed. "I am, too. You've made my day, Mr. Randall."

I'd been so busy listening to the tune, I hadn't noticed the time, but I noticed it now. I was going to have to hurry if I wanted to make it to the airport. I handed the watch back to Gert.

"I'm just curious. How much is it?"

"Fifteen hundred."

I'd have to ask Mom if she knew where Dad's was.

I'd gotten into the Fury when my cell phone rang. It was Kary.

"David, I have a few minutes before my next class. Are you looking for anything else besides information on these four names you gave me?"

"Not at the moment."

"If I can't find anything here, I'll check the public library."

"That sounds good, thanks."

"And we should tell Cam we're working together. He can probably guess, but there's no reason to keep this a secret."

"I'll tell him."

I closed my phone with a little twinge of guilt. I didn't think there was anything Kary could really do to help me on this case, but I'd been wrong before, and besides, why would I want to derail any chance of spending more time with her? "We're working together" sounded mighty good to me.

Camden and I looked a lot better by the time we arrived at the airport to meet flight sixteen twenty-two from Orlando. I made sure everything matched because my mom always dresses up, even if she's going to the grocery store, and everything has to match. Many days I was snagged at the front door and ordered to march upstairs and change my shirt or socks before I was properly color-coordinated to go to Elbert Falls Elementary. Camden was not color-coordinated, but then, he never is.

"Davey!"

I had to look twice to make sure the startlingly vibrant woman was my mother. Gone was the salt and pepper hair. My mother's hair was now a rich auburn shade and cut in a short style with jagged little bangs. Gone was the color coordinated two piece suit with frilly blouse she'd always favored, as well as what she called sensible shoes. She had on high heels, a tight skirt, leopard-print blouse, and several gold chains and strings of pearls that dangled above a bright red belt.

Her hug brought me out of my stupor. "Mom, you look great. I almost didn't recognize you."

"Thank you, dear. A little something different, don't you think?"

It wasn't just the clothes. She seemed more alive than I'd seen her in years. "A lot different." I was having trouble processing her new look. Camden cleared his throat. "Oh, Mom, this is Camden. Camden, my mother, Sophia Randall."

She took his hand in both of hers. "I was so sorry to hear about your friend. How are you doing?"

"I'm okay, thank you."

"I know this is not going to be the happiest Christmas for you. Thank you so much for letting me come visit."

"It's my pleasure, Mrs. Randall."

"You must call me Sophia."

I'd been concerned about what Camden might have picked up from their handshake. I didn't want him to see something in her future I couldn't handle. Mom can handle anything. I wasn't worried about her. But if Camden saw death or a lingering disease, I didn't want to know. However, he gave me a glance and shook his head slightly, as if to say, nothing serious.

"Thanks, Sophia. How was your flight?"

"Oh, very nice. I sat by the most interesting young lady who was flying to a dog show. She had two little longhaired dachshunds in a carrier under the seat. They were the cutest things and very well behaved. I wish Grady could've seen them."

She hadn't been here five minutes and already mentioned Grady. I almost bit my tongue. Grady's the man she's been seeing for about a year. I can't stand him. I know she's lonely. I know he's a good man who treats her well. I know she has no immediate plans to marry him. Yet something about him makes my stomach curl. Seeing my mother always brings back memories of Dad. Even now, after all this time, I find it easier to ignore the memories. It's like a mental bulldozer that slides across my brain, pushing all that aside. I don't want her to be with another man. Ironic, isn't it? I used to hop from one woman to another like a rabbit on speed, but Mom can't have any fun—at least, I don't want to hear about it.

"How many bags did you bring?"

"Just a few."

Did Grady help you pack? Oh, shut up, I told myself.

We waited at the baggage carousel for her luggage. Even her suitcases were different. She'd traded in the matching green leather set for bright pink bags with zebra striped trim. I checked the tags twice to make sure they were hers, and Camden and I hauled everything out to the Fury.

She patted the hood. "Davey, you still have Henry's old Plymouth. What a treat."

"Can't do without it. Hop up front, Mom. It'll take us about thirty minutes to get home."

Parkland was ready for Christmas. Mom admired the silver bells, golden stars, and large plastic ornaments dangling from every telephone pole and street lamp. I drove down Main Street so she could see the shops outlined in white lights and the store displays featuring electronic elves and carolers. She was equally taken with 302 Grace all decked out in holiday finery. "What a lovely old house," she said.

We'd done our best to straighten up the place, but despite our efforts, it still looked like bachelor pad meets college dorm.

Mom smiled and made nice comments about how warm and welcoming everything looked.

"It smells so good in here, cinnamon and evergreen. And look at your tree!" She admired the candy canes, the strings of popcorn and cranberries, and the paper chains that somehow had escaped Cindy's reign of destruction. "Such nice old-fashioned decorations. Did you boys bake the gingerbread men?"

"We tried to help Kary until she ran us out of the kitchen. She let us put the eyes in, though."

She eyed the small stack of presents under the tree. "I haven't done my shopping yet. I thought I'd wait and see what everyone would like."

It took me a moment to process this. Mom always had the Christmas shopping done months before, warning me upon pain of death not to snoop in closets and under the beds. "Well, there are loads of places to shop in Parkland."

"Yes, I'll make sure there's a giant pile of presents by Christmas Eve."

Camden and I heaved her suitcases up to the second floor and put them in one of the empty rooms. Camden had pulled out the best cream-colored towels, sheets, and bedspread. I'd put a big red poinsettia on the bureau.

Mom set her pocketbook next to the flowers. "This is beautiful."

Camden opened the adjoining bathroom door. "You have your own bathroom, Sophia, and here's the closet. If you get cold, there are some extra blankets right here on the top shelf."

"Thank you. If you boys will excuse me, I'm going to freshen up a little."

We went downstairs to the kitchen. Camden took a large plastic cup from the drain board and filled it with ice. He poured in some tea.

"Okay, what's going on?"

"I'm floored. She looks like—I don't know."

"She looks fantastic."

"Yes, but, where's my mom? I know women go through the change, but this is ridiculous. I mean, she looks—"

"Sexy?"

"Yes, damn it. It's freaking me out."

"And?"

"Isn't that enough?"

"Who's Grady?"

"She's thinking of him that hard?"

"No, you are."

I reached in the fridge for a cola. "He's this guy she's been seeing for about a year. He lives in the same apartment building. I guess I get tired of hearing about him." I sat down at the counter. "I met him once. He's a real milksop. My dad was all man, you know? Hunting, fishing, drinking, sports. Grady's a creampuff. I could mush him under one thumb."

"But you wouldn't want your mom to sit at home alone all the time."

"No. I'm glad she has someone her age to talk to. He's just—" How to explain it? "He's just in my dad's place. It was always Sophia and Henry, and now there's this stranger, this weak, mealy-mouthed stranger making time with my mom." I took a big drink. "There, I said it, and I'm proud."

"You going to tell her how you feel?"

"No, thanks, doctor. I believe our time is up."

"You going to tell her how you feel about Kary?"

"An even bigger no. She'll want to fix things. I'm warning you now. That's all she does."

"So do you."

"What?"

"Want to fix things."

"No, I want to find things. There's a difference."

He looked at me, eyebrows up. I started to tell him how I'd like to fix him when Mom came into the kitchen carrying a newspaper. I couldn't get over her new look.

"So, Mom, what made you decide to change your style?"

"It's wild, isn't it? I wasn't sure about the leopard print, but now I love it. I think I'll make it my signature look."

Sophia Randall, Leopard Woman. "Okay."

"And I never realized how much fun it is being a redhead. You ought to try it."

I hadn't noticed, but she had on gold hoops and a gold cuff bracelet. What happened to the little pearl earrings and the modest watch?

Steady, I told myself. She's going through a phase, that's all.

She toured the kitchen. "This is charming. I love the green and white and all the little farm touches." She admired the cow-shaped clock and chicken dishcloths, the salt and peppershakers shaped like eggs with legs. Then she peered out the bay window at the backyard. "And this is a wonderful view."

"Would you like something to eat?" Camden asked.

"No, dear, I had a snack on the plane. Now, don't feel you have to entertain me." She opened the paper. "I've been looking through the paper, and there's a craft and fashion show at your memorial auditorium. You can drop me off, or I can call a taxi."

At least this part of my mom was the same, always taking charge. "I'd be happy to take you," I said.

"Davey, I know you don't want to wade through all that. I'll be fine on my own. You have work to do, don't you?"

"Maybe Kary would like to go," Camden said.

I thought at first he'd lost his mind, but then reconsidered. What better way for Mom to become acquainted with Kary? They were going to be in the house together the whole holiday, and it was going to be obvious how I felt about Kary.

"That's a great idea," I said. "Mom, Kary will be home in a little while, and I'll take both of you to the show."

She refolded the paper. "Good. Now what have you boys been up to lately?"

I'd told Mom an abbreviated version of my last case. I'd left out the parts about fighting with a deranged woman who wanted to skewer me with a boat hook and jumping into a freezing lake to save Camden from drowning.

"Just helping people find things, Mom."

"Are you on a case now?"

"I'm trying to find some missing jewelry." I didn't say, and I'm going to solve Jared's murder.

"What about you, Camden? I believe David told me you worked at a clothing store?"

"Yes. Tamara's Boutique."

"Oh, that sounds like my kind of shop."

"It is. Tamara makes a lot of the dresses herself."

"That can't be very exciting for a young man. Or are you into fashion?"

Camden reached for the sugar bowl. "It isn't exciting. That's why I like it."

I explained the situation. "Camden doesn't need any extra vibes during the day."

"Oh, that's right. David told me you were psychic. I knew that. So you're saying the dress shop is a calm environment?"

He spooned sugar into his already sweet tea. "Tamara gets about three customers a day."

"I have to confess I never put too much stock into psychic pronouncements."

"That's okay. Sometimes I don't believe what I see, either."

I stood up. "I'm about to make a psychic pronouncement."

Mom looked surprised. "You are?"

"I predict that Kary will walk in the door in about five minutes."

Camden grinned. "Don't let him fool you, Sophia. Kary's nearly always home by four."

Kary was home by four. I met her at the front door. "Come meet my mother."

When I introduced her, the two women beamed at each other in instant friendship.

"Mom wants to go to the craft and fashion show this afternoon, Kary. Would you like to join her?"

"That would be perfect. I've got a few more things on my Christmas list."

"Good," Mom said. "Let me get my pocketbook, and I'll be ready."

As soon as Mom had gone upstairs, Kary said, "Your mother is not at all what I expected."

"Me, either."

"She looks like she just stepped out of *Marie Claire* magazine. What do you mean, 'me, either'?"

"She never looked like this before. She used to look like a normal mom."

"Well, maybe this is what a normal mom looks like these days. I think she looks fabulous. I've got to ask her where she got those shoes." She turned to Camden. "Cam, I'm sure David's already told you I'm helping him on this case. We're going to solve Jared's murder, and then maybe these horrible visions will stop."

I hadn't told Camden yet, but wisely he didn't let on. "As long as you don't put yourself in any kind of danger."

"Don't worry. I won't do anything foolish. I'm on the research side."

"Well, I appreciate your help." His glance to me was full of humor. "And I'm sure Randall appreciates your help, too."

Chapter Five

"Who is He That Condemneth?"

Camden and I dropped the ladies off at the auditorium. My head had finally stopped spinning.

"Okay," I said, "setting aside the fact that my mother has been replaced by some friendly fashionista, I've come up with a stealth plan to avoid Jordan and solve Jared's murder. We stick to the back roads. We approach this case from a different angle. What else was Jared into besides old cars? Didn't you say something about a comics convention?"

"Yeah. And come to think of it, where are his comics? I don't remember seeing them at the house."

"Who would know about them?"

"Let's try Comic World. That was his favorite place to shop."

Comic World was a small brightly colored shop in an ugly strip mall laughingly called Fair Oaks, squeezed between a dry cleaner's and a shoe store. An electronic version of "Jingle Bells" blared overhead. The owner was at the desk, bent over a drawing, his tongue in one corner of his mouth as he filled in tiny strokes. He looked up, his thin reddish hair in meringue-like peaks, his goatee clinging to his chin like the last drop of syrup in the bottle.

"Cam, you have to see the latest issue. Look! Here you are: the Psychic Kid."

He turned the drawing so we could see. The Psychic Kid looked like a beefed-up version of Camden, with plenty of spiky white hair and enormous eyes, a kind of cross between Sonic the Hedgehog and an anime hero.

"Look! He kills with his eyes."

"Good choice, Tor. This is my friend, David Randall. Randall, Tor Noris."

"Call me Tor." He eyed me. "So what's your job?"

"I'm a private investigator."

"Radical! Detecto-Man!" He grabbed his pencil and started sketching.

"Before you get too carried away, I'm investigating Jared Hunter's murder, and I need to ask you a few questions."

Tor's peaks of hair seemed to wilt. "Oh, man, that was awful. I couldn't believe it. Murdered in his own garage. This town's crazy."

"When did you last see him?"

Tor stroked his little goatee. I was surprised it didn't come off in his hand. "Let's see. He was in here last week to pick up the latest 'Phantom Archer' and to do a bit of trading. Left me some boxes of comics to go through."

"You have all of them?" Camden asked.

"Yeah, pretty much."

I knew some comics were worth a lot of money. "What kind of comics? Anything valuable enough to get killed over?"

Tor paled. "Good God, no. Jared had mostly one-hit wonders and stuff by local talent. He did have some old Disney and Gold Key that are kind of rare, but nothing worth dying for."

"Do you have his comics here?"

"They're in boxes in the back."

"Mind if we have a look?"

Tor took us to the storeroom in the back and left us while he waited on customers. Three long white boxes sat on the worktable. I started with the first box. The comics were bagged and arranged neatly and alphabetically by title from "Arachno-Man," "Beast," and "Conan," through "Donald Duck," "Elf Mage," and "Junior Jungle."

Camden thumbed through the second box. "These might be of interest to another collector, but there's nothing really valuable here."

The third box started with "Super Slug" and finished with "Wasteland Warrior." I don't keep up with comics, but even I could tell these weren't in the same class as Superman and Batman. "I thought there might be a one of a kind treasure in here, something someone would kill for."

"Not unless the murderer's a big fan of 'Betty and Her Pets.' The complete collection's in this box."

I imagined a comic called "Betty and Her Pets" featured a cute girl and kittens. Camden held up a copy. Well, the girl was cute, but spectacularly endowed, and her pets looked like happy snakes. "Betty's quite the animal lover, I see."

We went back to the counter. Tor finished with a customer. He reached under the counter for another sketchbook. "Cam, did I ever show you Marlin Man? You'll like this. Got him in here somewhere." He flipped through the pages. "Yeah. Bitchin' car. He parked it out front one day, and I got a good sketch of it." He opened the book on the counter.

There was the Marlin in excellent detail and Jared standing beside it in a classic hero pose, arms folded, chest out, a cape billowing behind with "MM" in fancy script.

Camden swallowed hard. "That's really nice."

"You want it?" He tore it out of the sketchbook. "I can do another."

Camden took the drawing. "Thanks."

"What was the occasion?" I asked.

He shrugged. "Nothing. A favor for Alycia. They were an item, you know? She liked the guy and his car. And he was a collector, so she talked comics with him a lot." He closed the sketchbook. "So Detecto-Man's on the case? What's the deal? Didn't they catch the guy that did it?"

"Not yet."

"Told you, man, the city's crazy. Find any secret clues in the comics? The titles spell out the name of the murderer?"

"Nothing that easy," I said.

"Have you seen Alycia lately?" Camden asked.

"Nope. But I got a cool picture of her." He turned over a page of his drawings. "Right here."

He'd drawn Alycia as a tall, fierce-looking woman. Her powers included something called Super-Grip Strength, which I thought would be handy for dentures, and she had the ability to call forth tigers from the jungle.

"I do all my friends this way. It's the highest form of flattery. Look, Cam." He piled some comics on the counter. "I've got the latest 'Marvelette' and 'Super Sumo.' Oh, check out 'Cherry Girl Blue, the Forever Saga.' Great cover, huh? I've got 'Long River Warrior Six' and the new 'Jerk Basket.' And Wendy's been asking about you."

He tossed this last comment in so casually, I thought it was another comic book title, but Camden shot him a glance.

"Wendy Riskin?"

"You remember her, don't you?"

"Vividly."

"What about that blonde you were seeing? Ellin, was it? Still seeing her?"

"Yes. I'm not sure she's seeing me, though."

"I know for a fact if you call Wendy, she'll be glad to see you."

"Wendy?" I said as we stepped outside the store.

"Probably the most spectacular redhead you're ever likely to see in this lifetime. She teaches aerobics at the Parkland Health Club."

"So how did you meet?" Camden's idea of exercise is raking the yard.

"She's a big anime fan. She was in the store one day and told me if I had black hair, I'd look exactly like Keiichi in 'Oh, My Goddess.' I told her she looked exactly like Ryoko from the 'Tenchi Muyo' series, and thus a great friendship was born."

"Sounds like she wants to be more than friends."

"Well, I told her about Ellie."

"But is that going anywhere?"

"Doesn't seem to be, does it?" He unfolded Tor's drawing of Jared as Marlin Man. "The answer's got to be in there somewhere."

"In that picture?"

"In the comics."

"But if they're not worth anything."

"They must have been to someone."

"What about that car? You don't see Marlins every day. Maybe somebody wanted it."

"But it's still in the garage. If he was murdered for the car, wouldn't it be gone?" Camden refolded the picture. "I don't understand any of this."

"We'll figure it out."

I'd parked across the street, and as we approached the car, I saw a piece of paper fluttering under one of the windshield wipers. "Don't tell me I've got a ticket. I thought parking was free on this street."

The piece of paper wasn't a ticket. It was a warning written in sharp black letters.

"I know you're looking for me. Leave me alone or you'll be sorry."

I didn't have to let Camden touch the paper to know this was from Alycia Ward.

"First Jordan and now Alycia. I'm a popular guy. You getting anything?"

He held the paper and looked around. "There are a million places she could hide."

"What about her old neighborhood? Would Tor know?"

We went back into the comic shop. Tor seemed to recall that Alycia lived in the Timberlake subdivision in Parkland's east side. Camden and I drove over to have a look.

Like most places in Parkland, Timberlake was misnamed. There was no lake and a shocking lack of timber. The houses were neat if unremarkable. Most of them were decorated for Christmas. We saw inflatable Santas and snowmen families waving from lawns and rooftops, bushes and trees draped with colored lights, and fancy wreaths on doors and mailboxes.

A group of women waited at the corner bus stop. Camden rolled down his window and asked if anyone knew the Ward family.

One of the older women pointed up the street. "Used to be some Wards that lived up on Forest Lane. That's the only ones I know. They moved away years ago."

Camden thanked her and we drove all the way up and down Forest Lane until he shook his head. "If her family isn't here anymore, she wouldn't have a place to go."

"And if she's involved with murder, they might not take her in." I turned the car around. "So why is she still in town? If she had anything to do with Jared's death, you'd think she'd get as far away as possible. And why warn me off?"

Camden looked down at the two pieces of paper, Tor's sketch of Jared and Alycia's note. "I don't know, Randall. I just don't know."

◇◇◇

We swung back by the auditorium and picked up Mom and Kary. They had their hands full of shopping bags and brightly colored feather boas around their necks.

"Aren't these wild, Davey? We just had to have them. And I found the perfect pillow for your Aunt Thomasina's sofa. You know how particular she is. She'll love it. And your cousin Louie will love this tie. Look, dice and playing cards. That's Louie, isn't it?"

Kary held up one of the shopping bags. "Wait till you see what Sophia bought for me."

Oh, my lord, I thought. There is no telling what's in that bag. And here I thought my mother would be a good influence on Kary.

"And we got the cutest shoes. We'll model them when we get home."

At home, my worst fears were realized. Sophia's gift for Kary was a leopard print blouse. The shoes were what my second wife

Anita referred to as go to hell high heels, fire engine red with black straps. Mom and Kary strutted around the blue arm chair and green sofa as if they were on the catwalk, flipping the boas. All we needed was a pole.

"Wow," Camden said, which I thought was a masterful understatement.

"Let me go put on my new blouse," Kary said. "Back in a minute."

Mom unwound her boa and put it over the sofa where Cindy immediately attacked it. "We bought some supplies to make cookies, too. You won't mind if I take over your kitchen, would you, Cam?"

"Please do."

She went around the corner. I rescued the boa before we had shredded feathers everywhere. "Thank God she's going to make cookies. I thought my entire mother was gone."

"You need to chill," Camden said. "She's just having fun."

"Fun? Now she's got Kary doing it."

"Doing what?"

"Acting like—well, you saw them. How would you like it if Ellin was dancing around in high heels and a feather boa?"

"Aside from the fact it would be the end of the world as we know it, I'd like it very much."

I thought I was calm until Kary came back in her new blouse, which revealed more than I was ready for. I pointed out a potential problem. "Your button's undone."

She glanced down. "It's supposed to be like this."

"Well, then, it's," I groped for the right word, "Impressive."

"Thank you. Your mother has excellent taste."

Kary went into the kitchen to help Mom with the cookies, and I went into my office to give myself a talking to. Mom and Kary both looked fantastic. Why couldn't I relax and enjoy their transformations?

After a while, I heard them laughing. I wandered into the kitchen to see what was so funny. The counter was covered with flour and dough. Two cookie sheets were full of Christmas cookies: trees, stars, bells, and Santas.

Kary was washing her hands. "David, your mother's told me all about how you were as a little boy."

"No wonder you're in hysterics." I chewed a bit of left over cookie dough. "When will these be ready to eat?"

"In about ten minutes." She dried her hands. "Sophia, I'm going to practice a little."

"Go right ahead, dear."

Kary went to the piano and began to play some Christmas tunes. Mom gave me a glance I couldn't quite interpret.

"All right, Davey, what's going on? I see how you look at Kary."

"That's one of things I wanted to talk to you about." Might as well come to the point. "I'm in love with her."

She gave me a long stare. "You're serious."

"For the first time in my life."

"Well," she said. "Well."

"I know it's crazy."

Mom looked toward the island. She looked at Cindy's well-chewed cat toys, the scattered newspapers, books, the television, the furniture, as if looking for clues to the mystery. She finally looked at me.

"What are you going to do about it?"

"I don't know. I've been trying to figure it out since I met her."

Another long view of the room. "How old is she?"

"I know she looks young, Mom, but there's only six years difference."

This brought her gaze to my face. "David."

"Bogart was forty-five when he married nineteen year old Bacall."

"David, honestly."

I heard the dismay in her voice. "This is the one. I promise. Kary is the one I've been looking for."

"You said that about Barbara. You said that about Anita, too."

"I was wrong."

"This house," she said. "These people. What exactly are you doing here?"

"I'm doing what I want to do. I'm finding things."

Her mouth trembled slightly and she pressed her fingers against it. Then she said, "David, you must forgive yourself. You did all you could."

For a moment I could see Lindsey's sweet forgiving smile. I'd had that wonderful dream in which I knew she didn't blame me, but it was still difficult not to blame myself.

"When did you last talk to Barbara?" Mom asked.

"At Lindsey's funeral."

"David, that was years ago."

"She doesn't want to have anything to do with me."

Mom leaned back against the counter. "I had no idea things were this bad."

"It isn't bad. I'm getting along just fine."

"What, here? But what kind of life is this, hunting for some lost jewelry and wanting to marry for a third time to a woman who needs to have her own life, not get all caught up in yours. Honestly, if your father were here—"

"He'd be proud of me."

She stopped to consider this. "Yes, he would, the old hound. He'd find all this immensely romantic. A detective, a beautiful woman, psychic overtones. Such interesting friends you have, dear. By the way, Cam seems a bit peaked. Is he coming down with something?"

"Camden's naturally pale, Mom, and he's having girl troubles." I paused a moment. "You've been talking to Kary. Did she say I was a dirty old man and she couldn't stand my drooling advances?"

"No, she wanted to know what you were like when you were little."

"You didn't tell her the Mickey Mouse story, did you?"

"Well, it's priceless. I should've sent it in to *Reader's Digest*."

"Mom."

"And don't get me off the subject. The last thing you need in your life is another relationship."

"I guess I could say the same thing to you."

"What are you talking about?"

It had slipped out, and now I had to go on. "I'm talking about Grady. How serious are you about him?"

"David Henry Randall, I cannot believe you are putting my friendship with Grady Sipe on the same level as your latest fling."

"Well?" I said. "How serious are you?"

"I'm not serious at all! We're having fun. And the fact that we're sleeping together is none of your business."

That brought up a mental picture that seared the inner lining of my brain. "Mom, for heaven's sake."

"Just because I'm old doesn't mean I don't have feelings. You think the sex drive turns off at fifty? Sixty? I'm still a very attractive woman."

"Yes, you are, but—"

"Let me finish. I could have any man I wanted in Bay Ridge Apartments. I like Grady's company because he treats me like a lady. We have a lot in common. I'm not going to stop seeing him just because it makes you uncomfortable to think of your mother as a sexual being."

"Gah! Stop! Okay, I'm sorry. Quit talking like that."

She grinned. I'd always been told I look like my dad, but that grin was pure me. "Your father was not the only one who enjoyed himself, Davey."

"Mom, please."

"Oh, the whole time we were married, I was faithful to him, despite all his little flirtations and carrying on. I loved him very much. I forgave him very much." She paused for a moment. I couldn't even guess what she was feeling. During my younger years, they were always laughing and teasing. I really never knew all the complications of their relationship. "When he died, what amazed me the most was the way the world kept going, as if nothing had happened, and I guess in the grand scheme of things, it was nothing." She paused again, as if she still couldn't believe it. "I was the one who didn't want to go on, but eventually, I did. I moved away from all those memories, all that cold Minnesota weather, to Florida to be near your Aunt Thomasina. You remember what I told you? 'It doesn't matter where I move. I'll never be warm again.' But I'm thawing out, Davey, and Grady is helping me." She put her hand on mine. "He'll never replace your father. No one will. But he's bringing me out of the cold."

I wasn't sure what to say. "You know I want you to be happy."

"Good. I'm setting you an example of how you ought to be."

"But I am happy."

"Remember who you're talking to. I know you better than anyone, and you are not going to have another dismal Christmas."

"I hadn't planned on a dismal Christmas, and by the way, it's a little hard to remember who I'm talking to when you look so different."

"Unlike a certain son of mine, I decided not to get stuck in a rut." She ruffled her new hair. "It's amazing what a change of style can do. I am movin' on, honey, and you should, too." Before I could say anything else, she said, "Now, about Kary. What do her folks say about you?"

"Her mother and father haven't spoken to her in years. When she got pregnant, they threw her out. I think it's against their religion to be forgiving."

"Are you telling me she has a baby?"

"No, she lost it, and now she can't have children."

"My heavens."

I knew that look. Kary was about to become a Project. "She doesn't like to talk about it."

"I'm not going to pry, Davey, but what do you mean, her parents threw her out? Do they live in town?"

"We could see them right now if you want to. They host a never-ending Bible Hour on Church TV."

"They're televangelists?"

"Yep. Too saintly for me."

"And they've disowned their beautiful daughter. How saintly is that?"

"I don't even try to understand it."

"Cam doesn't have parents, either. How did you end up in this orphanage?"

"Lost causes, Mom."

She smiled. My dad had made a living listening to lost causes in his bar. Often he'd come home and plop a big bag of money on the kitchen table and say, "Here's to lost causes, may they never be found." "Have you inherited your father's Listening Face?"

"Sometimes I feel it slipping on."

"Is that why you insist on keeping this detective agency?"

"I'm doing some good."

"When's the last time you talked to anyone about Lindsey?"

I could almost hear the clang of an iron door as I shut myself against the emotion. "That's not necessary."

"Oh, I think it is. That's one reason I agreed to come visit this Christmas. You and I need to talk."

"Not now."

"When?"

Not ever. "I don't know. Just not now."

She gave me a long considering look. "Well, then, let's see about getting some dinner started."

Chapter Six

"But Thou Didst Not Leave His Soul in Hell"

Mom and Kary had also bought supplies for Mom's special meat loaf, mixed bean salad, and cornbread. I was helping Camden set the table when Brooke Verner came in with a suitcase and went upstairs.

I couldn't believe it. "Excuse me, but is Ms. Verner moving in?"

Camden looked guilty. "Well, I thought about it some more, and since Rufus and Angie won't be back until after New Year's—"

I set the last knife down with a clank. "Oh, this is just great. Why in the hell didn't you tell her no?"

"But it's Christmas."

"Don't tell me you feel sorry for that harpy." I knew he did. It doesn't take much of a sob story, and I'm sure Brooke had a beaut. "Damn it, why do you keep attracting these warrior women? I need peace in my life."

"It's only for the holidays."

"It won't end. We'll be stuck with her forever."

"She said she'd be out by the end of the month."

"Just because you spent every Christmas in a Dumpster doesn't give you the right to foist this harridan on me."

He raised his eyebrows. "'Foist' and 'harridan'?"

"I've been practicing."

"Having women chase you never bothered you before."

"That was B.K. Before Kary."

"Brooke won't be in the way. She needs a place to sleep at night, that's all."

"And have you thought of Brooke plus Ellin? You might as well declare our peaceful island living room a nuclear testing site."

"Let's just get through dinner, okay?"

Ellin arrived as Brooke came back downstairs. Camden made all the introductions.

"Brooke, this is Randall's mother, Sophia, visiting us from Florida. This is Fred Mullins, and Kary Ingram, who live here with me, and I believe you've met Ellin Belton. Everyone, this is Brooke Verner. She works for the *Herald*. She'll be staying here for the holidays."

Someone had taken Evil Brooke away and replaced her with a kindly clone who smiled pleasantly. "It's a pleasure to meet everyone, and thank you for sharing your home."

We all sat down at the dining room table. As I expected, Mom's meat loaf and cornbread went over well with the crowd. Even old Fred couldn't find anything to gripe about. Everyone was so nice and polite, I thought I'd stumbled into an episode of *Masterpiece Theater*. Occasionally, Brooke would catch my eye and give me a grin as if to say, isn't this cozy?, but the rest of the time she behaved as if she were the star pupil at Miss Proper's Boarding School for Young Ladies.

Talk centered around Mom and how she liked Parkland.

"It's a wonderful city. So much to do! And such nice weather, too. In Florida, I miss the seasons, but I certainly don't miss those awful Minnesota winters, although it was always nice to have snow for Christmas. Do you ever have a white Christmas here?"

Ellin passed the salad bowl to Kary. "Every now and then. I can remember two or three."

Kary took some salad and passed the bowl to me. "You remember I did some student teaching in a third grade class? Well, we saw some of those kids at the crafts fair. They were giving a gymnastics demonstration."

Mom laughed. "You should have seen those little girls cart wheeling and turning flips. They were wonderful."

"They said they had a big meet coming up next week, and Sophia and I would like to go, but I wasn't sure what your plans were for you and your mom."

"I don't really have anything special planned," I said. "Whatever you want to do is fine with me."

"You'll have to come see the Psychic Service Network," Ellin said. "We're taping our Christmas specials, and we have a fascinating woman who can predict the weather for any holiday you can name. She calls herself Meteora."

This sounded like something I'd like to see. "Meteora, Goddess of Weather?"

Ellin was determined to be polite. "Not exactly."

"Have you booked a couple of wise men and some particularly bright stars?" Her eyes were beginning to flame, so I decided not to be a jerk in front of my mother. "Mom, I'll be happy to take you by the studio tomorrow."

"Thank you," she said. "Ellin, I don't know very much about the paranormal. I'm afraid I'll bore you with questions."

"Not at all, Sophia. I'll be glad to show you everything."

I could tell this invitation did not include me.

After dinner, Brooke went upstairs to get settled in, Kary went out with some of her friends to go caroling at rest homes, and Ellin went back to the network to schedule an angel visitation or something. Mom insisted on helping Camden clean up.

I finally got in touch with Boyd Taylor, and he said I could come by his house tomorrow. He was anxious for me to hear his side of the story. I told him I'd be very interested in his side of the story. I'd hung up when I heard a crash and a thump. Then Mom called, "David!"

I ran back to the kitchen. Mom was attempting to help Camden up off the floor. He was blank-eyed and trembling. A huge smear of tomato sauce spread across the counter and sink and down the cabinet.

"Blood," he gasped. "Too much."

I got him to his feet. "It's okay. You just spilled some sauce."

"Jared. Oh, my God, help him."

Mom stared at us. "What's he talking about? What's wrong?"

"Camden, it's okay. It's over. Mom, get him some tea and put plenty of sugar in it."

I steered Camden to the dining room and sat him down at the table. He put his head down on his arms and began to cry. I kept telling him it was okay, but he sobbed and hiccupped until Mom brought a glass of tea. She sat beside him and hugged him.

"Cam, honey, take it easy. My goodness, David, what's the matter?"

"He keeps seeing a friend's murder in wide-screen Technicolor."

"Oh, dear, how awful. How often does this happen?"

"More often than we like. I guess seeing all that sauce set him off."

Camden raised his head and blinked at us, confused. "Am I crying?"

I passed the box of Kleenex. "Like a baby."

He wiped his face. "What the hell?"

"Tell me what you saw."

"The usual. Jared lying in an ocean of blood, the murderer hacking away." He shuddered, and Mom patted his arm. "Blood gushing. Sorry, Sophia."

"Go ahead, dear. It helps to talk these things out."

"Not this one," he said. "It keeps coming back. And this time, I felt an overwhelming sadness. I don't know where all this is coming from." He banged both fists on the table. "Why won't it go away? It's driving me crazy."

"Calm down," I said. "We'll figure it out."

"Before or after I'm completely insane?"

Mom gave him another hug. "I'll clean up the sauce. You drink your tea and try to relax."

She went to the sink. Camden wiped his eyes and ran his hand through his hair. "Randall, this has got to stop."

"It will. First thing tomorrow, I'm talking to Boyd Taylor. Maybe he's psychic, too. Maybe he's sending you all this shit."

We went to the island. Camden put his tea on the coffee table and lay on the sofa with one arm over his eyes. Mom sat in the wicker chair near-by. "You don't have to baby-sit, Sophia," he said.

"Nonsense. I have reading to do."

"I'm really sorry. It's this talent. I never know what it's going to do."

"You must have loved your friend very much."

"Jared and I were friends, but I'd only known him for a short time. That's why I don't understand this intense reaction."

"Maybe because his murder was so violent?"

"I've seen much worse things in my life, unfortunately."

"It must be hard for you."

He sat up and reached for his glass of tea. "I'm usually able to handle things. Then something like this comes along and knocks me over. No wonder Ellie doesn't want to hang around."

"Your pretty girlfriend? Why wouldn't she want to hang around?"

He took a drink. "It's complicated."

Mom gave me a sidelong glance. "Any more complicated than David having the hots for Kary?"

This made Camden grin. "I see where Randall gets his tact."

"Thanks a lot, both of you." I sat down in the blue armchair. "Go ahead and tell her about your screwy love life, Camden."

He set his tea back on the table. "Ellie can't decide if she loves me or my psychic ability. You see, she doesn't have any psychic talent, at all, and she's crazy about that kind of stuff."

Mom leaned over and patted his cheek. "Then she's an idiot, because you are very lovable."

I don't think I'd ever seen Camden blush. With Mom in control of the situation, I went upstairs.

Brooke Verner was in my bed.

Fortunately, she was still dressed. She leaned back against the pillows. "I stopped by for a little advice."

"And I'm giving you some: if you want to live, stay out of my room."

She swung her feet off the edge of the bed, but didn't get up. "I want to catch the Avenger."

"So catch him."

"I need your help."

"Nope."

"Why not?"

"Because I don't care. I don't care if you catch him. I don't care if he continues his reign of terror. As far as I'm concerned, he's a nut having a good time at the city's expense. Eventually, he'll slip up, get caught, and have to pay for his crimes. End of story."

"Aren't you the slightest bit curious?"

"I'm busy right now. Will you leave?"

She leaned on one of the tall bed posts. "There's a reward for his capture. Ten thousand bucks. Can you believe it?"

"Ten thousand for some fool in a cape? No, I can't believe it."

"I'll split it with you."

"The only split I want is for you to split from my room. Now."

"All right, all right." She took her time getting off my bed. "Party pooper."

"I wouldn't think you'd want him caught. Once he's off the streets, you won't have anything to write about."

"You think that's all I can do, chronicle this guy's escapades? I'm a damn good writer. I can make a story out of anything."

"Apparently so. Why don't you try doing some good for a change?"

"Oh, like Chance Baseford, I suppose?"

Chance Baseford's the theater critic for the *Herald*. His picture can be found in any dictionary under "pompous ass."

"What's he got to do with this? He writes reviews."

Brooke made a face. "He thinks he's so much better than anyone else, and I happen to know he got his start at the *Galaxy News Weekly*, a world class rag."

"He hasn't exactly kept that a secret."

"I wish he hadn't told everyone. With that kind of dirt, I'd win a Parkie for sure."

"A Parkie?"

"The *Herald's* top news award. Only I'd deserve mine. You know what Baseford's are for? For writing nasty things about musicians and artists, for destroying careers. He thinks I'm useless, but I'm going to show him."

"How? By making up stories about the Avenger?"

"By proving the Avenger is real."

"I have to hand it to you, Brooke. You've got a nice little scam going."

Brooke's eyes glittered. "This is not a scam! This is a legitimate news story. I don't care what you or anyone else thinks."

"I don't think anything about it." Although I was thinking Brooke might be the Avenger to scare up her own news. "Get out of my room."

"So you really don't care?"

"I really don't care."

"And you're not going to help me?"

"I'm not going to help you."

She finally left, still huffing and glittering. Then someone who I would love to have in my bed stopped in the doorway, Kary, home from caroling, and not as full of the Christmas spirit as I would have imagined.

"David, I can't find a thing on Susan Carlyle or Morris Otto. Are you sure they have anything to do with Jared's case?"

"Well, I wasn't sure, but I guess now you've proved they don't."

She gave me an uncomfortably long stare, as if she suspected I'd sent her on a wild goose chase. "One of my friends remembers an Alycia Ward who used to work at Fancy Feet Shoes in Olympia Mall, but she kept coming in late and got fired. This might not be the same Alycia Ward we're looking for. Boyd Taylor works at Ben's Garage on Emerald Street."

"Thanks."

Another long pause. "These are actual suspects, right?"

"Yes."

"I really want in on this, David."

"I really want you in, too."

"Then don't you think it's about time you gave me a little more information?"

"I promise as soon as I know something, I'll let you know."

I'm not sure what she planned to say next because Mom came along.

"Oh, excuse me."

"No, that's all right, Sophia," Kary said. "I was just leaving. Good night."

"Good night, dear. David, Cam's asleep, and I'm going to my room to make a phone call. I'll see you in the morning."

"Okay, Mom. Good night."

She didn't say who she was calling, and I didn't ask. I figured I'd made enough women mad for one evening.

Chapter Seven

"Behold and See If There Be Any Sorrow"

There was a memorial service for Jared the next day, so I dropped Camden off at the funeral home chapel and told him to call when he needed a ride home. Ellin invited Mom to tour the PSN and watch a taping of "Ready to Believe," so I took her to the studio. Mom looked as surprisingly different as the day before in her tight black slacks and silky black blouse with leopard print buttons. She even had on large designer sun glasses trimmed with little rhinestones. I felt like I was like chauffeuring a famous movie star to the premiere of her latest film.

After escorting her into the studio, I went to talk with Boyd Taylor. As Jordan had said, there wasn't enough evidence to hold him for Jared Hunter's murder, but Taylor was angry and upset over being a suspect in the case.

Taylor was a big rough-looking man, six three, easily over two hundred pounds. His reddish hair curled around a high forehead. His gray eyes peered out over bags of wrinkles, reminding me of an elephant's eyes. He met me at the door of his small brick home on Worth Street, invited me in, and offered me a drink.

"Beer okay?"

"Sounds good."

"Camden couldn't come?"

"Did you want him to?"

"I don't know. I been thinking about it." He rooted in his refrigerator and handed me a can of Miller. "Lawyer I spoke to says I'm crazy to even try. He says any sort of psychic testimony's not going to hold up in court, but I figure Camden could tell who the real murderer is."

I still had my doubts about Taylor, but if he wanted Camden to come check out his vibes, that didn't sound like he had anything to hide. "You know Camden?"

"Seen him a couple of times at Jared's. I didn't kill Jared Hunter. I came over to see about the Marlin. He'd been talking it up at work, even brought photographs. I wanted to see the car."

"What time was this?"

"Around nine."

Camden had wanted to go to Jared's at nine, and it had taken maybe fifteen minutes for us to over from Grace Street.

"You didn't see anyone else?"

"No. I saw he was dead, so I ran into his house to call for help. Then I heard a car drive up. I thought it was the killer coming back, or maybe the police, so I decided I'd better get out of there."

"If you didn't do it, why run?"

"I been in trouble before. I didn't want no cops to find me with a dead body. But if Camden's clairvoyant, he'll know I didn't do it. I want you to get him over here. He can prove I didn't kill Hunter."

"Like you said, that won't hold up in court."

"Then you gotta take him back to Hunter's house and see if he comes up with any clues. He's got to be able to see I didn't do it."

"He's seeing things, all right," I said. "He's reliving Jared's murder at least once a day. What if he's getting these thoughts from you?"

"That's impossible. I didn't do it."

"Then who did? Who hated Jared that much? Did he piss somebody off at work?"

"No, no, we all get along good at the store, except for old Reese, and he don't get along with anybody, but he's eighty-five years old and can't pick up a wrench, let alone stab somebody. Just get Cam to go over to Hunter's and see what he can find out."

Going back to Jared's was probably the last thing Camden needed to do. "That's not going to happen. What if he comes here and talks to you?"

"Yeah, sure, anything." Taylor leaned against the sink and took a big swig of beer. "I seen how that big cop looked at me. It's only a matter of time before they haul me back in. They want to pin this on somebody, and it's not going to be me."

I looked around the dim kitchen. Christmas hadn't come to Boyd's house. A brown card table was set in one corner with three folding chairs. I could see into the living room, which was just as dismal. An old console TV sat in front of a greenish sofa. Scattered beer cans, potato chip bags, and newspapers provided that lived-in look. I saw several comic books on the floor. "Are you a comic book collector, too?"

"I got a few, but I'm not that much into it."

"Would Jared have had anything worth killing for?"

He took another drink. "A comic book, you mean? That's crazy."

"Some comics are valuable."

"Maybe he wasn't killed because of a comic book, or a car, or anything. Maybe it was some insane person walking by. I heard of that before. You leave your back door open, and some nut walks in and kills you. It happens. Why would I just stop by to kill somebody? I didn't do it." He finished his beer and crushed the can.

The crushing reminded me of the photograph in Jared's house. "I saw a picture of you and Jared and Alycia Ward. Are you dressed as the Incredible Hulk at a comic convention?"

He looked blank. "The Hulk? Me? Nah, I don't dress up. Must be somebody else. Will Camden come here?"

"I'll ask him."

The can was now about the size of a quarter. "Damn it. Somebody's got to believe me. You're a detective, aren't you? Can't you find out who killed Hunter?" His little eyes were pleading.

"I ain't got much money, but if you can help me, you can have whatever I got. You want to catch this guy, don't you?"

Yes, I did. Whether or not the murderer was capable of broadcasting severe visions, he was still out there somewhere.

I set my empty can in the sink. "I'll see what I can do. I want to talk to the people at your garage first."

Taylor's face sagged with relief. "That's great, thanks. It's Ben's Garage on Emerald. Don't let Old Reese bully you."

Old Reese was old, about as old as Fred, and just as cheerful. He was changing a tire on a Chevy truck.

"God Almighty, what a terrible thing to happen."

"Do you know of anyone who would've hated Jared that much?"

He tugged at the tire. "No, sir. Hunter was an asshole, but everyone who works here is an asshole, except for me. They don't know nothing."

"No one came by, looking for him? No arguments? No complaints? Women?"

He paused and straightened. "Well, now, there was one woman came by looking for him. Reason I remember is because she was a black woman about six feet tall. Looked mighty fierce, too."

The missing Alycia. "Did she say what she wanted?"

"Wanted to talk to Hunter, but he didn't want to talk to her. I remember hearing him tell her he wasn't in on what she wanted to do. She made a big face and said something like, 'Are you too chicken?' And he told her he wasn't doing stuff like that anymore."

"What kind of stuff?"

"Beats the hell out of me. She did have a really nice ass, though. She looked better going away."

"When was this?"

"I don't remember. Not long ago."

"Did she ever come back, wanting to talk to him?"

"Not that I know." He screwed up his little wizened face. "You think she had something to do with his murder?"

"I don't know. What do you think?"

He shrugged. I left this fount of information and spoke with some of the other men. Several remembered seeing a tall black woman, but no one had overheard any conversation between this woman and Jared. All of them expressed regret that he'd been killed.

"He was a good guy," one said. "A good mechanic. It's a real shame."

"What about Boyd Taylor? Did he argue with Jared over the Marlin?"

"Yeah, they had their differences," another man said, "But Boyd's not the kind of person who'd kill somebody."

In my experience, I'd found out that for love, money, or plain uncontrollable rage, anybody could snap.

"They were in the same Auto Club, right?" I asked. "When does it meet?"

"Every Friday night at Best Buys," the first man said.

Tomorrow was Friday. I thanked them and went on to my next stop, the offices of the *Parkland Herald.*

◇◇◇

I didn't want to talk to Brooke Verner about the Avenger because I had a suspicion she might be the Avenger. I figured Chance Baseford would have some information. I knew he'd have an opinion. I don't like Baseford, but I'd done him a favor once and didn't think he'd mind if I stopped by for a brief chat. When I tapped on his office door, he looked up from his computer and reared back in his chair, giving me the full glare.

"What do you want?"

"Good afternoon to you, too." I made myself at home in the chair in front of his desk.

Baseford's broad fleshy face went pink with annoyance. He tossed back his mane of white hair in a gesture that I'm sure sends waves of horror through timid dancers and painters trying to make it in Parkland, but I'm not that easily impressed by theatrics. "Every time I see you, it means trouble. What could possibly bring you to my office?"

"I'm mounting a new production of 'Swan Lake' and need your advice on the tutus. Should they be full length, or those little skirty things?"

"Very funny."

"No, really, I'm opening an exhibit of modern art at the Little Gallery, and a bad review from you will send hundreds flocking to see what's so terrible."

"Did you just stop by to mock me, or is there a purpose to this visit?"

"Brooke Verner and the Parkland Avenger."

Baseford made a gesture with both hands as if flinging something gooey away. "Obnoxious upstart. Tabloid mentality."

"That's where you got your start."

"In those days, it was different. We dealt with actual facts, not bizarre space fantasies. True, we may have stretched those facts, but there was always a kernel of truth in those stories. Nowadays, things are outrageous. If Brooke Verner thinks she's going to turn the *Herald* into another *Weekly Moonbeam*, she's sadly mistaken. This Avenger nonsense, for example. I'll bet you any amount of money you choose she's making it up."

"Eyewitnesses have seen the Avenger."

"Probably her stooge. She needs to investigate herself and her reasons for this charade. It's a cry for help."

I looked at the row of awards on his bookshelf. "She's shooting for one of those."

Baseford was too articulate to say, "As if!" but his eyebrows said it. "It's highly doubtful her work is up to Parkie level."

I got up for a closer look. "What are these for?"

"Mine are all for excellence in feature writing. Other people have won for investigative reporting, design, editorials. Brooke Verner's work fits none of these categories. We don't give Parkies for Fake Superhero sightings."

The awards were shaped like ovals rising from scrolls. They looked like piles of rolled-up newspapers going up in flames. Baseford had six Parkies from various years, as well as a selection of plaques of all sizes.

"These are voted on by *Herald* employees?"

"And the public. A week before the awards are decided, we run a ballot in the Sunday supplement."

"When will the next bunch of Parkies be handed out?"

He checked his desk calendar. "Next Tuesday, the twenty-third. You see what she's up to. She thinks this sensational story will garner her the popular vote. Well, I think our readers are above this kind of hoax."

I sat back down in the chair. "I don't know. You remember that pitiful granny last fall? A lot of people fell for that."

In October, an elderly woman had come to the *Herald* with the world's most pathetic sob story. She'd lost her life savings to a con man who'd promised to pave her driveway so she could finally maneuver her wobbly walker out to her failing Oldsmobile and drive to the market for the meager cans of cat food she shared with her ancient tabby. Pictures of Grandma and Sugar Baby had been on the front page for a week. Contributions poured in. The *Herald* raised almost five thousand dollars for this old lady until another reporter discovered she was perfectly hale and hearty and actually lived in Pine Village, an upscale retirement condo.

Baseford looked pensive. "I see what you mean. But an old woman claiming to live on cat food and an idiot in Spandex leaping from the rooftops are two different things. Perhaps, after being fooled once, our readers will be doubly cautious." He glared. "If you see Brooke Verner, tell her she'd better be doubly cautious, too. We won't tolerate that kind of deception here."

"You'll see her. Doesn't she work here?"

"Her office is as far away from mine as possible. I have no idea when she comes and goes, and I don't want to know. The last time she was in here, I told her to go away and never return."

I was disappointed he didn't say, "And never darken my door again." "She stopped by to bask in your presence, like me."

"She stopped by to gloat, the horrid creature. Thought she had some big scoop about me working in the tabloids. When I told her to go ahead and print whatever she liked, she deflated like a cheap balloon. Everyone knows that story. Why, I doubt there'd even be a *Parkland Herald* if not for my first efforts."

Give Baseford a chance, and he'll claim responsibility for creating the universe. "So you told her to go away."

"And did she go? No, she hung about like a bad smell, asking me all sorts of impertinent questions."

"Maybe she wanted the benefit of your great knowledge."

"She wanted to know my sources." Again the eyebrows went "As if!"

"You're not likely to tell her that."

"I'm not likely to tell anyone that! You must have some idea of how important good sources are and how you must protect them. She seemed to think they would know about this Avenger. I told her to go down to the state mental hospital and check herself in. She'd find all the faux superheroes she liked right there. She finally went away. The next thing I know, Galvin is printing Parkland Avenger stories on the front page, above the fold, mind you! Not only do I have that nonsense to contend with, I also have that ridiculous litany of discontent taking up valuable space in what used to be a quality newspaper."

"Are you talking about 'Your Turn'?"

He sneered as if smelling a bad smell. "If I were editor, that's the first thing that would go. I don't care how many readers it's pulling in. Do they even proofread that nonsense?"

"How many, actually?"

"Galvin says we've had over two hundred new subscribers."

"People must be hard up for entertainment."

"Well, thank God that line is down today. I'm sure the repairman will say it's a case of too many fools trying to call in at one time. Of course, a brain-damaged chimpanzee could make up better stories." He turned back to his computer. "I have a deadline. Go talk to Galvin. I've had quite enough of you for today."

I took his advice and went to see Ralph Galvin, the editor of the *Herald*. Galvin's a tall, wiry man full of energy. It was unusual to see him sitting at his desk. He was checking off dates on a large calendar full of appointments and meetings.

He grinned around the peppermint stick in his mouth. "That Brooke's kicking up quite a dust, isn't she, Randall? Got Baseford's tail in a crack."

"You think the Avenger's out there?"

He took the peppermint stick and set it in a clean ashtray on his desk. "Somebody's out there, and it's creating plenty of stories. I told Brooke to watch her step, though. I'd hate to have to sue her for fraud."

"She seems to want a Parkie pretty bad. Is there money involved?"

"Nope, just the trophy."

"She said something about a ten thousand dollar reward for information about the Avenger."

He looked through papers on his desk. "Yeah, we had someone offer that. Let's see, here we are. Fella by the name of E. Walter Winthrop."

I'd heard that name before. "Winthrop? Of Winthrop, Incorporated, a company that makes alarm systems?"

"Not any more. Says here they're into computers now."

I took the piece of paper and read, "E. Walter Winthrop. Winthrop, Incorporated. Computer Systems for Home and Office." The address was in the northern part of Parkland, an industrial park called MegaSystems.

"They give any reason why he's offering this reward?"

Galvin shrugged. "Hey, you've lived in this city long enough to know there is no 'why.' People do crazy things for no reason at all."

"But this Avenger isn't helping out. He's just getting in the way."

"Whatever. As long as Brooke Verner brings me stories that sell newspapers, I'm not really concerned over a deluded guy's motives. He's not a serial killer, unfortunately."

"Unfortunately?"

"What we need are more sensational murders like that Hunter case." He made a face at the candy in the ashtray. "Some days I think I'd kill for a cigarette." He glanced up. "Hey, don't look at me in that tone of voice. You know what I mean: if it bleeds, it leads."

"Yeah, too bad more people aren't dying for the *Herald*. So you're not concerned about another Sugar Baby fiasco?"

He picked up the peppermint stick and put it back in his mouth. "Nope."

"Speaking of Jared Hunter, I understand there was a problem at the museum not long ago, and your son was involved."

He smacked his hand on his desk. "My son had nothing to do with that! Someone on the police force has it in for me, and they thought they'd try to involve my family. That break in was all Hunter's idea, and if his criminal friends came back to get him, then good riddance."

"Did your son know Jared?"

"Hunter was a bad influence. I told Bert not to deal with him."

"And he listened to you?"

"Yes, of course."

"I'd like to talk to Bert."

Galvin's eyes narrowed. "You're pals with that policeman, Finley, is it? There's absolutely no reason why you should be talking to anyone in my family. It's none of your business. So if you don't mind, I've got a newspaper to run. The door's right there. Use it."

Clearly I wasn't welcome at the *Herald*.

Chapter Eight

"Let Him Deliver Him"

Camden called to say the service was over. I picked him up, and on the way to MegaSystems, I filled him in on my morning activities.

"The fellows at the garage remember Alycia stopping by a short while back. According to one of them, she gave Jared a hard time about not being in on something. Called him a coward."

"In on something? That sounds shady."

"I thought so, too. Then I visited Baseford and got an earful about Brooke. How dare she even think of winning a Parkie was the gist of his conversation. Ralph Galvin only wishes the Avenger was Evil Avenger so he could sell more papers and told me I'd better not come anywhere near Bert because, like the police, I am evil, as well."

"So where are we headed now?"

"Winthrop, Incorporated. That's the guy who's offering a big reward for information about the Avenger. It's also the company who made Petey Royalle's alarm system."

At Winthrop, Incorporated, a very pretty young secretary was happy to tell us the history of the company. Winthrop, Incorporated started in the early nineteen hundreds as a bank, and then became a securities firm. Later, the company branched out into alarm systems, but had jumped on the computer bandwagon, finding it much more profitable.

"We haven't manufactured alarm systems for thirty years, sir."

"But it's possible some of those systems are still working?"

"Oh, yes, sir. It was a quality product."

"What about repairs?"

"We offer a replacement system through another company, Guardian Electronic." Her hand hovered over the phone. "Do you have a system that needs repair? I'll be happy to call them for you."

"Not at the moment. Is there anyone here who knows how the old systems work?"

"I doubt it, sir. Most of the employees here are recently out of college. We have a few senior members, but they're mainly on the board. We have some displays, though. Would you like to see them? Down the hall and to your right. There's coffee, too, if you want some."

I thanked her and we went on our short self-guided tour. The walls were lined with old brown pictures of the first Winthrops. Here was the first building, the first horse and buggy delivery service; here were pictures of solemn men around a table and in front of another building at a ribbon cutting ceremony. Newer color photographs showed the present building, latest models of computers, and a smiling couple who must have been Mister and Mrs. E. Walter. There were also framed awards and citations from the Better Business Bureau and Parkland Chamber of Commerce.

Camden and I went back to the secretary.

"Was there anything else, sir?"

"If I wanted to speak to a senior member, who would that be?"

"Mister E. Walter Winthrop, Senior, would be able to answer any of your questions. Shall I make an appointment for you?"

E. Walter Winthrop, Senior, would be able to see me tomorrow at three. Camden and I thanked the secretary and got back into the Fury. I had every intention of interviewing more of Petey's employees, but when we got to Royalle's Fine Jewelry, I noticed yellow police tape across the street at Carlene's record shop. Carlene Jessup carries every kind of recording, old and new, and I can usually find something, even some on the Stomp Off label, a company that specializes in my favorite traditional jazz.

Now the large front window was shattered, letting in the chilly December air. When we came in, Carlene was cleaning up broken glass. She straightened. Carlene's slim and almost as tall as I am.

"Hi, David, Cam."

I brought the trashcan over so she could dump in the glass. "Are you okay? When did this happen?"

"The police say early this morning. Thank goodness I had to take my cat to the vet. I would've gotten here right in the middle of the robbery."

"What did they take?"

She set the broom and dustpan next to a shelf. "About fourteen hundred dollars."

"You had that much in the drawer?"

"No, it was in the safe. He didn't get anything out of the drawer." She led me to the back of the shop to a little room off to one side. A large old-fashioned safe sat in the corner

"It's not much of a safe," Carlene said. She gave a little tug, and the door swung open, revealing an empty shelf. "The lock's been broken for years. But that's not the problem. There's only one way to get back to this room, and it involves a hidden panel. I'm the only one who knows where this panel is, so this has always been a secure place. How did the thief know? Can you get anything from this, Cam?"

"I'll try." He touched the shelf and the door and all down the sides of the safe. "Nothing here. I'm sorry. Let me check the rest of the store."

"Who owned the building before you?" I asked.

If she'd said Winthrop, Incorporated, it would have made my life so much easier.

"I bought it from Moore's Hardware."

"Any angry customers? Strange people lurking around the store? Any of your employees unreliable?"

She sat down at her front counter and pushed back her long light brown hair. "David, I've never had any trouble. As for strange people, I get all kinds in here. My employees include my sister and my cousin. I trust them completely."

"But they don't know about the secret panel?"

"No. I haven't told anyone except you two." She looked out her broken window across the street to Royalle's. "First Petey's shop and now mine. What's going on?"

"Somebody likes shopping this end of town."

A young man came in, a pleasant-looking teenager with crisp brown hair cut so it would stand up like the spikes of a little mountain range. His blue eyes sparkled with excitement. "Carlene, you want me to help you clean up? Mister Royalle said I could."

"Thanks, Sim."

He picked up the broom and began sweeping with too much energy. "You think it could be the Parkland Avenger?"

"I thought he was a good guy," I said.

"He could have a dark side. I think it's way cool that Parkland has its own superhero."

"Even if he breaks into shops and steals things?"

"He may have been trying to prevent the crimes." He swept another pile of glass into the dustpan, dumped the glass into the trashcan, and wiped his hand on his trousers before offering it to me. "Hi, I'm Sim Johnson. Gert said you were the detective. I missed all the excitement at Royalle's 'cause I was off skiing."

"David Randall. This is Camden. What do you know about the Avenger?"

"Just what I read in the *Herald*. But he's bound to know the city inside and out, so he can be ready to stop the bad guys."

"He hasn't been very successful so far."

"But think about it. We weren't cleaned out at Royalle's. Maybe the Avenger surprised the crook before he could take more stuff. And Carlene, the thief didn't get the money in your register, did he? Why's this guy so picky? I think the Avenger shows up and scares him away."

Right now, it was as good a theory as any. "So how does the Avenger know where the thief's going to be?"

Sim picked a large piece of glass from the top of a cassette display. "Well, if he's a real superhero, he's out patrolling the city every night. Plus he's probably got this magical sixth sense about crime."

All this talk of superheroes gave me an idea. "You sound like someone who enjoys comic books."

He shrugged. "I've got a few."

"Know anything about them?"

"Yeah, I'm pretty good."

"You know Comic World in the Fair Oaks Mall?"

"I go there all the time."

"I need an expert's opinion on some comics. Would Mister Royalle let you have the afternoon off?"

Sim thought it over. "I promised him I'd help Carlene clean up, but I get off work at five today. Comic World's open till eight, if you want to go later."

"Meet me over there after work."

"Does this have something to do with the crime?"

"No, this is another case I'm working on."

I could tell Sim liked the sound of this. "Yeah, sure, I'd be glad to help."

"See you at five-thirty."

I asked Carlene if she wanted us to stay. She said her relatives were coming by with some plywood to patch the hole until she had a new window put in.

"I'll be all right, David, thank you."

Sim continued his sweeping. "And I'm here if she needs anything."

"I'll talk to you later," I told Carlene. "I think these two robberies are definitely connected."

◇◇◇

We went across to Royalle's. Gert Fagan was cleaning the glass cases and paused, her dust cloth in one hand, a spray bottle of glass cleaner in the other.

"Isn't that awful about Carlene's? Thank goodness she wasn't there. Is she all right? I told Sim to stay as long as she needed him."

"She'll be okay."

"I've been trying to think of anyone who might have a grudge against us," she said. "I've gone over our customer list and our special orders for the past two months. Everyone has been satisfied with his or her jewelry."

"So no one's come to the door to fling a defective bracelet at your heads?"

"That's right."

"No one casting longing glances at a ring he can't afford?"

"No one. It's very upsetting. Oh, J.C. is here, if you want to talk to her."

I expected J.C. Chapman to be a young man, but she was a severe-looking young teenage girl, her red hair pulled back in a tight bun. She wore no make-up and no jewelry. She had on a black dress and a black sweater. She came right up to me and shook my hand.

"I'm Josephine Clifford Chapman, but everyone calls me J.C., because I absolutely hate the name Josephine. I don't know what my parents were thinking, because there's no one named Josephine in our family. I've been a part-time employee here for the last four years. I'm very dependable, and everyone likes me. As you can see, I don't wear jewelry, so I'd have no reason to steal any. I'm not allowed to lock up, so I don't know where the alarm is, and neither does Sim, in case you're thinking he had anything to do with this. I really think you ought to be looking somewhere else for the criminal, because it isn't any one of us, and by the way, you're really good-looking."

"Thank you," I said. "No further questions."

J.C. gave me an approving nod and went back to the cash register. I caught Gert's eye. She was smiling.

"J.C. is very forthright."

"I appreciate that."

Our next stop was Boyd Taylor's house. His sagging face brightened when he saw Camden.

"Didn't think you'd come."

He stood aside to let us enter his depressing little house. The debris hadn't changed. He pushed a pile of newspapers off the green sofa.

"Have a seat. Get you guys a beer?"

"No, thanks," I said. Camden shook his head.

Taylor looked at me and then at Camden. "I don't know how this works. You need to go into a trance or something?"

"I'll just sit down for a minute." Camden sat on the arm of the sofa.

Taylor's eyes gleamed with hope. "You gotta know I didn't do it."

"I'm not sure of anything."

"I had no quarrel with Jared. I came over to see about the car. I was in the house calling for help when you came by. Didn't you sense that, or something?"

"Seeing Jared like that was a shock."

"Yeah, but you must've gotten some kind of vibe about the murderer. He must've just left." Taylor paced in front of the sofa. "Look, man, I'm desperate to even half believe this crap. Didn't you see anything that could prove it wasn't me? I mean, what's my motive here? Why would I kill the guy? And if I did, why not jump in the car and drive the hell away?"

Camden looked up at the craggy face. "I don't know, Boyd. I wish I did. Things are pretty confused right now."

Taylor looked around the cramped room in frustration. "Do you need a crystal ball? A Ouija board? What does it take?"

"What were you wearing that day?" I asked. "Sometimes he can pick up things from an object of clothing."

"My jacket, I guess."

He dug a battered-looking khaki jacket from a heap of clothes near the door. Camden took it, but after a few minutes, shook his head.

I could tell Taylor was getting frustrated. "Give him a minute," I said.

He ran his large hand over his face, pulling it down into more lines. "God Almighty."

"Give me your hand," Camden said. He held the large hand, stiffening slightly as he did. "It's okay. We're all under a little stress."

If he said Boyd's the murderer, I was ready to run, but he shook his head.

"The anger's there and a lot of sadness, but—"

He took so long to answer, I said, "But what?"

Camden's gaze was thoughtful. "But no blood."

Taylor sat back. "Told you I didn't do it."

"Boyd, we'll do all we can to help you," I said, "but you can't depend on any miracles from the Great Beyond."

"Yeah." He took a deep breath. "I thought—well, I have to try everything I can think of."

Once Camden and I were back in the car, I said, "He didn't do it, did he?"

"No. But you're going to have to prove it."

Chapter Nine

"And Thy Words Unto the Ends of the World"

Sim Johnson hadn't arrived at Comic World yet, but to my surprise, Brooke Verner was there, flipping through an issue of "Danger Woman."

"Brooke, what are you doing here?"

She put the comic back on the shelf. "Gathering clues. The Avenger's bound to be a comics fan. How else would he know how to dress?"

"I thought you knew all about the Avenger."

"I just report his moves."

I started to say something else when I heard Camden say, "Hello, Wendy," and I saw a gorgeous woman come down the aisle.

I'm often amazed by the women Camden knows, or who know him. Amazed, because he's settled on Ellin. Wendy Riskin was a tall sizzling redhead in a black form-fitting dress and black tights and acres of gold bracelets. She shook back a mass of magenta curls Medusa would've been proud to own and put all ten sharp little red nails on Camden's shoulders.

"Where have you been? I haven't seen you in ages. You are going to Flaming Panels, aren't you? I told everyone you'd be there, and don't give me any of your lame excuses about not driving. Tor, you'd better have the new 'Silver Wonder,' or I'm calling down all my powers on your pitiful little store."

Tor was already groping through the file cabinets. "It's here, it's here, hold on."

"And could we please have some decent music on in here? Sounds like somebody in the last stages of emphysema."

Tor wasn't going to argue with her about anything. "You can change it, if you like."

She strode to a small closet between two racks of comics, rooted through the CDs, found one she liked, and popped it into the player. Something electronic with a heavy beat echoed through the store. "That's better."

Camden introduced Miss Flame Thrower. "Wendy, this is David Randall. Randall, Wendy Riskin, also known as the Goddess of Destruction."

"Better believe it," she said.

"Pleasure to make your acquaintance, Miss Destruction."

She smiled and looked me up and down. "Pleasure's all mine."

"It could be."

"Oo, a flirt. You don't meet many of those these days. Everyone's so PC. Are you by any chance Cam's detective friend? Are you hot on the trail of a master criminal today? Perhaps a major fiend who wants to rule the world?"

"I'm looking for the Parkland Avenger."

"The Avenger?" She dismissed him with a wave of her red-tipped fingers. "Pooh, what an amateur."

Brooke turned. "An amateur? What makes you say that?"

"Skulking around at night. That's for babies. Skulking in broad daylight, now, that's more like it."

"Is that what you do?"

Wendy wasn't put off by Brooke's tone. "Yeah. I skulk. I'm a damned good skulker. Ask anyone."

"Do you know anything about the Avenger?"

"If I did, I wouldn't tell you. You'd rat on him."

"You're wrong. I'm on his side. I think it's about time someone upheld the law in Parkland."

Wendy laughed. "Seems to me this guy's just getting in the way. Maybe you oughta hire someone more competent."

"Hire someone? You think this is all a set-up?"

"Sure, why not? Some doofus runs around in a cape, you write the stories, get some publicity. Sounds like a set-up to me. Not a very original one."

By now, the women were eye to eye and snarling.

Wendy's comic book flapped in Tor's shaking hands. "Take it outside. Wendy, please. My other customers."

She looked around. "What other customers, Tor? Are you counting those two nerds in the back, hoping to find a 'Superman Number One' in your bargain sacks? Let me finish off this skinny twerp."

Brooke swelled. "I'm not afraid of you."

"Big deal."

"Maybe you're protecting someone. Maybe you're the Avenger."

"I'd like to see you prove that."

Wendy was definitely fit and she knew all the superhero lore. Still, reports indicated the Avenger was a man. Reports written by Brooke. Were Brooke and Wendy in this together? Judging from the dirty looks, I'd say no.

"Whoever this guy is, he's really stupid. He's getting in the way." Wendy took the comic book Tor held out like a peace offering. "Give me that." Then she gave Camden a kiss that left every male in the store reeling. "Sayonara, boys." She sauntered out.

Camden steadied himself on the counter. "I don't think Wendy is the Avenger."

Brooke glared after Wendy. "With all that extra weight, she'd never be able to leap from rooftops."

She made her exit as Sim burst in. "Sorry I'm late! Where's the stuff you wanted me to see? Hi, Mister Norris."

Now that the dueling divas had left, Tor calmed down. "Afternoon, Sim."

"I'm going to look at some comics for Mister Randall, if that's all right with you."

"They're in the back."

I took Sim to the back and waited as he carefully inspected each one of Jared Hunter's comic books. Occasionally, he'd make a remark like, "Wow, 'Tales of the Styx,' number thirty. You don't see that every day," or, "I used to have this!"

When he finally came to the end, I said, "What do you think?"

"Well, it's a nice collection, but I know lots of guys with better. I don't think this guy was real serious. He bought what he liked. There's no theme or anything. He doesn't have just superheroes or DC or Marvel. He's got a little bit of everything."

"What would you guess a collection like this would be worth?"

He looked at the boxes, frowning in thought. I could see him mentally adding. "I'd say about five hundred dollars. The 'Danger Ranger' is in mint condition, and 'Betty and Her Pets' is an acquired taste, if you know what I mean, so, depending on who wants them, maybe six, seven hundred, tops. How come you didn't get Mister Norris to price them for you? He's an expert."

"I wanted a second opinion." And someone who wasn't directly involved with Jared Hunter.

Sim looked flattered. "You ought to see my collection. It beats this one all hollow—although, I wouldn't mind having the 'Tales of the Styx.'" He dug through the boxes until he found the comic. "Think anyone'd mind if I read it?"

"No, go right ahead."

I went back to the counter. Camden was looking through more of Tor's sketches.

"Find anything?"

"Sim thinks the collection's worth about six hundred dollars. That sound right?"

"Yeah, the kid's got a good eye."

"You planning to sell it?"

"Thought I'd keep most of it. There's a show next month in Asheville, so I'll probably sell some of it there."

Sim came up to the counter. "Guys, this is kinda funny." He held up "Tales of the Styx." "What's this supposed to be?" He opened the comic. A torn piece of paper was stuck inside.

I pulled it out. The paper had a faded imprint of lines and arrows. "Well, at first glance, it looks like part of a map. Know what this is, Tor?"

He gave the paper a glance. "No."

Camden and I went to the back with Sim. We opened all the comic bags and looked through each comic, but we didn't find any more pieces.

"A map to what?" Camden asked. "You think it came with this particular comic, and you were supposed to collect all the pieces?"

"I would've remembered a contest like that," Sim said. "It must belong to guy who brought in these comics. You could ask him."

Camden had to look away.

Sim lowered his voice. "Did I say something wrong?"

I put the comics back in their bags. "The man who owned these comics was murdered. I'm trying to find out why."

Sim dropped the comic he was holding. "Murdered? Over these?"

"We're not sure."

"But there's nothing valuable here, not really, unless this is some kind of treasure map, and then you'd need the rest of it."

We went back to the counter. "Mind if I take this?" I asked Tor.

He was sketching and didn't even look up. "Go ahead."

I thanked Sim for his help. He said he'd keep an eye out for any more clues. "Sim's on the trail, but Tor didn't seem very interested," I said as Camden and I got into the car. "You getting anything from that paper?"

Camden held the piece of paper for a long while. "It really is part of a map." He turned the paper sideways. "The writing here says 'Old P.'"

"Old Parkland, maybe? Now that would be interesting, considering most of the recent break ins have been in the Old Parkland district."

"Randall, I can't believe Jared was planning a series of robberies."

"First let's find out if this really is a map of Old Parkland. Don't you think Mom would enjoy a trip to the history museum?"

"That's a great idea."

I got out my phone. "I have another great idea. I'll ask Kary to do some research on Old Parkland at the library."

"If you don't ask her to do something soon, she's going to be breaking down doors and taking names."

"I'm not sure how deeply I want her to get involved."

"She's already involved."

"The library should be safe enough." Kary must have been in class because her phone went to voice mail. "Kary, I need whatever information you can find on Old Parkland. A map would be especially helpful. We found a piece of map in one of Jared's comics. Thanks."

Camden gestured for the phone, and when I handed it over, he added, "It's a real clue this time, Kary."

I took my phone back. "And not busy work, I promise."

At the studio, Camden paused to talk to Bonnie and Teresa, the two attractive women who take turns hosting the PSN television shows. I found my mother in Ellin's office doing her specialty: interfering. When I heard their topic of conversation, I paused just outside the doorway to listen. Mom was trying to play Cupid.

"Why in the world are you hesitating, dear? It's obvious he's crazy about you."

Ellin sounded a lot calmer than usual. "I don't know. I know in my heart he's the right one for me, and I want to make this work. He's just so different from what I had in mind."

"Different in what way?"

"In every way. I've always had this idea of the man I'd marry, and Cam doesn't fit a single characteristic."

Mom laughed. "Oh, I see. Yes, I always planned to marry a man just like Cary Grant."

"I take it Randall's father wasn't like that?"

"Not at all. Henry was never serious. Sometimes I wanted to smack him, but he would've laughed at that, too. He was a big cheerful man, not at all brooding. Handsome, very lively and talkative. I suppose it was from all those years tending bars and talking to the customers. My goodness, how I miss all that chatter. I never thought I would, but I do."

I do, too, Mom.

"He sounds like a wonderful man, Sophia."

"Yes, I was very lucky."

"I wish Cam had a little more drive, more ambition. He seems content to stay where he is in life."

And what's wrong with that? I thought. At least he's content and not all squirrelly like you.

"Is there someone else?"

Yeah, I'd like to hear the answer to that question. It didn't surprise me that Ellin mentioned her work.

"No, not unless you count the PSN. I've built this network up from nothing, and its success means a great deal to me. It's the one thing I've really accomplished on my own, and how I look had nothing to do with it."

"How you look?"

"Being the youngest and only blonde in a family of brunettes has been impossible. 'Well, of course you got an A, Ellin. All you had to do was bat your eyes.' I could never get beyond my appearance. No one could. But the network is all mine. I wish Cam would be more supportive."

"In what way?"

"He could be a huge star. Every time I manage to get him on a program, there's a terrific response. Our ratings shoot way up. But he never wants to be on TV. I don't understand it. We could build a whole series around him, but as I said, he has no ambition. He likes everything to be exactly the same. He eats two brown sugar Pop-Tarts and drinks a glass of Coke for breakfast every single morning. He works at Tamara's, comes home, does some repairs on the house, reads, watches TV, eats supper, and then looks out his telescope for an hour before he goes to bed. I know his early years were chaotic, but this is taking things to the other extreme."

"There's something to be said for a calm routine life."

Amen, Mom. You tell her.

"Except when Randall involves him in some ridiculous case."

Oh, I knew eventually we'd get around to Evil Me.

"Sorry, Sophia, but your son manages to find the stupidest crimes, like songwriters back from the dead, and here's Cam, stuck in the middle because he won't say no. Oh, he'll say no to me, but with Randall, it's always how far and how high."

As Mom chuckled, I made my presence known. "Hi, there. Ready to go home?"

"Davey, we were just talking about you."

I grinned at Ellin, who tried to look pleasant in front of my mother. "Yes, Randall, we were just saying what a good influence you are on the world."

I gave her my most modest look. "I try. Mom, let me treat you to the best hot dog in town."

"Sounds wonderful," she said. "See you later, Ellin."

I took Mom to Janice Chan's. Janice owns and operates one of the few restaurants left downtown. Her specialty is hot dogs. The little brick building was full of fragrant steam that clouded the windows. Janice saw us come in and gave me a nod. She was occupied, as usual, with four customers at once. As soon as she'd scooped three hot dogs in a bag for one man, handed another bag to a second man, plopped a fully loaded dog in front of a large woman, and set a tray full of hot dogs and slaw onto one of the small tables for a family, she came up, smiling and tucking her long black hair behind one ear.

"Janice, this is my mother, Sophia, visiting from Florida. Mom, this is Janice Chan."

Janice took her pad from her pocket and a pencil from behind her other ear. "Pleasure to meet you. What will you have?"

"Two all the way, hold the onions on one. Coke or coffee, Mom?"

"Coffee, please."

Janice was back in a few minutes with our order. As I bit into the juicy hot dog surrounded by mustard, slaw, chili, and onions, I wondered how in the world Alycia fit into these crimes. She was just as elusive as the Parkland Avenger. Come to think of it, maybe she was the Parkland Avenger. And this map. Did it have anything to do with this case?

"Davey." From Mom's tone, I could tell this wasn't the first time she'd said my name.

I gave her my attention. "Sorry. Thinking about my case."

"These cases of yours don't sound like very much."

"They never start out that way. By the time I solve them, usually they've gotten way out of hand."

She wiped mustard from her mouth. "I don't like you putting yourself in danger. All this about murders and people running around like Batman."

"That's what makes it interesting. Another hot dog for you?"

"No, thank you. This is very good, but one is enough."

I wanted to change the subject before I got a lecture about my dubious career. "Parkland has a really good history museum. Sound interesting? We could go tomorrow."

"Yes, I'd like that."

We ate for a while and I thought of something else I wanted to ask her. "Mom, whatever happened to Dad's pocket watch, the one that played 'Twelfth Street Rag'?"

She wiped traces of chili off her fingers. "My goodness. I haven't thought of that in years. I suppose your Uncle Louie has it. Why?"

"I always thought it was neat."

"You want me to call Louie? Do you want it?"

I couldn't hide my expression.

"Of course you want it. You don't have that many things of your father's, do you? I'll call him as soon as we get home."

"I remember every night after reading me a bedtime story, he used to take it out and let it play. Maybe that's why I like jazz."

"Maybe that's why you like people. You had a father who read to you every night. You were damn lucky, David Henry Randall."

I leaned over to kiss her cheek. "I still am."

Chapter Ten

"All We Like Sheep Have Gone Astray"

I brought Mom home and she went upstairs. Kary got home a few minutes later. She sat down at the kitchen counter, accepted her Diet Coke, and told me her news.

"I got your message, thanks. I talked with the reference librarian at the public library. Most of the older historical documents aren't in the general collection, but she said she'd look in all of them and see what she could find."

"That's great, thanks. It'll save me a lot of time."

"What have you found out?"

I'd learned my lesson. I was going to be straight with her from now on. "I had a talk with Boyd Taylor. He says he's innocent, and so does Camden. The guys at Ben's Garage remember a woman fitting Alycia Ward's description who came to see Jared and basically called him a coward for some reason. And as I told you earlier, we found a piece of a map in Jared's comics he left at Comic World."

"And you think this map will help connect all these incidents?"

"Or at least explain some of them." I took the little scrap of paper with "Old P." on it out of my pocket and showed it to her. "When are you going back to the library?"

"Tomorrow afternoon."

"Take this with you and see if it matches anything they have."

"I'll be very careful with it."

"And my apologies for being elusive."

"'Elusive.' That's what? Ten points?"

"Camden would give me only five for that one." I felt myself relax. I hadn't realized how tight my shoulders were, hoping she'd accept this apology.

"You said a woman fitting Alycia's description stopped by the garage. What does Alycia look like?"

"She's a tall black woman, attractive, athletic."

"Were she and Jared a couple? Why do you think she called him a coward?"

"I don't know. The guys at the garage said he didn't want to talk to her."

"They must have quarreled."

"If that's the case, it doesn't look good for Alycia."

"Camden believes Boyd Taylor is innocent?"

"He said Boyd didn't do it. But you know Camden's impressions won't work for Jordan."

"That leaves Alycia. Maybe it was a crime of passion."

That would explain the many stab wounds. "Or somebody wanted it to look like one. The problem is, we don't know very much about Jared except he was a few years ahead of Camden at the Green Valley Home for Boys. He could have made a lot of enemies. 'Old P' could be a drug dealer for all we know."

"Wouldn't Cam have picked up on that?" She reached for the phone book. "Have you called Green Valley?"

"That's something else you could do."

She turned to the Yellow Pages. "Where's Cam? How's he been today?"

"He was okay, but I left him at the studio. Ellin said she'd bring him home. We'll see what sort of state he's in then."

Kary paused for a moment in her search. "She really loves him, you know."

And I really love you, I wanted to say. I love the way you're all fired up about solving this case. I love the way you believe the best in everyone.

She turned a few more pages. "By the way, where's Sophia?"

"She's upstairs." Talking to Grady, no doubt. I unclenched my teeth. "I thought I'd treat everyone to my famous chicken pie tonight."

"Excellent idea. Oh, here's the number." She punched it in and listened for a while. "Their office is closed for today. I'll try again tomorrow." She hung up the phone. "Anything else?"

"Marry me."

"Besides that?"

"Accept my proposal."

"Or that?"

"Become Mrs. David Randall."

She patted my arm. "You'd better get started on that pie."

The next morning, I found Brooke Verner sitting in my office, filing her nails and looking as if she owned the place.

"Out," I said.

She got annoyed. "What is with you?"

"Pardon the pun, Brooke, but you're bad news. I don't want to have anything to do with you or your schemes."

"Not even if I have information that will help your case?"

"Such as?"

She waggled a finger. "Huh-uh. You've got to give me something in return."

I could think of several things. My expression must have conveyed this, because she shivered in mock fear.

"Oo, the big bad detective is going to get rough, is he? Then you'll never find out what I know about Jared Hunter."

"Withholding evidence always goes over really big with the Parkland PD."

She put her fingernail file away and fluffed her hair. "You help me find the Avenger and I'll tell you."

"But you already know who the Avenger is. You're paying someone to leap around at night so you can write your stories."

"Why does everyone assume I'm that stupid?"

"Because you want a Parkie award, and I think you'll do anything to get one."

She tried to look uninterested, but she couldn't fool me. "Why would I want one of those ridiculous plastic statues?"

"Why do I want you out of here? Because it would make me happy. Scram."

She got up and huffed out, pausing at the door to say, "I suppose you don't care who killed Jared Hunter."

"Any information you have would be highly suspect."

A few minutes later, Camden looked in. "Was Brooke here?"

"Yes. I'm going to have to sleep with her to get her off my back."

"That conjures up an interesting picture."

"You know what I mean. Don't women understand that when a man says no, he means no?"

"Where are you going today?"

I checked my calendar. "Mom to the museum, Winthrop at three, Auto Club tonight."

"I've got to get a Christmas present for Ellie."

"You mean you haven't done that already?"

"She's been deciding what she wants."

"Besides the moon? How about a ride down to Royalle's Fine Jewelry? When do you have to be at work?"

"One."

"No problem. We can stop by after our museum tour. I need to talk to Petey, anyway."

He started out and then came back. "Oh, Lily says she might be able to help with the Avenger case."

"Don't tell me: she shared a saucer with him."

"A member of the ASG also belongs to the SHS."

ASG stands for Abductees Support Group, an organization of deluded souls who believe they've been taken up in UFOs. Camden's neighbor, Lily Wilkes, is the founding mother and guiding light. "Do I really want to know what SHS is?"

He was enjoying this way too much. "Superhero Society."

"You mean Parkland has its own Justice League?"

"They meet every Friday at four thirty. You can easily fit them in today."

"You're making this up."

"No, I'm not. Lily says they'll be delighted to talk to you. They're very concerned about the Avenger."

"So he's not one of them? He's a rogue Avenger?"

"Lily says they feel he's giving superheroes a bad name by not cooperating with the police."

If there's any sort of deviant in Parkland, eventually I get to shake his hand. "Where do they meet?"

"They're at Lily's today."

"Great. I'll pick up a mask and a cape while I'm out. Is my mom ready to go?"

"She's reading the paper."

"If you can call it that," Mom said when I walked into the island. "What in the world is this 'Your Turn' section? Are these letters for real?"

"I'm afraid so, Mom. Parkland at its best."

"But it's so ridiculous. Listen to this one: 'You are not putting the landfill near Sherman Glen because of the buzzards and rats. You are putting it there because you think we won't protest. Well, I protest hardly.' Do you suppose the poor soul meant 'heartily'? Doesn't anyone proofread these? Oh, and I love this one. 'A big thank you to the man who stopped and helped my daughter-in-law change a flat tire on the highway this past weekend. What a kind jester.' At first, I thought they meant a fool in cap and bells was out changing tires, and that I wanted to see. They meant 'gesture.'"

Baseford had fumed about the lack of proofreading, but I thought the jester was pretty funny. "I can't imagine how that one slipped by."

Fred squinted at the paper. "And what's this about voting a tax on cigarettes? They didn't let me vote. I smoke, and I ain't paying no taxes. See if I vote for Hoover again."

She tried to explain. "Fred, Herbert Hoover isn't president anymore."

"Kennedy, then. I like him. He's all for the space program. When are we gonna get into space, that's what I'd like to know."

"Fred, you're already into space," I said. "Let's go, Mom."

Parkland has several museums, but the one I was interested in was the Parkland Museum of History, which chronicles the rise of the city from railroad stop to bustling metropolis.

As we paid for admission, Mom said, "You boys don't have to stay. I can look at exhibits by myself."

"I don't mind," I said. "I haven't seen this museum."

"Me, either," Camden said.

We started with prehistoric Parkland, a wilderness full of deer and bears and an obscure Indian tribe that no longer exists. Then we moved on to Early Parkland, a muddy stop on the road called Park's Hollow. Museum artists had sketched three small buildings and a barn located where Main Street runs now. The next exhibit was called "The Railroad Years." Life comes at last to Park's Hollow. Faded photographs showed groups of serious-looking men standing in front of an old locomotive, more men hammering away at the tracks, other men posed in the front porch of the Park Hotel. One of the informative posters told us that Park's Hollow grew from thirty-five people to over two hundred in just a month, the town was formed, and a great-great grandson of the original Park family, Charles Park, was elected mayor. There was a large display of Civil War artifacts and weapons, including information on the Underground Railroad, General Nathaniel Greene, and a famous battle near the river, where several members of the Park family fought valiantly and died. On May 15, 1887, the town was officially called Parkland.

The next display was devoted to Charles Park and his family. We saw photographs, articles of clothing, and personal items, including Mister Park's pocket watch.

"That reminds me," Mom said. "Louie says he doesn't have your father's pocket watch. He doesn't know where it is."

"That's okay."

"No, it isn't. I really want to know what happened to it. I'll call Thomasina. Maybe she knows where it is."

Parkland progressed through the ages, growing steadily through the Twenties, taking a hit in the Thirties, going to war in the Forties, booming in the Fifties.

Camden pointed to a photograph. "Here's old downtown. It hasn't changed much, at all. There's Royalle's, and Moore's Hardware, and the bank."

I was more interested in a collection of old blueprints and schematic drawings. "This is a pretty detailed map of the old shoe store and the cafe. Do you see one for Royalle's?"

"Just this photo."

The drawing for the shoe store showed every detail, including what looked like a tunnel connecting it to the shop next door. "I think a drawing like this could be very handy."

While Mom checked on Parkland in the Sixties, Camden and I went in search of a museum employee. The young woman at the front desk directed us to the curator's office. The curator, a thin scholarly looking man, looked up from a pile of old photos, and smiled.

"Can I help you?"

"Do you have the old schematic drawings for other buildings on Main Street?" I asked. "Or possibly a map? I'm interested in Royalle's Fine Jewelry and Moore's Hardware, specifically."

"I wish we did," he said. "There used to be a whole set. We had all of them stored in the back, but when it came time to put them on display, most of them had crumbled. Sometimes, despite all our best efforts, paper items are too fragile. And unfortunately, a lot of things were destroyed during the robbery."

"What can you tell us about that?"

"About a year ago, a couple of people broke in. We're not sure what they were after, but they didn't get away with anything. The police caught one of them. However, they made a huge mess. As you can imagine, we have hundreds of items in the back waiting to be catalogued." He gestured to the stack of photos. "Here's an example. People donate items, and we have to sift through them to see if there's anything of historic value. Well, we came in the next morning to find practically everything in the department on the floor."

Jared's unfortunate brush with the law. "Did the thieves get anything valuable?"

"No, thank goodness. We have Charles Park's gold cufflinks, lots of jewelry, old money that's very rare, antique guns and swords. They didn't come anywhere near those items. We were lucky these robbers were so clueless. The paper you're looking for probably got crushed underfoot when they tried to get away. However, you might try the city offices or the courthouse. A lot of times they have duplicate records."

We thanked the curator and found Mom all the way up to the Eighties. "This is fascinating, Davey. Did you know your old movie theater was once a vaudeville house and then a disco? Seems to me you and Barbara enjoyed dancing."

"We did for a while." We enjoyed a lot of things for a while: dancing, hiking, being a family. That was over and gone.

We reached the last exhibits. Mom admired the display of Parkland Now with the three tall buildings people like to call skyscrapers. "Well, here we are: Modern Parkland. It's a lovely city."

"With plenty of room, if you want to stay."

"That's sweet, dear, but I'll be heading back to Florida."

And to Grady, I thought, but I didn't say it. "Camden needs to get Ellin a Christmas present. Do you mind if we stop by the jewelry store?"

"Do I ever say no to a jewelry store?"

Royalle's was crowded with Christmas shoppers. Gert, J.C., and Sim all greeted me. I introduced Mom and Camden and told Gert we needed a gift for Camden's girlfriend. While she showed him an array of glittery things, Mom checked out the rings. I showed Camden the pocket watch.

"This is like Dad's." Sim got it out of the case for me. I opened it, and "Grandpa's Spells" rang out. "Dad's played 'Twelfth Street Rag.'"

Mom took the watch for closer inspection. "Somebody in the family must have it. This is going to worry me until I find out who. How much is that one, Davey?"

"Fifteen hundred."

"Oo, my. Put it back."

Camden looked at the tray of rings. I knew he wanted to buy one. "Go ahead and do it."

"An engagement ring at Christmas is so romantic," Gert said, "and we have these beautiful little gold boxes."

He shook his head. "I'm not sure."

"Are you kidding? You know she'd take it."

"Maybe."

"Now, don't rush him," Mom said. "It's huge decision. You ought to know that, David."

Camden reached for one of the sapphires, and then stopped. "I'd really like to choose one she's picked out."

"So drag her in here," I said.

Camden smiled at Gert Fagan, who was poised to wrap up his choice. "Thanks, but I need to think about it some more."

"Of course," she said.

No sale at Royalle's today.

There was a burst of laughter at the other counter. Sim had gone to the back and returned dressed as an elf. Not to be outdone, J.C. appeared in a Santa hat that spelled out "Merry Christmas" in flashing lights. The customers laughed and made admiring comments. Petey looked cheerful and relaxed.

Gert chuckled as Sim attempted an elf dance. "They knew Petey needed a laugh today."

"The hat's a nice touch," I said.

Petey came over, and I introduced him to Mom. While she was enjoying more of Sim's antics, I told Petey what I'd found out so far.

"I think the robbery at Carlene's rules out your employees," I said. "Do you have any blueprints or drawings of this store?"

"My dad has all that stuff. He keeps saying he wants to write the history of Royalle's."

"What's under the store?"

"A basement, but it's very old. I keep some things down there, but nothing valuable. Cleaning supplies, light bulbs, extra cardboard boxes."

"Is it possible there's a tunnel connecting Royalle's to another store?"

"A tunnel?"

"Mom and I were touring the museum, and I saw a map of this area of town with several tunnels."

"I've never heard of any, but if they exist, my dad would know about it."

"I'd like to talk with him."

"Let me write down his number. Oh, and I talked with several other jewelry shop owners in town. They don't remember a Jared Hunter, sorry. Maybe he had another source for his jewelry."

Maybe he stole it, I thought, but I hoped that wasn't the case.

Mom came back, still beaming at the kids. "They look adorable. David, you used to dress up as an elf, remember?"

"No, Mom. I've blanked out that time of my life."

"I'd like to hear about that," Camden said.

"Forget it." Petey handed me a piece of paper with his father's phone number. "Thanks, Petey. Mom, are you ready for lunch?"

"I'm always ready for lunch."

I told Petey I'd check with him later, sent Camden a look and a message that said, "Mention the elf and die," and held the door for Mom. "Let's go to the Elms."

Chapter Eleven

"Lift up Thy Voice With Strength"

The Elms is one of my favorite restaurants. It's not too fancy. The tables are separated by palms and other plants, so you always have privacy. We managed to beat the lunch crowd and waited only a few minutes for a table.

Mom opened her menu. "Now we have to think of something for Ellin. Leave it to me."

I can see it now: a leopard print thong.

"I want to hear about Randall the Christmas Elf," Camden said.

Unfortunately, the Elms has a policy against strangling your friends at the table. "Did you not hear the special thought I sent your way?"

Mom patted my arm. "Oh, he was the dearest thing. You see, his father always dressed up as Santa and went through the neighborhood. When David was old enough, we dressed him up as a little elf and let him go along."

Camden gave me his most innocent look. "I don't know why you never shared this special Christmas memory. You wouldn't happen to have any pictures, would you, Sophia?"

"I'm sure I do. I'll send you one. That reminds me, I want to take pictures of everyone to show Grady."

I swear I could hear my back teeth grind. If I didn't change the subject, we'd be having a Grady lunch. "Isn't there anything at Tamara's Ellin would like?"

Camden wasn't sure. "Ellie tends to dress a little more conservatively. Besides, have you seen the prices on Tamara's stuff?"

"Don't you get a discount?"

"I can wear only so many pairs of stiletto heels."

"I thought you looked taller."

Mom had a few suggestions. "Perhaps something for her office. She's quite the career girl. A nice attaché case?"

"I was hoping to find something a little more romantic," Camden said.

The waitress came for our order. Mom decided on the grilled chicken salad. I ordered a club sandwich and fries. Camden chose a cheeseburger, and everyone had iced tea.

The waitress took our menus. "Be right back with your drinks."

Mom unwrapped her silverware from her napkin. "Well, there's always lingerie. Do you want to get that personal?"

I grinned. "They can't get any more personal."

Camden had to admit there was a nightgown at Tamara's he liked. "But it's all pink lace, very fancy."

"That sounds perfect, dear. She'll love it."

"You think so? That's how I see her."

"Trust me. After lunch, we'll go right out and buy it. And speaking of Christmas presents, David, what do you want? I have a few small things, but is there something special you have your eye on?"

Well, how about my old mother back? No, that wasn't fair. Hadn't I told her I wanted her to be happy? "Got everything I need, Mom."

"I think you could use a few more good shirts. What about you, Cam? Your wardrobe seems a bit thin."

I thought he might say, "A new brain, please," but he said, "I'm fine, Sophia, really. You don't have to get me anything."

"Well, I'm going to, anyway. And what would Kary like?"

A baby. A child. The one thing I can't give her. I passed Camden the sugar packets. "Anything that has to do with music."

"Good. I love to shop."

The waitress arrived with our tea. As soon as she'd gone, Mom settled back in her seat and folded her arms.

"All right, boys. What's going on with the murder case? Have you had another bad spell, Cam?"

He looked surprised. "Why do you say that?"

"You put five packets of sugar in that tea, and it's already sweetened."

I unwrapped my straw. "That's normal."

I got a sharp glance from her. "Well, something's happened. I can tell."

"We stopped by Boyd Taylor's," I said.

"Isn't Taylor the alleged murderer?"

How does she know these things? "We don't think he did it."

She took a drink. "You don't 'think' he did it? But he could have, right? And the two of you just wandered in to say hello?"

"Mom, you really don't have to get involved with this."

Whoops. Wrong thing to say.

Her dark eyes flashed. "Now you listen to me, David Henry Randall. If you insist on pursuing a potentially hazardous career, then you'd better believe I'm going to be involved. Finding things for people is one thing, but I told you at that hot dog place you don't need to fool around with murder."

When she gets like this, it's better just to nod and agree. "Yes, ma'am."

She turned to Camden. "What's your full name?"

He usually doesn't tell anyone, but she startled him. "John Michael Camden."

"John Michael Camden, this goes for you, too."

"Yes, ma'am."

"Where else did you go yesterday?" she asked me.

The waitress brought our food, so Mom had to wait until she'd gone before I could answer.

"We went by the comic book store. Jared left some comics there, and we looked through them."

"I know that's not all."

"Well, yesterday morning, I spoke with Jared's co-workers at the auto shop, checked out Winthrop, Incorporated, the company that manufactured Petey Royalle's burglar alarm, and talked with Carlene Jessup about a break in at her record store."

She stirred salad dressing into her salad and took a bite. "Do you think any of these things might be related?"

"The two break ins have similarities."

"How so?"

"At Petey's and at Carlene's, the burglar knew inside stuff, like how to disable the alarm and where a secret panel is to get in. I don't know how he or she is getting that kind of information."

"One of the staff, of course."

"I've talked to everyone at Royalle's. No one has a motive. They like working there."

"What about Carlene's employees?"

"Family members. No motive there, either. Don't you want to talk Christmas instead of crime?"

"Not really. If you boys are getting into dangerous territory, I think it's best to solve the mystery and get out. What did you find out at the museum?"

I turned to Camden. "You see why I could never get away with anything?"

"I think Sophia is psychic, too."

I gave Mom my attention. "We found out there are some tunnels underneath Parkland. It's possible the thief is using these tunnels to get into the stores. After lunch, I'm going to call Petey's father and see if he can tell me more."

"And when you find out about these tunnels, what then? Don't even think about going down underground. There could be whole tribes of murderers and thieves."

Well, of course, I'd want to explore, but I sure as hell wasn't going to say that. "I'll call Jordan Finley at the police department and let him take it from there."

"I didn't realize you worked with the police department."

"Jordan and I share information." When we have to. "He'll be the first one I call." After I'd had a look.

Thank goodness Mom isn't really psychic and couldn't hear my real thoughts. "All right. That sounds like a reasonable plan. Promise me you won't do anything foolish. You, either, Cam."

"We won't," I said. "Can we talk about Christmas now?"

"Cam, did I tell you about the time when Davey was four years old and mistook the Baby Jesus for Mickey Mouse?"

I groaned. "It was that halo thing. That plastic circle around the baby's head."

"No, you didn't, Sophia," Camden said. "I would love to hear that story."

"Can I help it if it looked like mouse ears?"

After lunch and many more embarrassing stories, I took Mom and Camden to Tamara's and then called Petey's father, Carlton Royalle, told him who I was, and asked about tunnels.

"Tunnels?" he said. "I think I'd know if there were tunnels under my shop."

"Petey said you might have some blueprints."

"I've got some sketches my father made back when Royalle's was first built. Where did you get the idea about tunnels? There'd be no use for anything like that."

"How about the stores on either side? Do you have sketches of those?"

"We weren't interested in anyone else's store. We had enough to worry about with our own. What's this all about? Aren't you supposed to be finding the people who robbed the store? You think they dug up from underground? What sort of fiction have you been reading?"

Growing up with crusty old Pa Royalle must have been a treat for Petey. "Just trying to eliminate all possibilities."

"Well, a person would have to be a dang fool to dig up under the store. For one thing, the basement's got a stone floor. That'll knock your head right good."

"I'd like to come by and have a look at your father's sketches."

"Come on, then."

I live with Fred, so I know grumpy. Carlton Royalle greeted me at the door of his gray stone house. He was a small, stoop-shouldered man with a pinched face. He motioned for me to follow him back to the kitchen where he had piles of paper stacked on the table.

"Here's the drawings. My father wasn't much of an artist, as you can see, but I don't reckon they'll help you, anyways."

He tried his best, but he couldn't out-grump Fred. "Thank you." I examined the worn paper with its shaky ink outlines. I could make out the store and the basement. Two lines in front represented the street. "What's this circle here on the side?"

Mister Royalle peered around me. "That's supposed to be a tree."

"And these two lines over here?"

"Used to be a street there, too."

He was right. The sketches weren't much help. "Petey tells me you're writing a history of the store."

"Trying to. Not a lot of people remember how it was back then."

"Have you been to the museum?"

"They tell me a lot of the papers crumbled up. It's too bad." He fixed me with a narrow gaze. "What are you doing about the robbery?"

"Talking to people, asking questions, trying to put clues together."

His sniffed. "You're about as useful as the police. What's my son paying you?"

"We're using the barter system. He's helping me with another case."

He gave me another hard look. "If you're through, you can see yourself out."

"Thanks." I was ready to leave. I took one more glance at the sketches. Was it possible that circle and two lines meant something else, something Carlton Royalle's father was trying to draw, or something he forgot to mention?

◇◇◇

I went back to Tamara's. The pink lace nightgown had been purchased and gift-wrapped. Camden was going to work until five, so I took Mom home. By then, it was almost three and time for my appointment with E. Walter Winthrop.

E. Walter's office was huge, but E. Walter himself was a tiny pale little puff of a man, dwarfed by the expanse of his desk. He did not shake my hand or offer me a drink. He spoke gruffly.

"What is this all about? I'm a busy man."

I was surprised he didn't have a squeaky little elf voice.

"I'm interested in one of your early alarm systems, like the one in Royalle's Fine Jewelry store."

"We no longer manufacture alarm systems. I can recommend Guardian Electronic."

"Is there anyone around who knows how the old systems work?"

"No. Why should there be? I can't imagine anyone using one any more, not when there are better, more efficient models on the market."

"Apparently, this one still works."

"We made a quality product. However, I'm sure the warranty expired on that one a long time ago." He looked at his watch. "Was that all?"

"You're offering a ten thousand dollar reward for information on the Parkland Avenger. Why?"

His expression darkened. "I think it's a crime that one deluded person is making a mockery of our fine city, that's why."

"A lot of deluded people live in Parkland."

"True, but they aren't making the front page every day." If he'd had a full height, he would've drawn himself up to it. "The Winthrops are a proud and established family in this area, Mister Randall. We find this kind of behavior insulting. If my offer of a reward can get this imbecile off the streets, I feel I will have done Parkland a service."

"If you feel this strongly, why not give the police department a donation to get some of the real criminals off the streets? Or help out some of charities in town?"

Now I'd insulted him. "You should have done your home-work. Winthrop, Incorporated, is a leading contributor to all the charities. I believe this conversation is finished."

"One more question, please. You have quite a nice display of the history of your company here. Do you have any old maps or blueprints of Parkland?"

"Only those associated with the buildings and offices of Winthrop, Incorporated. What could possibly be your interest in those?"

"Well, believe it or not, I'm trying to catch the Avenger, too."

He'd been on the verge of throwing me out. Now his little pale eyes gleamed. "Why didn't you say so?"

"It's an independent investigation. I don't want a lot of people to know."

He leaned forward. "I assure you I'll be discreet. What have you discovered?"

"I have an associate at the *Herald* working undercover." Boy, would she like to. "I think she has a direct connection to this guy."

"When do you expect results?"

As soon as I can wring it out of her. "Soon. And there may be some connection between the Avenger and some robberies downtown, but I'm not sure."

He pointed one tiny stick finger. "You find this Avenger, and I promise you, you'll get the reward."

"I'll keep you posted."

"Excellent. Good afternoon, Mister Randall."

On my way out, I stopped by the secretary's desk. "Excuse me, but your boss doesn't look a thing like his picture."

"Oh, he's been ill," she said. "He's a cancer survivor."

"That explains his interest in all the charities."

"He's very concerned about giving something back to the city."

"He seems pretty concerned about the Parkland Avenger, too."

"We hate to see anything about that character in the paper. We know Mister Winthrop's blood pressure will be off the scale."

"Any reason why he feels so strongly?"

"I have no idea. I think the Avenger's kind of funny, myself. Just somebody playing a joke."

"That's my theory, too," I said.

Back in my car, I had a call from Kary.

"I talked with a very nice man at Green Valley. He couldn't go into all the details, of course, but he said that Jared was brought there when he was a baby, like Cam. 'Hunter' was the name on his birth certificate. Both parents had died, and there were no relatives to take the baby. He said Jared was a good student and made friends easily, but he was never adopted and stayed until he was eighteen and then left."

Because of his tendency to stare off into space and see things that weren't visible to others, Camden had been hard to place until Hubert and Rosalie Camden took him in, but at least, he'd had a family of sorts.

"Did he stay in touch with the Home?"

"The man said he hadn't heard from him. I didn't tell him Jared had been murdered. I couldn't."

"That's okay. You didn't have to."

"Being a detective isn't easy, is it?"

"Unfortunately, sometimes it gets a little more personal than you'd like."

"Well, I'm hoping to find something useful at the library today. See you later."

I closed my phone and sat for a while, thinking. Camden had mentioned once that as a child, how puzzled he'd been that no one wanted him until Hubert and Rosalie decided they'd keep him, strange behavior and all. No one had wanted Jared, and this had to be upsetting. So, wouldn't he have been the one full of anger, the one who would stab and kill?

Nothing made sense. Yet.

Chapter Twelve

"We Have Turned Ev'ry One to His Own Way"

If the Avenger was one person playing a joke, then the Superhero Society was a whole pile of people playing a joke. I knocked on Lily's door at four thirty, and a tall man wearing red long johns and a red plastic belt let me in.

"I am Keltar, the Incredibly Gifted. I perceive that you are Camden's friend, David Randall, sent by the High Council to offer us guidance in the distressing problem of the Parkland Avenger."

"You perceive correctly, Keltar."

"Come in, come in. We've just started."

There were six people sitting in Lily's living room, having tea and cookies, all dressed in what I'm sure they imagined were superhero outfits, although the general effect was of slumber party crossed with the tackier aspects of glam rock. I hadn't seen this many sequins since Kary's last beauty pageant.

Lily Wilkes is our neighbor, a lovely and petite yet completely delusional young woman who is convinced she's been abducted by aliens many times. She was dressed in her usual grab-bag attire, a shapeless plaid jumper over a flowered shirt and a pith helmet decorated with a large pink bow over her unusually white fluffy hair. "David, I'm so glad you could come. Let me introduce you. You met Keltar, the Incredibly Gifted. This is the Mad Shadow, Spiral Man, Destiny's Arrow, The Hook, Free Form, and Last Nerve."

I couldn't tell if The Mad Shadow was male or female. It was wrapped completely in black with only the eyes showing. It nodded. Spiral Man was a lanky fellow in green with spiral antennae. He waved a wand. Destiny's Arrow was a large woman dressed in Robin Hood style, complete with bow and arrows. She looked me up and down, smiled, and said to call her Destiny. The Hook had both hands, but held a nasty-looking instrument that might have once been a harpoon, which he shook in my direction.

"I'm the Hook of Justice. Once you're in my grasp, you can never get away."

This left Free Form and Last Nerve. Free Form was a young woman, all glitter, with glittery wings and a shiny face sprinkled with more glitter. As for Last Nerve, he was a nerdy-looking man all in silver with a determined expression.

"Last Nerve here. When you get to me, you've had it."

"Nice choice," I said. "Very original. How can I help you folks?"

Destiny's Arrow moved over on the sofa and patted the cushion next to her, inviting me to sit down. "We want you to catch the Avenger. While we realize he's doing some good out there trying to stop crime, but he's making it harder for the rest of us to be taken seriously."

This was a true test of my ability to keep a straight face. "So all of you want to stop crime, too?"

"Yes, of course. We don't just sit around having tea. We want to do some good in the world. The Avenger has become a laughing stock. How do you think that makes us feel?"

Well, if you're not embarrassed to be seen in public in that outfit, I can't imagine how you feel. "It must be difficult."

Last Nerve gestured with his cookie. "Mister Randall, we truly believe in the principles set forth by the High Council: Truth, Honesty, and Freedom for All. We're trying to make this world a better place. We don't need upstart Avengers prowling the streets. Something must be done."

"Do any of you have an idea who the Avenger might be? A former member of this group, perhaps?"

The Hook used the end of the harpoon to scratch his head. "We've been considering that, and we're pretty sure he isn't one of us."

"This is a small, select group," Lily said.

I gave them another look. Physically, none of them matched the Avenger's description, not even the black-clad Mad Shadow. He or she was too dumpy.

Keltar cleared his throat. "We have an idea—or rather, I should say, I have an idea. We plan to patrol the streets every night, catch this Avenger, and discover his identity. Then we shall threaten to expose him if he continues on his misguided path."

I could just see Jordan's reaction to this crew. "That might not be a good idea." Keltar drew himself up, insulted. "The police are not real happy with the Avenger. They'd be inclined to arrest you for interfering."

"But we want to do something!" Free Form said. "It's really really important."

I looked around at their earnest, goofy faces and at the Mad Shadow's eyes gleaming hopefully behind its mask. "Okay, there might be something you can do." I accepted a cup of tea from Lily. The SHS leaned forward. "You're all superheroes. You know what it's like. Help me understand what makes a person choose this kind of life. You have to be special, I know that. What's a typical day for a superhero in Parkland?"

They exchanged glances. "Well," Keltar said, "I can't speak for my fellow crime-fighters, but my day begins with a morning jog, followed by a shower and a good breakfast. Then I resume my duties at an accounting firm where my true identity is a closely guarded secret. After putting in a full day's work, I am free to pursue my superhero activities, which include neighborhood watch and the recycling of discarded cans and plastic bottles I find on the streets."

The others had similar stories. Spiral Man, Last Nerve, and the Hook had office jobs. Free Form worked in a beauty salon.

Destiny worked at home, and the Mad Shadow declined to reveal any information. I was beginning to get the picture. All of these people were loners, all were only marginally attractive, nobody was in good shape, and underneath all the vinyl and glitter, they were all annoyed their world view wasn't shared by the masses. This wasn't the way things were supposed to be, dagnabit, so they were going to set things right, even if it meant running around in funny costumes.

"So, as far as you know, you're the only true superheroes in town?"

They conferred.

"Do we count Virtue Vixen?" Destiny asked.

Spiral Man's antennae wobbled as he shook his head. "She's way behind in her dues. I'd say no."

Free Form was more sympathetic. "Come on, guys, she's my roomie. Just because she missed a few meetings."

"Talk to her, then," Keltar said. "Is she taking this seriously, or not?"

"I don't know."

"I thought you told me she was always complaining about the outfit."

"She complains about my outfit. She says it's too flashy. Just because she dresses with no imagination whatsoever."

The others looked back at me. "I wouldn't count on the Vixen. We're the only ones," Destiny said. "But we're always looking for possible recruits. You could join."

"No, thanks," I said. "I'm allergic to Spandex."

"Then tell us what we can do to stop the Avenger." Keltar lowered his voice. "I'm beginning to believe he may have gone over to the Dark Side."

I warned them again about getting in the way. "Keep your super senses alert. Any clue you can find is going to help."

Lily saw me to the door. "They're really sincere about this, David."

"So am I."

"And we need to keep their identities secret."

"They didn't tell me their real names, Lily."

"Oh," she said. "Okay, then."

"Make sure they don't try to help."

"They really want to help."

"They can really help by staying out of the way."

The Mad Shadow came up and nudged my elbow. "You should speak to Vixen."

Even the Shadow's voice didn't give away gender. "Why's that?"

"She always wears yellow and red, like the Avenger."

"Do I sense a little superhero jealousy here?"

The Shadow managed to look affronted. "Despite my name, I am a force for good."

"Where would I find this Vixen? That's not her real name, is it?"

"Her name's Emmajean. Ask at the beauty salon. Hair's Looking At You."

"You, too."

"No, no, that's the name of the place. Downtown on Third." The Shadow made a few darting glances right and left and scurried back to the living room.

"My," Lily said. "What do you think of that?"

I gave Lily my standard answer after an afternoon at her house. "I have no idea."

Hair's Looking At You was a small beauty salon wedged between a defunct video arcade and a hardware store. When I opened the door, the smell of hair-curling chemicals and hair spray made my eyes water. All three women in the salon looked as startled as if I'd reached up and snapped off the soap opera whining in the corner. The one sitting under the dryer dropped her *Glamour* magazine. The one sitting in the chair getting a haircut gave a little jerk and almost lost part of her ear. The woman cutting her hair said, "Oh, my goodness, don't jump like that."

I hadn't meant to cause such a reaction. "Sorry, ladies. I'm looking for Emmajean."

The woman cutting hair lowered her scissors. "She isn't here. She works every other Tuesday. What's this all about?"

"I'm an old friend in town for a few days. Thought we might get together."

She eyed me. "I'm sure Emma would like that. You want to leave your number?"

"Sure."

She came to her desk and tore a piece of paper off her appointment book. I wrote my name and phone number. I added, "Lily and Keltar send their love."

"I'll put it at her station," the woman said.

"Thanks." I noticed a stack of newspapers and magazines covered one small table. "You ladies been keeping up with the Avenger?"

The woman under the dryer's face wrinkled with disapproval. Looked like she'd been under there long enough. "Lot of nonsense."

"Some college boy playing a prank," the woman getting her hair cut said. "My nephew had to run around town in his underwear for some fraternity initiation."

The beautician continued trimming. "I don't know. This Avenger must be for real."

"What makes you say that?"

She looked surprised that I would question her. "Because it's in the paper. Look here." She put down her scissors and reached for a newspaper on the counter. She folded it back to an article on the front page.

"Parkland Avenger Sighted" the headline read. I skimmed the rest of the article, noticing it had been written by Brooke Verner. "Parkland's self-appointed superhero, the Parkland Avenger, was seen near Buncombe Street last night. Witnesses report he was wearing his traditional yellow and red, with red cape and mask. When greeted, the Avenger gave a salute and then disappeared into the night. 'I feel safer knowing he's out there,' one witness said. 'You can't count on the police to be everywhere.'"

Oh, I'll bet Jordan loved this.

I handed the paper back to the beautician, who said, "Why would they print it in the paper if it wasn't true?"

"Well, sometimes not everything in the newspaper is true."

This had obviously never occurred to her. "That doesn't make sense. Why have a newspaper full of lies?"

"I don't mean out and out lies like the sun is green, or Germany won World War II. I mean sometimes the facts get a little blurry or opinionated, like in 'Your Turn.'"

"But those are real calls phoned in by real people with real concerns. That's probably the most honest part of the *Herald*."

Her buddies agreed with her. "I called in a complaint, myself," the woman under the dryer said. "The garbage men were coming around my neighborhood at six in the morning making the awfulest racket. I called 'Your Turn,' and the route got changed. Now they come at a much more reasonable hour."

And wake up another neighborhood at six.

The woman getting a haircut put in her two cents. "My cousin called, too. Asked about all those foreigners coming in, if there was going to be room for the children in the schools, and how waiting in line at the post office was getting to be a problem."

I wasn't sure how or if these things were related. I tried to get the conversation back on track. "Anything in 'Your Turn' about the Avenger?"

"Oh, he averages five or six calls a week. Most people say he's doing the city some good."

"Sometimes he just gets in the way, though, doesn't he?"

"Not every time."

The door opened. In walked a tall young woman all in black. Her skin was a rich tan, her light brown hair was a complicated series of braids and beads, and she had a ring on every finger. She was carrying two brightly colored shopping bags and a black gym bag.

"Emmajean, you weren't on the schedule today," the beautician said.

"I know. I stopped by to work on my tan."

"Well, this is lucky. This gentleman's an old friend come by to see you."

Emmajean looked me up and down. "I don't know that he's an old friend, but he sure as hell can be a new one."

"Hello, Emmajean. I'm David Randall. The SHS sent me."

She made a face. "Oh, gosh. What do they want?"

"They say you're a little behind on your dues."

The other three women were leaning forward to listen. Emmajean took my arm. "Come on. We'll talk in here."

She led me to an adjoining room. Three open doors revealing coffin-like tanning booths lined one wall. A worn beige sofa took up the other. "Now look, whoever you are. I came by to stretch out and relax in one of these booths and keep my nice summer tan. I don't need any grief from that bunch of leotard-wearing wackos."

"No problem. I'm trying to get some information on the Parkland Avenger. I thought you might be able to help me."

She sat down on the sofa and put her shopping bags aside. "Oh, that's another nut. What are you, a reporter?"

"Private investigator."

Emmajean wasn't impressed. "I can save you time and money. The cops'll catch that idiot before long."

I sat down, too. "I'm a little confused. The SHS called you Virtue Vixen. If you feel this strongly against the group, why did you join in the first place?"

"Well, to start off with, it was fun. We had a lot of laughs making up names and costumes. Then Dwayne—that's Keltar, by the way—began all this crap about doing good deeds and bringing criminals to justice. Now they're all too serious for me. So they sent you to collect my overdue dues?"

"No, I wanted to talk to you."

"You're talking."

"You're no longer a member of the SHS?"

"That's right. No more will Virtue Vixen shine her light upon the unwary."

"And you have no idea who the Avenger might be?"

"You met the gang. What do you think?"

"None of them fit the description. And neither do you, although you seem to be in great shape."

"Thank you. I run, lift weights, and I'm on the gymnastics team at the Y." She indicated the black bag. I saw "PGT" on the side in bold white letters. "Parkland Gymnastics Team."

"Just in case the call should go out for Virtue Vixen?"

She grinned. "I'll be ready. No, I'd never dress up and go running around the city at night. I'm not that stupid. Parkland's not as bad as some big cities, but it's still foolish for a woman—for anyone—to wander some of those streets after midnight."

"So you don't think one of the SHS is taking this a little too seriously?"

"They're all talk and no action, believe me." She stood up and brushed her hands on her skirt. "I've got to be at the Y in an hour, and I really need to spend some time in the tanning booth. I'd love to talk to you some more—as long as it's not about superhero nonsense. I'm usually busy weeknights. The gym team is practicing for a meet on January 12. Saturdays are free, though. What's your schedule like?"

In my Before Kary days, I would've encouraged an attractive woman like Emmajean, but I was staying all business. "I'm pretty busy with my caseload, but if you hear anything else about the Avenger, give me a call."

◇ ◇ ◇

Fred scowled at me when I came in the house. Now what did the old coot want?

"What's your problem?" I asked.

"Who's this new woman?"

At first, I thought he meant Emmajean. "Have you suddenly become psychic, too?"

"This new woman in the house, bustling around, always in the kitchen telling me what to do."

"Fred, that's my mother, remember? She's here for Christmas."

I didn't think it was possible, but Fred's wizened features puckered further in. "Christmas? Damn it, there's another reason to get rid of that useless holiday. Strange women in the house."

He kept muttering to himself as he walked up the stairs, passing Camden coming down. Camden was in his one and

only gray suit, white shirt, and burgundy tie. I could tell he'd combed his hair, but it was already straying.

"How come you're all cleaned up?"

"Kary has three tickets to the Parkland Ballet's production of 'The Nutcracker.' Two of those little third graders she student taught are in it, so I told Sophia and Kary I'd escort them. I knew you were going to the auto club meeting tonight and probably wouldn't want to go to the ballet, anyway."

"Your psychic powers continue to astound me."

"The ladies are getting ready. Could you give us a lift to the theater?"

Camden doesn't drive. He says there are too many psychic distractions, and seeing how some people drive in Parkland, I have to agree with him. "As long as I don't have to go in." I followed him to the kitchen. "Anything left for dinner?"

"Yeah, there's some chicken and mashed potatoes."

Two pieces of chicken were in the oven, wrapped in foil, alongside a baking dish half full of mashed potatoes and green peas. I got some tea out of the fridge and took my dinner to the counter. Camden opened a Coke and joined me.

"So how's everyone in the SHS?" he asked.

"They're all busting a gut to help me in my investigation."

"That's not good."

"I think I convinced them to stay put. It's quite a crew. There's the Hook of Justice with his faithful harpoon, Keltar the Incredibly Gifted, a fairy named Free Form, and an Angie-sized woman who likes to call herself Destiny's Arrow. My personal favorite is the Mad Shadow."

"Did he say why he was mad?"

"I'm not even sure it's a he."

"I don't think they'll get in your way. They like to play dress up, but that's as far as it goes."

"Nobody knew the Avenger. Nobody looked like him, either." I ate some potatoes. "E. Walter Winthrop would gladly strangle the SHS if he knew about them."

"Not too keen on superheroes?"

"Not too keen on anything."

Mom and Kary came in, turning gracefully so we could get the full effect of their finery. Mom had on a sleek black dress with a leopard jacket, black heels, and loads of gold jewelry. Kary looked radiant in a royal blue dress that hugged her perfect figure. She'd put her gold hair up in some fancy bun and stuck some little jeweled pins all around. Her lipstick was a light rose pink, her perfume a sweet smell like honeysuckle. Chicken clogged in my throat. I almost said, "I'll go with you." Almost. I swallowed. "You two look fantastic."

Mom gave me an impish smile. "Sorry you can't go."

"Gotta work tonight."

"Cam, dear, you look so nice. You should dress up more often."

"Thanks, Sophia, but this is it."

I checked my watch. "When do you need to be there?"

Mom readjusted an earring. "We have about thirty minutes. Cam, do you have the tickets?"

He patted his suit pocket. "Right here."

"Oh, you know, I think I'll take my other pocketbook. I don't need one this big. Be right back."

She went upstairs. Kary said something to me, but I was still so spellbound by her appearance, I had to ask her to repeat it.

"I said the librarian made a copy of that little scrap you gave me. She thinks she may have a map that matches it, if we could stop in some time tomorrow."

I managed to say, "Sure. You look amazing. Did I tell you?"

"Yes, you did, thanks. And we need to talk."

"Talk?"

"A serious talk. When I get back from the ballet."

You're finally going to say yes! "All right."

I guess I would've continued to stare stupefied all night, but Mom returned with her pocketbook, and she and Kary decided to sit in the island to protect their outfits. Camden watched them go and then turned his gaze to me.

"They're getting along fine."

"Told you she always wanted a daughter."

"She knows how you feel about Kary."

I met his deep gaze. I could almost feel him strolling about in my brain, opening doors and looking through the cabinets.

"You truly love her, and it's changing you."

I didn't get a chance to ask him if it was changing me for the better.

It had to be.

◇◇◇

After dropping Mom, Kary, and Camden off at the Parkland Auditorium, I went over to Best Buys, a large used car lot. The members of the Auto Club had parked all their vintage and remodeled cars in the large area in front and stood around, talking shop. I admired a shiny red Chevy Corvette and a 1958 two-toned Ford Fairlane. I spoke with a man named Jeff Abilene.

Jeff was a lanky fellow with a hound dog face. A huge ring of keys dragged at the pocket of his jeans. He regarded me sadly. "Still can't believe what happened to Hunter. I heard the police think Boyd Taylor did it, but I can't believe that, either."

"Taylor was interested in the Marlin, right?"

"And as far I know Jared was going to sell it to him."

"Was there anyone in the club who didn't get along with Jared? Maybe someone who wanted the car?"

"Boyd was the only one who wanted it. As for Jared, everybody got along with him all right. Only time I saw him ever get riled was when somebody brought up something he'd done about a year ago. Something about getting caught breaking into a store, maybe. It was a sore point with him, 'cause he said that was over and done, and he didn't want to talk about it. Said he'd been an idiot, and it ruined his chances of getting a decent job. Seems some of his buddies talked him into it and then backed out when things got serious."

Could this be why Alycia Ward called Jared chicken when she talked to him at Ben's Garage? Was she trying to get him back into the gang? "So, as far as you know, that's the extent of his life of crime?"

"Yeah, said he'd never do anything that stupid again."

"Did he actually steal something?"

"I don't know. You think this has got something to do with his murder?"

"That's entirely possible."

"Do you know a woman named Alycia Ward?"

"She came around a few times. She and Jared were friends."

I stayed around a couple of hours, admiring cars and talking to the men about Jared. All seemed sincerely sorry about his death and angry about the violent murder. Everyone said Boyd Taylor was not the murdering type. And no one had seen Alycia Ward.

But I got to see Alycia Ward up close and personal.

I returned to my office and was typing up my latest notes on the case when I heard an odd noise outside. I knew it wasn't Fred because it was almost nine thirty and he went to bed at nine. I pulled back the curtain. A shadow detached itself from one of the large oak trees and moved toward my car. The light from the candy canes lining the front walk revealed a tall black woman slipping a piece of paper under the Fury's windshield wiper.

Enough with the threatening letters. I ran through the island and the kitchen to the back door and came around the corner of the house just as the woman stepped back from the car.

"Alycia, wait!"

She bolted, scattering gravel and leaves as she sprinted down Grace Street. She was fast, but I knew a few short cuts through the neighbors' yards. I nearly tripped over some unexpected Santa in a sleigh and brought down a whole section of wreaths on someone's fence, but caught up with her as she headed for the park. She abruptly halted and I ran right into her outstretched arm. Alycia must be made of iron. It was like running into a metal pole. I was staggered for a moment and managed to snag her ankle. She fell, and we rolled around a while before she finally gave up.

"All right! All right! Get off of me!"

I sat back, but I didn't get off. "Will you calm down and listen? I'm trying to help you."

"You're going to make things worse!"

"Explain how that's possible."

"I will if you'll get off of me."

"I will if you won't run away."

This grudging truce accepted, I got up and helped her to her feet. In the dim light from the streetlights, I could see Alycia Ward had a long lean athlete's build. Her hair was short and curly, and her eyes were filled with apprehension.

"Why send me those warning notes?"

"Because if you found me, you'd turn me over to the police. They think I killed Jared."

"Did you?"

"No!"

"Where were you that night?"

"I don't have to tell you anything."

"Stop thinking of me as the enemy. I want to find Jared's killer, but I'm not working with the police."

She eyed me as if wondering if she could trust me. I must have looked sincere enough.

"Here's the problem. The night Jared was killed I was by myself in the Motel 6, so I don't have any sort of alibi. The night before, I'd been over at his house, but we had a quarrel, and I left, otherwise I would've been there. The next thing I know, he's been murdered, and I'm a suspect."

"Who hated Jared that much? What had he done?"

"Nothing! There must be some nut case out there running around killing people. That's another reason I'm scared. Just drop this whole thing, you hear me?"

"Does this have to do with the museum break in? What do you know about that?"

"A stupid prank. A mistake. I can't see any connection there."

"When you came by Ben's Garage, you called Jared a coward. What did you want him to do? Another stupid prank?"

"Does that even matter now?"

"It might. What did you quarrel about?"

"Our usual problem. He never really wanted to take any chances, and I was all about having adventures. If we'd been in a comic, we would've been Spontaneous Girl and Caution Boy."

"What about his comics? Worth anything?"

"Not really."

"There was a piece of a map in one of them. What's that all about?"

At the mention of the map, she closed off. "I have no idea."

"Since you're a woman who likes adventures, were you at the museum that night with Jared? Was Bert Galvin in on this little caper?"

She backed away. "I need to stay hidden, and you need to quit looking for me. You found me, okay? Now leave me alone."

"You said you were scared. Are you afraid Jared's killer is looking for you?" Her hesitation was all the answer I needed. "Alycia, I've got a friend on the police force. He'll hear your side of the story. If you need protection, he can protect you."

"By locking me up? I don't think so."

"Then come to Camden's house. It's a safe place. You can stay there while we figure this out."

I might have convinced her, but a squad car came down the street, and her face hardened. "You bastard!"

"I didn't call the cops," I said, but I was talking to empty air. Alycia disappeared into the darkness of the park. The squad car pulled up to me. The window slid down, and Jordan stuck out his head.

"You taking an evening stroll?"

He hadn't seen Alycia. I swung my arms and stretched. "Yeah, just needed to clear my head."

"Well, lock your doors next time. I stopped by to see how Cam was doing, and the whole place is wide open. Only thing I heard was Fred snoring like a bandsaw. Where is everybody?"

"Camden, Kary, and my mother went to see 'The Nut-cracker.'"

He gave me a closer look. "How come you're out here without a jacket?"

"Just a short stroll. I was on my way back."

"Any leads on Alycia Ward?"

I'd told Jordan I'd let him know if Camden had any contact with Alycia. Well, Camden hadn't. I had. And Jordan was being so ornery about this case, I wasn't in the mood to share any info. Not yet.

"No." If he could tell I was lying, I didn't care. I could be just as uncooperative as he was.

He gave me another long look, rolled up his window, and drove away.

◇◇◇

Around eleven, I went back to the Parkland Civic auditorium and picked up Mom, Kary, and Camden. As much as I wanted to tell Camden about my close encounter with Alycia, I was more anxious to hear what Kary wanted to talk to me about.

Mom was beaming. "What a wonderful show. You would've enjoyed it."

Kary showed me a program. "My students did such a good job."

"Glad you liked it. Now about that talk."

"Let's step out on the porch."

The night air was chilly, so I grabbed my jacket from the hall tree. Kary still had on her coat. Up and down Grace Street, Christmas lights twinkled from porches and rooftops, and Christmas trees sparkled from windows. A neighbor had synchronized his lights with music, so a frantic version of "God Rest Ye Merry Gentlemen" was flashing all the bushes and lawn ornaments in his yard. Across the street, another neighbor's plastic Nativity scene glowed, one Wise Man leaning against another and the sheep upside down.

Kary folded her arms. She didn't look like she was going to say, "Yes, I'll marry you. It has been my goal in life to become Mrs. David Randall." I was in for a serious lecture.

"David, you have got to understand something. I am not going to be the Velma of the Randall Detective Agency."

"Velma?"

"From 'Scooby Doo'? The girl with the glasses? The one who does all the research and has all the answers?"

"I never saw you as Velma."

"I do not need protecting. I'm not this helpless little girl. I'm not—" she stopped and then said, "I'm not Lindsey."

I couldn't say anything. My emotions ran back and forth as erratically as the neighbor's lights, which were now dashing up and down the yard to—ironically—"What Child Is This?"

What child is this. Kary wasn't a child. She wasn't my child. Was I trying to make her into Lindsey? Was that what I'd been doing? Was I still trying to atone?

Kary put her hand on my shoulder. "You're trying to keep everyone safe. I understand that. But you have to understand that for the first seventeen years of my life, I was so sheltered, I could barely exist in the real world. I had to get away from all that, and now that I have, I don't ever want to go back."

This wasn't the time for me to explain that my idea of protection was not the same as her fundamentally Christian family's idea.

"You have to see that sometimes I can't help but interpret your concern differently. Sometimes I feel smothered."

"I definitely don't want that. No smothering."

"I'm glad to research things for you, but if I'm going to be on your team, I want to take a more active part in your investigations."

"Okay."

"I mean it."

"I promise. If there's something else you can do, I'll tell you."

"You'd better," she said, "or I'll find something else on my own." She kissed my cheek. "Good night."

She went back inside. I stood on the porch until the music cycled back to "God Rest Ye Merry Gentlemen." For a few moments, the lights blurred. I wiped my eyes. I knew in my heart Lindsey had forgiven me, but I never wanted to lose anyone ever again. Hanging onto Kary too tightly would only drive her away. I had to let go.

When I came in, Mom and Kary had already gone to bed, and Camden was in the kitchen. I took a beer out of the fridge.

"I've just been told, in no uncertain terms, that I'd better start treating Kary like the Daphne she is, not the Velma."

Camden tugged his tie loose. "I believe you are speaking Scooby?"

"Yes. Guess that makes me the dog." I sat down at the counter. "I ran into Alycia this evening. Literally."

"She was here?"

"Leaving another love note. I chased her down and managed to get her to talk to me. She's sure the police are after her, and she's afraid Jared's killer is after her, too."

"Does she have any idea who that is?"

"I don't think so. I might have learned more, but Jordan drove up and she ran away. He didn't see her, and I didn't tell him."

"Find out anything at the auto club?"

"All the guys at the auto club liked Jared. Said he only got mad when the break-in was mentioned. He couldn't have been making much at his job. He was going to sell his beautiful old car. Maybe the idea of knocking over a few stores was appealing. Maybe he got in touch with some of his criminal pals, and when he had second thoughts about the deal, one of them killed him."

"Or maybe a criminal pal got in touch with him."

I took a drink. "Here's an idea. What if Alycia's the criminal pal? She came by Jared's workplace looking for him. She told Jared he was chicken. I think she was planning something he didn't want anything to do with. She told me she was all about adventure. She was Spontaneous Girl and he was Caution Boy. Maybe the museum break in was her idea of fun, and Jared was the only one who got caught."

"Then wouldn't he have been angry with her? And if he refused to go along with her next plan, would that be any kind of motive to kill him? And I know she didn't."

"That's where my idea hits a snag." I took a bag of chips from the cabinet. "'Valley of Gwangi' is on tonight, if you need an antidote to 'The Nutcracker.'"

Camden tossed his empty Coke can into the recycle box by the back door. "It was all right. I like the music, and your mother really enjoyed it."

"I've got to think of something for her to do tomorrow. Any suggestions?"

"Oh, she and Kary already have something planned. There's a cooking demonstration at the shopping center and some sort of fashion show. They've been talking a lot. It's good for Kary to have someone like Sophia to confide in."

Since Mom had already delved into Ellin's love life, I could only imagine what sort of advice she gave Kary, or if Kary even mentioned our relationship.

"Anything I should be concerned about?"

"They've mainly been talking about Kary's teaching career and children."

Well, of course Kary would be talking about children. Damn.

We took our seats in the island and turned on the TV. "The Valley of Gwangi" is one of our favorite movies, and we'd gotten to the part where a cowboy wrestles a pterodactyl when Brooke came in. She was surprised to see us.

"Are you two still up?"

"You're still up," I said. She looked flushed, her hair in tangles, and her clothes askew. "Did you get lucky, or was there a bear party down the street?"

She tried to straighten herself. "It's gotten windy out. Well, good night."

As she hurried up the stairs, Camden and I exchanged a look.

"Windy?" he said.

"As in a lot of hot air. Wonder what she's been up to? A midnight assignation with the Avenger?"

"Guess we'll read all about it in tomorrow's *Herald*."

Chapter Thirteen

"The Crooked Straight and the Rough Places Plain"

We read all about it, all right. The front page was alive with news about a third break-in in the old Parkland shopping district. Trilby's Antiques, two doors down from Carlene's shop, reported the theft of a valuable collection of coins and jewelry, as well as a set of china, three Civil War era knives, and a Faberge egg. The thief or thieves had entered through a trap door in the ceiling.

I'd gotten ambitious and cooked bacon and eggs this morning. "I'll bet this was a secret trap door known only to the Evil Avenger and his minions."

Camden had chosen his usual brown-sugar Pop-Tarts and Coke. He dragged himself over to the toaster, looking heavy-eyed. "'Minions.' Five points."

I brought my plate to the counter where we'd spread out the newspaper and sat down on a stool. "Speaking of minions, why aren't you getting anything on the Avenger? Planning to become his sidekick? The Parkland Avenger and the Psychic Kid?"

"I don't know."

Unfortunately, when it comes to his own future, Camden doesn't see much. "You must be planning to run into him soon. Give Brooke Verner my regards."

The editorial page of the paper was filled with letters to the editor, half of them decrying the Avenger's antics, the other half pleading with the Avenger to stop the crime wave. The editorial was about Parkland's downtown district and how these thieves were destroying our priceless heritage.

I crunched into a piece of bacon. "Looks like everyone at the *Herald* is bucking for a Parkie."

Camden rubbed his eyes and yawned. "Was the Avenger out and about last night?"

"Not unless he was robbing the antique store. Want to go check Brooke's room?"

"Not unless you want to give her the wrong idea. She's still asleep."

I forked up more egg. "Exhausted from protecting the city, and speaking of exhausted, you don't look too chipper, yourself."

The Pop-Tarts popped up, and he put them on a plate. "Nightmares."

"Let me guess: bloody nightmares."

He pushed his hair out of his eyes. "Deep, dark bloody nightmares. I could hardly breathe."

"Ellin needs to sleep with you every night."

"I'd love to have her sleep with me every night."

"Well, tell her, you dope. When's the last time she was over? Last week, was it? You got her a new little nightie for Christmas, but Christmas is five days away. You're not going to last. Tell her you're dying."

Mom bustled in, already dressed and looking ready to take on the day. By now, I was almost used to her new hairdo and jewelry, but the leopard print poncho over black leggings made me rock back a little. "Good morning, boys. What's for breakfast? David, that smells delicious. Cam, what on earth is that? Are you drinking Coca-Cola? No wonder you don't sleep at night."

"I'm sorry, Sophia," he said. "Did I wake you?"

"I'm a very light sleeper, dear. I heard you rolling around up there."

Camden glanced at me and grinned wryly. We both knew that took care of the Ellin sleepover. "Sometimes I have nightmares. It's nothing, really."

She patted his hand. "Does this have to do with the tomato sauce incident the other day?"

"I'm afraid so."

"Davey, what are you doing about this?"

"I'm trying to solve the mystery, Mom, but it looks like I've got another robbery to investigate, too." I showed her the newspaper.

"Trilby's Antiques. That's down by the jewelry store, isn't it? This thief must like the neighborhood."

I took a drink of coffee. "That's what I'm hoping to find out."

Kary came in, looking angelic, as usual, in her pink pajamas and white robe. "Good morning, everyone. Do I smell bacon?"

I put my coffee cup aside. "I can have your order up in a few minutes, ma'am."

She sat down at the counter. "Thanks."

"How would you like your eggs?"

"Scrambled, please."

"Two over easy for me, Davey." Mom sat down beside Kary. "I thought we might go by the cemetery today."

Even after all this time, it still feels like someone kicks me in the stomach. The car accident that had taken Lindsey can replay in my mind as if it just happened. "No, thanks, Mom."

"I found a lovely little arrangement at the crafts show."

"I'm really busy today."

There was a moment of uncomfortable silence. Then Kary said, "I'll be glad to go with you, Sophia. My Beth is buried in the same children's area. I have the nicest wreath with little angels. When would you like to go?"

I kept my eyes on the frying pan, knowing Mom was watching my face, but she spoke calmly to Kary.

"Any time that's convenient for you, dear."

I put Kary's eggs on a plate and added two strips of bacon. When I handed her the plate, I wanted to say thanks, but couldn't talk around the lump in my throat. She smiled her beautiful sympathetic smile. I couldn't have asked for a better Christmas present. I cleared my throat.

"Two over easy coming up."

◇◇◇

It took me a while, but I got my emotions all settled and locked back up before heading out to the courthouse. I've used the resources of the county courthouse before. They provide a wealth of information, as long as you're polite to the clerks, which isn't a problem. The clerks like to think they're in charge when actually most of the info is available to the general public. I like to deal with Dixie Sonoma. She's a big brunette woman with a good sense of humor, and she likes to flirt. Today, she had on a bright red Christmas sweater decorated with ornaments, a green skirt, and a big pin shaped like a candy cane.

"What is it today, David?"

"Two things."

"Only two?"

"One may be a challenge."

"Let's start with the easy one."

"Please check your files for Jared Hunter. He broke into the history museum about a year ago."

Dixie's fat little fingers flew over her computer keyboard. It took her about five minutes to locate Jared's record.

"Here we go."

I read the brief report. It was approximately what Jordan had told me. At one o'clock am on July 10, Jared Hunter of ten sixty-five Willow Avenue was apprehended by Parkland police, who answered an alarm at the Parkland Museum of History. Another suspect fled the scene. Hunter was unarmed. Felony charges were dropped at the request of Ralph Galvin, head of the museum board.

If Ralph's son Bert was part of this crime or prank or whatever it was, why didn't Jared say so? If Alycia Ward had something to do with it, why did Jared protect her, as well?

I must have been deep in thought because Dixie nudged me. "What's your hard question?"

"I need a map or schematic drawing of the old Parkland district."

"That's easy, but we'll need to take a little trip."

The Parkland courthouse was built in the Thirties and someone decided elevators wouldn't work within the existing structure, so there are lots of stairs. I followed Dixie up two flights to an office marked "Historical Records." I expected to find a dusty gnome hunched behind a battered desk, but the office was bright and modern, with sleek furnishings and a light green carpet.

"What are you looking for?" Dixie asked.

"I'm looking for a map of the old Parkland district, specifically old drawings of Royalle's Fine Jewelry and Moore's Hardware."

The room was filled with filing cabinets and cabinets with long flat drawers. Dixie went to one of these and pulled out several drawers until she found the one she wanted.

"This is all I have."

Under sheets of protective plastic were photographs and pencil drawings of Main Street, Parkland, as it appeared over the years. They were mostly copies of ones I'd seen in the museum. "No blueprints? Nothing that would show how the buildings were constructed?"

"No. We used to have something like that, but it crumbled before we could restore it. It was on a piece of brown paper, very old and creased. The last time I saw it, I was going to show it to an electrician who was going to rewire one of the shops. He wanted to make sure he didn't overlook anything or leave anything that might cause a fire. When I took it out, it disintegrated." She closed the drawer. "Have you tried the library? They might have a copy. Or the history museum?"

"The library's my next stop," I said. "Thanks for your help."

On my way to the library, I stopped by Trilby's Antiques.

No one at Trilby's Antiques wanted to talk to me. The owner was furious with the police and anyone else who looked like a detective for failing to protect his store.

"This is ridiculous!" He stood in his doorway as if daring me to come a step further. "Doesn't anyone see a pattern here? Are we all going to be robbed before something's done? First Royalle's, and then the music store—why weren't there extra patrols on this street? Do I have to sit in my store every night with a shotgun?"

"Did your alarm system fail?"

"How was I to know there's a trap door in the ceiling? How did the thief know about it? Coming in that way, he didn't trip the alarm."

"How long have you been at this location?"

"Ten years. Ten years without a minute of trouble, and now this. Clear out! I don't want to talk to anyone."

He slammed the door, setting the police tape trembling in the breeze. I thought about waiting until he had calmed down and trying to speak to him again. Instead, I called Kary.

"Can you meet me at the library?"

"I was just about to call you. I'm on my way."

She didn't mention anything about the visit to the cemetery, and I definitely didn't ask.

As I drove to the Parkland Public Library, I thought over my information. By now, I was pretty sure Jared Hunter and Bert Galvin had been looking for and had possibly stolen a map that showed secret entrances to most of the old buildings on Main Street. Why they needed this, and who was working with them remained mysteries, but someone had hidden a map of some kind in his comic books.

Kary met me in the reference section. "They don't have the original map, but they have a copy, and Mandy is making me one."

In a few minutes, the reference librarian brought us four pieces of paper which she arranged like the pieces of a puzzle. "We don't have paper big enough, so I did each section. It goes together like this."

We taped the edges, and I had my very own key to downtown Parkland, or at least the part I was interested in. There was

Royalle's Fine Jewelry, alarm system and all, Moore's Hardware, now Carlene's record store, including the secret panel, and the store that now housed Trilby's Antiques, complete with trap door. On the map, the antique store had originally been Hagerty's Feed and Grain. There were tunnels, passageways, hidden doors, and a maze of underground rooms. A burglar's paradise.

"Mandy, do you have any idea why there are all these odd doors and passageways?"

Why did I ask? Of course she knew, and if I'd thought about it, I'd have known, too. "During the Civil War, Parkland was a major stop along the Underground Railroad."

"That's right. I saw something about that in the museum. So these were hiding places."

"Yes, and if there was trouble in one place, you could sneak along the tunnel to another place and get out."

And I bet someone was using these tunnels to rob the stores and get out. "Has anyone else asked you about this map?"

"A police officer came by and looked at it. I told him what I told you."

"No one else?"

"No. Most people don't know about all the things we have here in the library."

That was true. I should have come here first, and poor Jared Hunter could've saved himself a lot of trouble and probably his life if he'd only come to the library.

Kary and I thanked her and took our copy of the map to another table to examine it closer.

I pointed to Royalle's, Carlene's record store, and Trilby's Antiques. "These three stores have been robbed. I think somebody else has a map like this, a map that shows all the neat secret rooms."

"They'd have to know their history, wouldn't they?"

"Yes, they would."

"So what was Jared doing with a map like this?"

"My guess is he was using it to steal things. He'd already been caught breaking into the history museum."

"If I were a thief, a history museum wouldn't be my first choice."

"Mine, either. Unless he really wanted this map. Or someone wanted it, and Jared got sucked into the scheme."

Kary went to the shelves to look. I sat down and stared at the map. Come on, give me a clue. Give me something to go on here. If the thief or thieves were hoping for a big score, why take only a few items from each shop? Royalle's was loaded with expensive jewelry, and the antique shop had tons of rare and valuable things.

"This might help." Kary put a large book entitled *Parkland: City of Promise* on the table. "There's quite a lot about Parkland during the Civil War."

I started to read when my cell phone beeped.

It was Tamara Eldridge. "First of all, don't panic. It's not as bad as last time, but he's still shaky. He said you were at the library, so I hope I haven't interrupted anything important."

"Just a little research. I'll be right there." I closed my phone. "Camden's had another little spell. See if we can take this book with us."

Mandy apologized and said *Parkland: City of Promise* had to stay in the library.

"You go take care of Cam," Kary said. "I'll see what I can find out from this book."

Chapter Fourteen

"And the Rulers Counsel Together"

Camden met me at the door of Tamara's Boutique. "I'm okay. It was just a little tremor, not a full earthquake."

"Any blood?"

"More like I couldn't breathe. It's okay now."

He looked pretty white. Behind his back, Tamara made all kinds of signals, shaking her head and indicating it was not okay. I thought some overly sweetened food might help.

"Let's go get some lunch. Tamara, can we bring you anything?"

"If you go up to Chunky Chicken, you can bring me the regular garden salad and some tea, thanks. Take your time."

"Feel like walking?" I asked Camden.

"I'm all right."

Chunky Chicken's across the shopping center. We walked to the restaurant, ordered a salad for Tamara, sandwiches for us, and tea all around. Camden picked up a double handful of sugar packets. I flipped some straws out of the dispenser.

"I found some details at the courthouse of that crime Jared wouldn't discuss with you. It was indeed the museum robbery."

"To get the map."

"Yes. You remember the curator said the robbers made a big mess? I think they were covering their tracks. I think they specifically wanted the map, and if they crushed a lot of paper, the folks at the museum would assume the map was destroyed. They swept up the remains and didn't try to put all those pieces back together."

"Good grief." He ran his hand through his hair. "I wish he had confided in me."

"This morning you said you couldn't breathe. What's going on?"

"It felt like I was choking, but at the same time, it felt good, if that makes any sense."

"Not really."

"It was very strange. More like a feeling of accomplishment."

"Oh, so you were happy you were able to choke."

He shook his head. "It's two separate things. I don't know how to explain it."

"You're getting two messages at once, maybe."

"But from the same source, whatever that is."

"Someone who's choking and enjoying it."

Our order was ready. The girl handed over the bags and seemed relieved to wait on the next customer.

As we walked back to Tamara's, I said, "No blood this time?"

"It's still there, but kind of in the background. The choking thing is more important now."

"More important?"

"That's what it feels like. Do any of these visions make sense? Ever?"

"Don't get worked up. We always manage to figure them out."

"I don't want to choke."

"Who does? We'll deliver the salad, eat our delicious Chunky Chicken specials, and then I need to get back to the library."

This made him grin. "Tamara didn't believe me when I told her that's where you were."

"I now have a copy of the burglar's map, and I should be able to thwart his next move. I've also found a scholarly tome that may reveal All."

"'Thwart' and 'tome.' Go to the head of the class."

"See what going to the library does for me?"

Tamara thanked us for the salad and insisted Camden go home.

"I can handle things," she said. "You go have lunch and relax."

I was surprised he didn't argue with her. We went to the Fury and spread our lunch out on the front seat. Camden often remarks there's enough room for a seven-course meal in my car.

I unwrapped my sandwich. "You want to go by the PSN and tell Ellin you're dying?"

"No, I'm okay. I need a little time to sort things out." He gazed off into space for a few minutes. "If I'm experiencing the killer's thoughts, then I must be connected to him or her in some way."

"Who do you know that's that vicious? I mean, you know a lot of screwy people, but this is extreme."

"I didn't know Jared until a short while ago. Maybe this is someone else from my past." His eyes got large, and I knew what was coming.

"Camden, don't even think it."

Too late. "Oh, my God," he said. "What if it's my father?"

"Your father is not a mass murderer."

"How do you know? We don't know anything about him except his name is Martin and he looks like me. What if I'm experiencing his thoughts?"

"Why would your father kill Jared?"

"Do murderers have to have reasons?"

"Most of the time they do."

"Unless they're crazy."

"Okay, so now your father is an insane mass murderer."

"Well, he probably is. Anybody who'd leave his wife and newborn child has serious issues."

"Get a grip. I'll solve this, okay? And you'll see that the killer is some creep who happens to be able to broadcast a little louder than usual."

I ate my sandwich. Camden took a few bites of his and set it aside.

"You're not going to brood in my car," I said, "or I'll dump you off at the PSN and let Ellin harangue you."

That got his attention. "'Harangue'? Can you even spell that?"

"I'm three words ahead of you now."

Kary called to ask about Camden and to say she'd gotten some good information from *Parkland: City of Promise* and was on her way home.

"We are, too," I said. "See you there."

Kary got home first and was waiting for us in the dining room where she'd spread the map on the table. Mom was also there, looking on with interest.

"There was a long section in that book on the Underground Railroad, featuring names and pictures of prominent Parkland citizens who'd taken part," Kary told us. "Under one picture, I found the name 'Ward.' According to local history, the Wards started out as sharecroppers, but eventually became one of the wealthier black families in town."

"Are they still wealthy?"

"The book didn't say."

"Camden?"

He shook his head. "Alycia never had a lot of money."

Kary had more. "I asked Mandy if she remembered someone named Alycia Ward. She did remember a very tall woman who was doing a report for college and needed some information about the Underground Railroad."

I knew it. "Did she ask about the map of old downtown?"

"No, she didn't."

Maybe she didn't need to. Maybe she already had her own copy, the copy Jared Hunter stole from the courthouse.

"Okay, maybe Alycia wants to be rich again, like in the good old days, and using her knowledge of the Underground Railroad hideaways, she's masterminding the thefts."

"I need a closer look at this map," Camden said.

We gathered around the table and bent over the map. Mom sat down and pointed to a section. "Is this Royalle's?"

"Yes, and I can't wait to show old Mister Carlton Royalle there really is a tunnel under his store," I said. "But it doesn't connect to any other tunnel. Royalle's is on one side of the street. Carlene's shop and Trilby's Antiques are on the other. If I were the thief, where would I go next?"

Camden ran his hand lightly along the paper. "This tunnel goes under Carlene's and several shops."

"Yeah, but does the thief need shoes, tropical fish, or his Avenger suit dry-cleaned? And why hasn't he hit the most obvious target, the Parkland First National Bank on the corner?"

"The tunnel doesn't go that far."

"And judging from what's been stolen, this thief didn't seem too concerned about making the big haul." I straightened. "Are we dealing with a very selective thief, or has he been surprised each night by the Avenger, as Sim Johnson suggested?"

"I'm not getting anything."

"This is a copy of a copy Mandy made for us. You probably need to feel the real map."

"You think Alycia has it?"

"I think Jared and his cohort broke into the museum to steal the map, which is crazy, because they could've gotten a copy from the library just as I did. I think Jared had it hidden away in his comics, and someone who knew this wanted it bad enough to kill him. It's possible Jared knew about this map through Alycia's research."

"What about Bert Galvin?" Kary asked. "Maybe he knew about the map."

"It was never clear if Bert was there, and Jared didn't talk." I carefully folded the map. "I need to find Bert. And here's another thing. I still wonder if these current break-ins are some sort of publicity stunt cooked up by Brooke Verner to win a Parkie. No one's been hurt, the stores weren't badly damaged, and lots of valuable stuff's been left behind."

"You think Brooke has Jared's copy of the map?"

"I'll ask her."

◇◇◇

I went to the *Herald* and found Brooke in the least likely place: Chance Baseford's office. He was in full rave.

"Does it mean that much to you, you stupid woman? Here, take it." He shoved one of the Parkie statuettes into her hands. "Take it!"

Brooke almost dropped the Parkie. "I'm not doing this for an award. I want respect. I want to be treated like a real reporter."

"Then report on something real."

"The Avenger's really out there!"

"Oh, he's out there, all right."

She slammed the award on his desk. "Listen to me! No matter what you think, there's a real Avenger."

"A copycat, like a serial killer."

"No! A real hero!"

"Oh, give it up, Verner. You've cried wolf so many times, you've got your own pack. This fellow's a nut, exactly like yourself, and if anyone gets hurt, you and your stupid scheme will be held accountable." He noticed me in the doorway. "You might as well come in, Randall. I need a witness that I awarded Brooke Verner a Parkie for the most ridiculous story of the year."

"Congratulations, Brooke."

Her glare was almost a full-force Ellin Belton glare. "You don't know anything about this, Randall."

"As much as it pains me to agree with Baseford, I think this scheme of yours is heading for disaster."

"It isn't a scheme! I'm reporting the facts!"

"Okay, what are the facts?"

She paced Baseford's office, gesturing wildly. "The Avenger has foiled three break-ins in the historic downtown section of Parkland. Royalle's Fine Jewelry is missing only a handful of items, the music store lost a little money, and Trilby's Antiques could've been wiped out. With alarms disarmed or bypassed, why did the thief or thieves stop? Because someone stopped them, and that someone was the Parkland Avenger."

Since Brooke's line of reasoning sounded very much like my own, I hesitated. Baseford asked the burning question.

"Why the Avenger? Why not some citizen out for a midnight jog, or a police car coming around the corner? Do you have to invent some exotic excuse for a thief's behavior? Proof, woman, that's what you need. Maybe Ralph Galvin is letting you get away with this, but I never want to see you in my office again."

Brooke was shaking with indignation. "I'll show you, you overgrown oaf. My exposé is going to blow the roof off this town."

"With clichés like that, I should imagine it would." He waved her out. "Shoo, shoo."

Brooke stormed past me without another glance. I followed her all the way to the other end of the building to her office. It wasn't as large or as cluttered as Baseford's, but she had her own desk, computer, and file cabinets. Tacked on one wall was a city map decorated with colored pushpins, no doubt indicating Avenger sightings. Brooke flopped into her chair and gave me another glare.

"What do you want, Randall?"

"Oddly enough, our theories coincide."

"Oh, so now you're a believer? You couldn't say so in front of Baseford? Give me a little backup?"

"I don't think there's an Avenger, but you're right about the thief being selective. I'm curious, too, why he's taking only a few things."

"Maybe he's re-decorating his town house."

I pulled out the folding chair in front of her desk and sat down. "Level with me, Brooke. Who's this Avenger, and what kind of deal have the two of you cooked up?"

"There's one way you can find out."

"Okay. Your place or mine?"

She sat back, looking disappointed. "I don't want that to be the only reason you sleep with me."

"Well, it would be."

She folded her arms and looked at me for a long moment before giving me a reluctant grin. "Damn you."

"Anything for a story."

"This isn't a story. There really is an Avenger."

"Yeah, sure. Are you using a map of Old Parkland's Underground Railroad to help him plan his daring moves?"

"The only map I've got is the one on the wall. What the hell does the Underground Railroad have to do with anything? People aren't fleeing to the North these days."

The latest *Herald* was spread out on her desk. Besides a headline on the antique store break-in, there was one stating, "Woman Attacked in Park." I read the details. A jogger had surprised a man trying to choke an unidentified woman. An unidentified black woman. The man had run off, and the woman disappeared. Police had no leads, no suspects. The crime had happened around midnight.

Brooke frowned at me. "What's your interest in that? You think the Avenger did that, too?"

"What time was Trilby's robbed?"

She checked her wall map. "The police aren't sure. The call came in after midnight."

I folded the paper and put it back on her desk. Could the unidentified black woman be Alycia Ward? Had Camden somehow intercepted her feelings and the feelings of her assailant? "If I were the Parkland Avenger, I'd be trying to save people from being killed instead of hanging around antique stores."

Brooke leaned forward again. "Parkland's a big city. If we work together, we could cover twice as much territory."

"No, thanks. I don't have any more room in my trophy case."

"I'm not doing this just for a Parkie."

"No, there's that ten thousand dollar reward to consider."

"And not for that, either. My journalistic reputation is at stake." I got up. "If you say so."

"I'll show you, Randall. I'll show all of you."

"You don't have to show me anything. I want to find out who killed Jared Hunter. If it turns out to be the Avenger, then hooray. If not, he can go on saving the city." I took another look at her map. For some reason, something one of the women in Hair's Looking At You said came to mind. I'd mentioned that the Avenger got in the way, and she'd said, "Not all the time."

"Brooke, when did the Avenger start avenging?"

She consulted her notes. "December 8."

"Is that when he got in the way of the police car?"

She looked again. "That's when he fell off the roof of the parking garage onto someone's car and dented the hood. December 15 is when he got in the way of the police car."

The night Royalle's was robbed. "You've still got copies of your stories, right?"

She went to her computer and opened her files. "Here."

I came around so I could see the screen. I'd already read the December 15 account about the Avenger's attempt to block the bank robbers' getaway car. "When was the next one?"

"December 18. He was spotted in the downtown district."

Carlene's shop was broken into on the 18th. "Witnesses reported a man in yellow tights and a red cape Thursday night in the vicinity of Old Parkland. The alleged 'Parkland Avenger' was seen as he leaped from a Dumpster in the alley to the top of the Mains Building." "Leaped," I said. "Sounds pretty agile. Did you see him do this?"

"No, someone called it in." Brooke pointed out the next story. "December 19, a sighting near Trilby's Antiques."

I read the first paragraph of the December 19 account. "Parkland's own superhero, the Parkland Avenger, may have prevented another robbery last night in Old Parkland. An eyewitness near Trilby's Antiques tells the *Herald* that a man dressed in yellow and red surprised someone on the roof of the antique shop. Both men disappeared before the police arrived." I glanced up. "How about this one?"

"I heard it on my scanner and went over there, but I missed him. What are you getting at?"

"I'm not sure. Your first stories report the Avenger as a dunce, but the other accounts make him sound pretty athletic. Half the time, he may be doing some good by scaring off thieves, but the rest of the time, he's Captain Klutz."

"So? Even a superhero has off nights."

"Well, the next time you see him, tell him to step up his game," I said. "I know some real superheroes who'd be glad to take his place."

Chapter Fifteen

"He Looked For Some to Have Pity on Him"

I thought we'd had enough drama for one day, but when I got home, there'd been another crisis. Camden was sitting on the sofa, Mom holding a damp cloth to his forehead, and Kary hovering with a glass of tea. Camden was about as white as he could be and taking short little breaths.

"Did you two spill some ketchup or something?"

Camden was trying to control his gasps. "No. This is different."

Kary got him to take a drink of tea. "It happened just a few minutes ago. He said something about being glad someone almost choked."

"I enjoyed it. It's the sickest thing I've ever felt."

Someone who's choking and someone else who's enjoying it. "A woman was attacked and almost strangled late last night, probably about the same time you were having that nightmare. Her attacker got away, and she didn't stay around to talk to anyone. The jogger who saw them said she was a black woman."

I didn't think it was possible, but he turned a shade paler. "Alycia."

"That's my guess. Another reason why you've been swimming in all this raw emotion. These are friends of yours, and when the bad guy keeps reliving his crimes, then so do you."

Mom looked up at me. "David, what are you talking about?"

"Somehow, he's tuned into the murderer's thoughts, Mom, and the victims', like Jared and possibly this woman who was almost strangled. Now, whenever the murder thinks back over his crimes, so does Camden."

"Oh, my God. How horrible. How can we stop it?"

Camden sat back on the sofa. "We've got to find him."

"'We'? Don't even think about it," I said.

"In case you haven't noticed, it's all I can think about. This guy's toxic brain waves are killing me, too."

"All the more reason for you to stay away from him."

"What if he starts planning to kill someone else? We've got to find him, or warn the next victim—I've got to do something."

"And spend the day twitching and sobbing? I don't think so."

"But now that I know what's going on—"

"Camden," I said. "No. Not this time."

"I totally agree," Mom said. "You're going right to bed."

"No, I'm okay. If I go to sleep, I'll have nightmares about the same damn stuff."

"Well, sleep down here, then, so we can look after you," Kary said.

Can anybody resist Kary when she pleads like that? Faced with her big brown eyes and Mom's stern glare, Camden agreed. "Maybe I'll lie down for a little while."

It didn't take him five minutes to fall asleep. Kary set the glass of tea on the coffee table and sat down in the blue armchair. Mom spread one of the afghans over Camden and then looked at me.

"What are you going to do about this?"

What was I going to do? "I need to find the Parkland Avenger. The way he's been on the scene makes me think he knows about the map, too."

"Shouldn't we call Ellin?" Kary said.

I thought of Ellin's reaction the last time she was summoned. "I'm not sure she'll appreciate that."

"I think she ought to know."

"You call her, then. Maybe she'll listen to you."

As Kary went into the kitchen to call, Mom sighed. "I don't know, David. It might be time to call the police, too."

Jordan would immediately take over and take all the credit, too. "This is my case, Mom."

"Has anyone actually hired you to find this killer?"

"Boyd Taylor's going to pay me what he can."

Kary returned to the island. "Ellin's on her way. And I noticed we're out of Pop-Tarts. I'm going to go get some more. I'll be right back."

"Thanks, Kary," I said. "Mom, come help me fix something to eat. We'll wake Camden after a while and load him up with sugar. He'll be fine."

Mom came into the kitchen with me, fussing about Camden's odd diet and the lack of fresh vegetables in the house. "He doesn't get enough vitamins. If they get married, will Ellin look after him? She seems obsessed with her job."

I sliced some of the leftover meatloaf. "There's no way you're going to fix that relationship, Mom. No one understands it, least of all me."

She got the tea out of the fridge. "Well, of course not. You're too busy with your own curious relationship."

I stopped slicing. "You haven't said anything to Kary, have you?"

"You think I want to scare her? Besides, she knows how you feel about her. She knows you want to be more than friends."

"And I'm valiantly hanging back until she's ready."

"Are you telling me you're actually showing some restraint? Let me check your blood pressure."

"Ha, ha."

"Seriously, David, you need to reconsider this."

"You back off and I won't say another word about Grady Sipe."

Mom filled Camden's large plastic cup with tea. "Grady Sipe is my age."

"You don't think you could fall for a younger man?"

"I suppose. But it's more than age, Davey. You've been through two marriages. You should have learned something by now."

"This time I'm going to make it right."

She set the cup down and put her arms around me. "I wish you'd come talk to Father Morgan."

"I don't need counseling, Mom. Besides, I'm not going to Florida just to see some old priest. We've got plenty of preachers here, and they all say the same thing: give it time." I felt grief swelling inside. If I didn't act quickly, it would overwhelm me. "That's not going to work with me. You can give me all the time you like. I'm never going to get over Lindsey's death. Never. The only thing I can do is push it to the back of mind every time it comes up and hope it stays back."

She didn't say anything. She gave me another hug. "Okay. How much sugar does Camden want in this cup?"

I did what I do best and pushed the rising emotion down. "Too much."

A few minutes after Kary returned with a fresh batch of Pop-Tarts, Ellin came in, looking concerned. Mom explained what happened and she and Ellin sat at the island, talking in low voices about what should be done.

Kary put the Pop-Tarts in the cabinet. She left one box by the toaster. "He'll probably want some when he wakes up."

Adoption: Is It Right For You? sat on the counter beside a stack of pamphlets from adoption and child care agencies.

Kary caught my glance. "It's a lot more expensive than I thought."

I told myself I should be happy about this, but I had a sudden mad desire to smooth the way for her. "It'll happen someday."

"I hope so. I don't like to think of myself as obsessive, but every time I see a mother with a baby, I stop and watch and imagine what it would be like to have a little life to look after. In stores, I'm always in the children's department, admiring the little clothes and toys. Just now, in the grocery store, I saw a father with his little girl, and when she hugged him, I could almost feel her little hands on his face."

I remembered hugging Lindsey and feeling her little hands softly patting my back. "My Daddy," she'd say. "My Daddy."

Kary straightened the stack of pamphlets. "I know it's going to be a long process, but it'll be worth it."

I couldn't believe how close to tears I was. I took a deep breath. Would I be able to help Kary fulfill this dream? Or would I be reduced to a blubbering mass of emotion every time she talked about children? Camden wasn't the only one who needed to get a grip.

Fortunately, Kary changed the subject. "But right now, our main goal is to find out who killed Jared."

"I'm pretty sure it's the same person who's sending Camden all the bad vibes. Did you find out anything about Bert Galvin?"

"Not a thing. But I have a plan."

"Kary—"

She held up a hand to stop me. "Remember what we talked about?"

"No smothering. Got it."

"Good. Now I know you and Cam have some kind of connection. Nothing there, either?"

"Sometimes I pick up on what Camden sends me, but I can't count on that. Usually it's a distress signal."

"He's better now that Ellin's here."

Camden looked pretty relaxed with Ellin holding his hand. She looked up as Kary and I came back to the island. She was sitting beside him on the sofa. Kary sat down in her chair, and since Mom was in the blue armchair, I stood behind it.

Ellin gave me one of her fiercest glares. "Jordan better be in on this."

"He's already on the case and has warned me off several times."

"This is serious, Randall."

"I know that. I'm doing all I can."

Her next words surprised me. "What can I do to help?"

"Do you remember hearing or reading about a break in at the museum about six months ago?"

"No, but I can ask at the PSN."

"Oh, everybody over there ought to know."

She was about to tell me something uncomplimentary when Camden woke, and Kary, Mom, and I decided to leave the two of them alone.

Mom followed me into my office. "You shouldn't tease her like that."

"It's okay, Mom. She can take it. You can chaperone if you like." I picked up my copy of the map. "I'm going out for a while."

She fixed me with a glare very much like Ellin's. "Just be careful. I don't want you trying to find those tunnels. The last thing you should do is snoop around underground."

I wasn't going to try. I was going to find the tunnels. And if I did, I was definitely going to snoop. "Yes, ma'am."

Chapter Sixteen

"All They That See Him Laugh Him to Scorn"

I went to Carlene's and hung around, talking music until closing time. Then she showed me the secret panel that allowed access to the safe. To her surprise and to my satisfaction, behind the panel was a doorway that led down into a tunnel. I was hoping to find the Avenger's lair, complete with Avengermobile, or better yet, run into the thief as he tried to rob another store. Of course, if the Avenger or thieves decided to work the Royalle side of the street, I'd be screwed, because the tunnels didn't run under the street. It was worth a look, though.

The tunnel was narrow, musty, and full of cobwebs. I had my copy of the map and a flashlight. I was thinking this might not be the smartest idea I've had when a sound behind me made me whirl around. A figure came closer. Wow, this was too easy. I hadn't been down here ten minutes, and I was going to solve something, or possibly get killed. Or had Carlene decided to join me for a little search and seizure in the dark?

In the dim light of my flashlight, the figure looked like a ghost. A small ghost, however, and one I'd seen before.

"Thanks, Camden. My heart needed a jump start."

He looked a lot steadier. "I was hoping I'd find you."

"You knew you could find me. Ellin give you some hot lovin'?"

"Not only that. She gave me a ride."

"And Mom let you out of the house? How did you manage that?"

"Well, I told her I was meeting you at Carlene's music store."

"You just didn't mention you were meeting me under Carlene's music store."

"I didn't want to trouble her with any unnecessary information."

"Ellin didn't want to come down here with you?"

"Business at the PSN."

"Sometimes that comes in handy. What about Kary?"

"She went over to Lily's."

Uh, oh. "She didn't happen to say what she was up to, did she?"

"No, and she's annoyed you don't trust her."

I had a feeling we would both catch a little hell when we got home. "Any particular reason you wanted to see the tunnels of Parkland?"

"You're going to need help."

I've learned the hard way never to ignore Camden's predictions. "Thief or Avenger?"

"I'm not sure, but someone's going to come down here."

"Are you up to this? Any blood or choking on the menu tonight?"

"You can always say, 'snap out of it.'"

"Yeah, we know how well that works." I shone the light on the map. "Let's try this way."

It gave me an eerie feeling to be in the tunnel, and I wondered if Camden was picking up any of the fear and desperation the slaves must have experienced as they tried to escape. I didn't remember a lot about the Underground Railroad, but my elementary school class had read a story about Harriet Tubman, a conductor on the Railroad, who made over a dozen trips and saved at least seventy people.

"You think Harriet Tubman came this way?"

"Probably not. If she did, some expert would've made this a historical site by now."

"Are you getting anything?"

He put his hand on the rough dirt wall. "I'm good, Randall, but not that good. That was before and during the Civil War, so we're talking 1850 to 1860 something, and I'm sure people were hurrying to get through. I get a slight impression of anxiety, but that could be from the thief."

We wandered single file under the shoe store, finding a passageway that led right up to the store. "Need new sneakers?"

"Not tonight," he said.

"This is actually kind of cool."

A few more turns and we were beneath the pet store. "Second floor: guppies, hamsters, snakes."

Camden stopped. "There wouldn't be any snakes down here, would there?"

"Doesn't seem too snake-like."

"Oh, brother. I never thought of that."

"You've been thinking too much already. Come on. If I see one, I'll get it."

"I really don't like snakes."

"No snakes. Just spiders."

"Spiders I can handle."

I looked up at the entrance to the pet store. "You know, these doors are kind of high. The thief must have brought his own stepladder."

"Or brought an accomplice."

"Let me boost you up and see if you can reach it."

"And have a snake fall out on top of me? No, thanks."

I measured the height. "If I take a running jump, I can get it."

"You don't actually want to break in, do you? I thought this was a fact-finding mission."

"The detective business isn't paying very well this month. I could use a few extra gerbils."

Camden didn't want to play burglar, but I convinced him to climb up on my shoulders and push on the door. It was solid as a rock.

He jumped down. "Guess the gerbils are sitting on it."

We went around several turns until we reached a larger room. From here, tunnels went off in three directions. I checked the map. "Okay, according to the map, the right hand tunnel leads out to the world above, the left-hand tunnel ends, and the one in the middle goes on down under one more shop."

"I vote for world above."

The tunnel became even narrower and a lot dirtier.

Camden peered at the passageway. "Can you squeeze through?"

"It'll be a lot easier for you." The tunnel floor slanted up slightly. "We're heading out."

At the end of the tunnel was a round piece of wood like a manhole cover. We pushed, and it opened. We crawled out and found ourselves in the alley between two abandoned stores and behind a pile of trashcans.

I dusted my hands. "So much for that. Where was the danger?"

For an answer, Camden pushed me back against the wall. I saw a shadowy figure coming down the alley. Camden and I hid behind the dumpster and watched as the figure pulled up the tunnel cover and wedged his way into the tunnel, but not before he stroked his chin in a familiar manner.

Camden and I looked at each other. "It's Tor," he said.

"Tor of Comic World. That's perfect."

"What'll we do?"

"First we plug the hole."

We found a heavy piece of wood next to the Dumpster and managed to roll it over on top of the tunnel cover. Then we ran out of the alley and all the way back down the street to Carlene's.

She let us in. "Are you guys okay?"

I ran past her. "Our thief's in the tunnel, and we're going to catch him."

"Oh, my God, David, don't go down there! He could have a gun."

"We'll be careful."

She didn't like the idea, but Camden and I went back, pressed the secret panel, and hopped into the tunnel.

Camden hurried along behind me. "Do we have a plan?"

"Let's ask him if he's the thief or the Avenger."

We waited under the shoe store until we heard Tor's footsteps. When he came around the corner of the tunnel, I turned my flashlight on in his face and said, "Hi."

Tor screamed like a girl and fell on his rear. "Don't kill me! Don't kill me!"

Camden stepped forward. "Take it easy, Tor. It's just us. What are you doing down here?"

Tor fought back hysterics. "What are *you* doing down here? Nobody's supposed to be down here! Nobody knows about this tunnel."

"Obviously you know about it," I said. "Care to tell us how you know?"

Camden pulled him up. "We're not going to hurt you. We just want to know what's going on."

Some people should not wear Spandex. The tight red and yellow outfit emphasized Tor's bandy legs and less than manly chest. Besides the yellow tights and red cape, he had on a red mask that hung off one ear. He caught his breath and blinked in the light from my flashlight. "I'm not here to steal anything, if that's what you're thinking."

I couldn't believe this guy was our superhero. "Are we in the presence of the Parkland Avenger?"

Tor shook with anger. "So what? Anything wrong with that? Somebody's got to do something about crime in this town."

"You found Jared's map in his comics." That's why he'd been so casual about it earlier.

"Nothing wrong with that, either. He left those comics to me."

"So you've been lurking under the city, hoping to foil the criminals' evil plans? You've been doing pretty good so far."

Tor had been putting up a brave front, but his courage was leaking fast. "You can't prove anything! No one will believe you. No one can stop the Avenger!" He turned and ran back up the tunnel.

Camden and I waited. After about five minutes, a rumpled and dirty Tor came back. He glared at us. "Let me the hell out of here."

I blocked his way. "We want the full story first."

"You can't keep me down here."

"So leave."

I knew he couldn't get past me. Defeated, he slumped against the wall.

"I'm trying to do my civic duty."

"Since when?"

"I'm not just a comics dealer. I care about this city."

"By running around in red and yellow undies?"

He folded his arms. "I don't have to answer to you."

"Okay, we'll go call the cops. You can answer to them."

As Camden and I turned to go, Tor caught Camden's arm. "Wait, wait. Cam, don't let him call the police. They'll kill me."

"Then stop fooling around and level with us."

He gulped a couple of times. "I was trying to impress Wendy."

Now things were making sense. I'd like to impress Wendy myself. "Did it work?"

He shot me a dark look. "Not yet."

"From the beginning, please."

"Okay, okay." He folded his arms again and leaned back against the tunnel wall. "She's always going on and on about how tough she is and how men today can't measure up to the heroes in comic books. When I heard about the theft at the jewelry store, I thought I'd see what I could find out. The map wasn't much help with that, but after the music store was robbed, I realized these tunnels connected. Maybe the thief left his dough down here, so I came to look. I was down here when the thief went into the antique store. I scared him off."

"Did you get a good look at him?"

"No, he rushed by. He was a blur."

"Now that he knows you know about the tunnels, why would he come back? Why did you come back?"

He returned to Avenger mode. "This is part of my nightly patrol."

"How does Brooke Verner fit into this?"

He answered way too quickly. "I don't know a Brooke Verner."

"Sure you do. Tall blonde with an attitude. She was in your shop the other day, arguing with Wendy. Said she was in to do some research on superheroes. I think she stopped by to give you your next assignment."

"Oh, no. This is all my idea. I'm getting all the credit."

Camden wasn't convinced, either. "So you took Jared's map?"

"Hell, no, man! I told you I found it in those comics he gave me."

I wondered how much Tor was involved. "Did you know Jared stole the map from the museum?"

"Yeah, I knew that. He was afraid if anyone found it, he'd be hauled back to jail."

"Who else knew about the map?"

"Me and Alycia and Bert. He's the one who thought up the robbery in the first place."

"How did Bert know about the map?"

Tor shrugged.

"And nobody thought to ask someone at the library to make a copy?"

Tor looked confused. "There's one at the library?"

"How do you think we found out about your secret tunnel?"

Tor looked at us nervously. "I've told you everything. You aren't going to turn me in, are you? I haven't done anything wrong. Who knows what the thief would've gotten away with if I hadn't been here?"

"You haven't told us everything. Where's Bert now?"

"He had some mental problems, and his father sent him off to a sanitarium somewhere. Now are you going to turn me in or not?"

"I'm not going to turn you in, but I think it's time for you to hang up your cape."

"Why should I?"

Camden tried another tact. "It's really too dangerous, Tor. That thief you surprised could've killed you."

I had to add, "And there's no way in hell you're ever going impress a woman like Wendy."

I think he would've taken a swing at me if he'd had the nerve. "What do you know about it, smartass?"

"I know if she gets a look at you in that getup, she'll never stop laughing."

He looked uncertain. "I have a duty to the city."

I thought of something else. "How does five thousand dollars sound to you?"

"Five thousand dollars?"

"Half the reward Winthrop's offering for getting the Avenger off the streets. You go home and forget this nonsense, I'll split it with you. What's Brooke paying you?"

"Two hundred a—" He choked on the next words.

I knew it. Brooke, you're one hell of a liar. "Five thousand and you quit risking your neck and the wrath of the Parkland Police Department."

He wavered. "You'll let me out of here, no more questions?"

"I might have a few more questions, but they can wait."

He tried to save what face he had left. "This really was my idea. That Verner woman took advantage of the situation."

"Yeah, you're a real pushover. Do you meet her at the paper, or does she always come to the store?"

He wasn't saying anything else about Brooke. "Let me out of here."

Camden and I went up to the music store first and distracted Carlene so Tor could slip out her front door. I thanked Carlene for her assistance.

She glanced worriedly toward the back of the store. "What about the thief?"

"False alarm. We blocked the tunnel, though, so he can't get in."

To make her feel safer, before we left, we blocked the tunnel on this side, too, and nailed some boards over it. Once in the car, Camden said, "We've got to talk to Alycia."

"Yep, I think she's the key to all this. And the mysterious Bert." I started the car and pulled out into traffic. "Can you believe that guy, running around like an idiot?"

"I have to say his outfit wasn't very flattering."

"I'm curious to hear what Brooke has to say."

◇◇◇

Brooke wasn't at the house when we got there. I expected Mom to be at the door ready to grill us on our nightly activities, but apparently she had gone to bed. I wanted to talk to Kary, but she'd gone to bed, too.

I flopped down in the blue armchair. "It's late. Brooke's still out stirring up trouble."

Camden sat down on the sofa and picked up the remote. "When she came in late the other night, she looked a bit rumpled, as I recall."

"You get that way leaping from rooftops. What's on?"

He turned the TV on to channel sixteen. "Looks like 'Mothra.'"

"Excellent choice. Why couldn't Parkland have a giant screaming moth instead of a dorky superhero?"

"All we have to do is find two tiny Japanese girls who know all the words to the 'Mothra' song."

Halfway through "Mothra," Camden fell asleep. I stayed up and watched the rest of the movie. There was no sign of Brooke, so I finally dragged myself up the stairs to bed. It was one of those nights when my mind wouldn't shut off and go to sleep. I listened to the New Black Eagles. I reviewed everything I knew so far about the case. I fantasized about Kary walking down the aisle in a wedding dress, to which my tired brain added a leopard print veil. But my thoughts kept drifting to Jared's sad little album filled with pictures of his imaginary family. At least I'd had loving parents, even if one was currently driving me crazy, and my new Grace Street family was a fine support system. But Jared had nothing, and it looked as if he'd died for nothing, too.

Chapter Seventeen

"But Who May Abide the Day of His Coming?"

Sunday morning, Brooke still wasn't home. Camden and I saw no reason to tell Mom or Kary about our underground adventure. They fussed a little bit about Camden going out when he wasn't feeling well, and he told them in all honesty that Ellin had been with him. For part of the evening, anyway.

Mom was pleased with Victory Holiness Church and chatted with everyone as if she'd been a member there for years. She and Kary must have done some more shopping because she was all decked out in a Christmas red pants suit with a leopard print belt, and Kary had on a tight black skirt and fancy green blouse. Several leopard patterned bracelets dangled from her wrist.

Attack of the Jungle Women. I had to stop thinking like that.

While Mom was admiring the candles and holly in the windows and talking to the family sitting behind us, I had a chance to ask Kary about her evening.

"Camden said you went over to Lily's. How's she doing?"

"Fine. She says to tell you hi."

Even though I knew this was foolish, I had to make the attempt. "You two talk about fashion?" As if Lily would ever be remotely fashionable.

"No. I was interested in the Superhero group that meets at her house."

Oh, my God. "You can't seriously be considering—"

Kary cut her eyes at me as if to say, stop right there. "I believe we've been through this."

"Yes, but—"

"Shh."

The service started and I had to shut up. We sang Christmas hymns and heard a Christmas-themed message, and Camden sang a solo about the Baby Jesus, and I didn't hear a word. Through it all, I was thinking, she can't possibly be planning to join the SHS.

After church and during lunch, Kary's warning glances kept me from bringing up the subject. Ellin stopped by to invite Mom and Kary to see an exhibit of Egyptian artifacts in the museum in Charlotte. Ellin was taking a film crew to do a feature on curses of the pharaohs.

"Afterwards, we can hit the malls," she said.

Despite Camden's objections, Mom was washing the lunch dishes. "That sounds wonderful. I have a few last minute Christmas gifts to buy."

"Ellin, I would love to go, but I have something I need to do today," Kary said.

"Maybe next time."

She went upstairs before I could say anything, but then, what could I say? No, don't do it? I won't let you? I forbid it? That would go over really well. Besides, I didn't know exactly what she was planning to do.

Camden took his usual seat on the sofa in the island. Ellin tugged off her blue coat and put it over the armchair. "I wish you'd come with us, Cam. You might get some interesting vibrations from the artifacts."

"Thanks, but I'm not in the mood to fight the Christmas crowds at the mall."

"You just don't want to go to Charlotte."

"Not really." He picked up a stack of Christmas cards that had toppled off the coffee table. "You're still planning to spend Christmas Eve with us, aren't you?"

"I don't know."

"You said your family opens gifts Christmas morning."

"With Kary and Randall and Sophia here, you're going to have your own family."

"But that includes you."

She didn't sit down. I paused at my office door. Here it comes: The Big Talk. "I care about you, Cam, I really do, but I have serious concerns about our future."

He looked up at her. "Our future looks great."

"Don't give me that. I know you can't see your own future."

"Well, what can I do to make it better?"

"I just wish you had more ambition. Are you always going to be happy selling clothes at Tamara's, or making bookshelves, or riding around with Randall, doing all sorts of stupid things?"

He straightened the stack of Christmas cards. "It's a little late for me to become a doctor or a lawyer. Hell, I never finished high school. It was hard to concentrate on Algebra Two or American History with the entire student body's hormonal thoughts racing through my head."

Now's the time for sympathy and understanding, Ellin. She remained behind the armchair.

"Well, there's a simple solution. You could always get your GED. You could always come back to the Psychic Service. I could get you a good job there. Everyone's always asking about you."

"I'm having enough trouble keeping my mind straight right now."

"Why don't you come talk about that on the show? Don't you think our viewers would eat that up? 'The Inner Thoughts of a Murderer.' It sounds sensational."

He looked at her, genuinely puzzled. "Ellie, don't you get it? It's not something I can turn off and on, and when it happens, it's awful. I usually fall over or scream and cry and black out. You want me to do that on TV?"

Finally she came around to him, but she didn't sit down. "I'd be there. Aren't you always saying I'm like some kind of eraser for the bad thoughts?" Her tone was just this side of pissed. "I'll hold your hand."

"You think that's the only reason I want you around?"

She didn't answer his question. "Would you please consider coming back to the service? It would solve a lot of problems."

"Ellie." He got up and took her in his arms. "I love you. The fact that you can help erase the visions is a bonus. If you want a future with me, then we'll have one, no matter what."

I'm not sure what she would've said or done at this point, because Mom came around the corner from the kitchen, drying her hands on her apron.

"All set! Let's go!"

Ellin pulled free and put on her coat. "We'll probably be late getting back."

"We need to finish this conversation," he said.

"Just think about what I said."

We saw the ladies out. As Ellin's car drove away, Camden sighed and sat back down. "I'll never figure her out."

"Don't even try."

The phone rang. "It's for Sophia," Camden said.

I went to the kitchen and answered the phone. "302 Grace, David Randall speaking."

"David, what a pleasure to hear your voice."

I'd know that milksop tone anywhere. "Hello, Grady."

"I know you're enjoying having your mother visit you for the holidays. I'm calling to wish her a Merry Christmas. Is she there?"

Hearing this guy's voice made me cringe. "She just left with some friends to go shopping in Charlotte. I'll tell her you called."

"That would be very nice, thank you. And how have you been? Are you still in the detective business?"

"Yes."

"It's doing well, I hope? Nothing too dangerous? Your mother worries about you."

"It's doing fine. In fact, I'm working on an important case right now, so I have to say good-bye."

"Well, it's been a pleasure talking to you. When are you coming to visit us in Florida?"

"Maybe next month. It depends on my work load."

"You know you're welcome any time."

"Thanks. Good-bye." I hung up and glared at the phone. "Visit us," my ass. Where did he get off saying "us," like he and Mom were a couple? "Come on, Camden. I need to read some comics."

Wendy Riskin was in Comics World, giving Tor a hard time about something called "Free World Two Thousand." She must have already made her musical selection because a jarring bass thundered from the speakers. She beamed at us, and Tor's eyes pleaded, don't tell!

"Hi, Tor," I said. "Thought we'd hang out a while this morning."

"Sure, sure."

Wendy draped herself around Camden. "I'll hang out around you. We can read the newest 'Ghost Vixen.'"

"Wendy," I said, "you know anybody named Bert who might have been friends with Jared?"

"The only Bert I know is on 'Sesame Street.'"

I gave Tor a break and waited until Camden and Wendy were further down the aisle. "Are you expecting Brooke this morning?"

He looked disgusted. "I was expecting her last night. She was supposed to meet me here and pay me, but she never showed."

"But the Avenger didn't foil a robbery last night."

"That doesn't stop her from making up stories. She still owes me, and, by the way, so do you. Where's my five thousand?"

"Thought I'd wait and make sure your superhero days were over."

"Yeah, they're over. It's not as glamorous as it looks."

Nothing could be less glamorous than Tor in his Avenger suit. "So you're back to the calm of the comic store?"

Before Tor could answer, Camden gasped and suddenly rocked back as if someone had punched him hard in the chest. Wendy was close enough to catch him.

"Whoa! What gives?"

"Shot," he said.

"Shot? Who? Where? We didn't hear any shot."

Tor leaned over the counter, open-mouthed. I helped Wendy sit Camden down. "He means someone was shot, and he intercepted the feeling."

Camden held one hand to his heart and breathed heavily. "Same one."

Wendy pushed back her tangle of red curls. "This person's been shot before?"

"This person's killed before," I said. "Anything else?"

Camden grimaced. "A really gross sense of satisfaction."

Wendy couldn't believe it. "Cam, are you linked to this killer?"

"Only when he kills."

"Cool!"

I almost expected Tor to leap up on the counter and declare, "This is a job for the Parkland Avenger!" but he didn't.

Wendy continued to gush. "This is amazing! It's like you have super powers. Can you tune into the killer and see who it is? Can you see his victim?"

"No, just what they're feeling."

"I've never seen you do anything like this. Does it happen often?"

"These episodes have been particularly intense. I can't figure out why."

"The killer must have a super strong mind. Oh, here, lean back on me till you catch your breath."

"It was Brooke," he said. "Brooke's been shot."

Behind me, I heard Tor gasp. "Is she all right?"

"I think so."

I hauled him up. "Let's go check."

Tor was shaking. "I could be next."

Wendy frowned at him. "Why do you think that?"

"Now's your chance," I told Tor.

He took a deep breath and revealed his secret identity. "Wendy, I am the Parkland Avenger."

We could hear her laughing all the way out to the car. I put Camden in the front seat. "You okay?"

"Sure. I've been stabbed, strangled, and shot. I feel fine."

"Is it the same man?"

"Yes."

"You're not getting anything else?"

"Just his happy thoughts. My God, this guy is sick."

As much as I wanted to solve this on my own, I wondered if this was the time to involve the police. "Do you want to call Jordan?"

"You know what he always says. Any sort of psychic information doesn't hold up well in court."

"Maybe he knows something that could help. But let's check on Brooke first."

◇◇◇

Jordan was at the emergency room desk when we arrived.

"What happened to Brooke?" I asked.

"The initial report is Ms. Verner's attacker was a random drive by shooting," Jordan said. "Someone opened fire in the parking lot of the *Herald*. She may or may not have been the target."

"Is she all right?"

"They tell me she's in stable condition."

Camden let his breath out in relief. "It's the same man, and it isn't Boyd Taylor."

Around us, the waiting room swarmed with crying babies, people clutching bloodstained bandages, people coughing. Jordan motioned for us to follow him outside to a quieter place away from the door. His frown deepened. "Okay, listen up. Everything in our investigation points toward Boyd Taylor. Cam, I believe you, but you know how my colleagues feel about psychic information. About the same way they feel about the Parkland Avenger."

"That's no longer a problem," I said.

Jordan raised his eyebrows. "Oh? You've decided to come clean?"

"As of last night, the Avenger's no longer avenging."

"I don't want to know how you know that, Randall. Besides, this latest attack is more pressing. Fortunately, Ms. Verner is still alive, and as soon as I hear from the doctors, I plan to ask her some questions. You, however, will not ask her any questions. You will stay away. Do I make myself clear?"

"Jordan, Brooke's a friend of mine," Camden said. "If she can help me find her attacker, then I'll need to talk to her."

Jordan steamed silently for a moment. "Have you got a picture of his next victim in your head, an address, anything?"

"No, unfortunately not."

More steaming. "You can talk to her, but only after I've finished."

◇◇◇

The doctors wouldn't let us see Brooke, so we went home. Camden paced the island.

"This is so frustrating. Why can't I see who he is, or something useful that would stop him, instead of getting all the reruns? There must be something I can do."

"You can stop walking around like that. You're making me dizzy."

He flopped down on the sofa. "Damn stupid visions."

"There must be a reason you're having trouble controlling them this time."

"It's because I'm submerging all my murderous tendencies."

"That's what I think of when I look at you: cold-blooded killer."

"I do not want to sit here and wait for the next toxic wave."

My cell phone rang. "Don't go surfing yet." I answered and heard a firm young voice.

"Mr. Randall, this is J.C. Chapman from Royalle's Fine Jewelry, if you'll recall. I have some information that—oh, be quiet, Sim, I know what I'm doing. Excuse me, Mr. Randall, but Sim Johnson seems to think I should tell Mr. Royalle this first, but I'm worried about what he'll say, so I thought I'd ask you."

"What did you want to tell me, J.C.?"

"Sim and I took some things down to the basement yesterday, and we had to move some boxes. I saw something sparkly, and when I picked it up, it was a ring. I'm almost certain it's one that was stolen, so if it is, that means the thief got in through the basement, only we didn't see how. So we started poking around and moving more things, and we found a—I guess you'd call it a cover, like a manhole cover, only made of stone. When we slid it back, we found what looks like an underground passage, which is amazingly exciting, only Sim thinks we should tell Mister Royalle, and I thought we'd better call you, and Sim says I should take the ring to Mister Royalle right away, but if it's a clue, shouldn't you see it first?"

The other tunnel! "Where are you right now?"

"I'm in the store, of course."

"Sim's with you? Who else is there?"

"Everybody's working today."

"Can they hear your conversation?"

"No, we're in the back."

"Stay right there. I'm coming over." I closed my phone. "That was J.C. at Royalle's. The kids found the other tunnel."

◇◇◇

We drove to Royalle's Fine Jewelry, found a parking place in the next block, and went in. Everyone was with a customer, but J.C. managed a wide-eyed look at me.

"I need to talk to J.C.," I told Petey, and he nodded.

I waited until she finished with her customer. Then she led me and Camden to one of the back rooms where the employees kept their coats and dug into a large black bag.

"Here's the ring. I'm not really sure if it's one that was stolen, but it looks like one of those. Should I give it back to Mister Royalle? What if he thinks I stole it? What do I do now?"

"I'll give him the ring and explain things." I was curious about the bag. It looked like the one Emmajean had. "Is that a gym bag?"

She turned it so I could see the white letters, "PGT." "Parkland Gymnastics Team."

"Are you on the team?"

"Yes, we were all state champions last year." Even though no one was around, she lowered her voice. "Do you want to see the tunnel?"

"That's why we're here."

Royalle's basement was neat and well-organized. J.C. pushed a large box aside and showed us the entrance. "Sim and I decided to cover it up again." She slid the round stone cover over, and we looked into the black depths. "What's it for? What could be down there?"

"It may be part of the Underground Railroad."

"Oh, wow. Really? That's cool."

"I'm surprised you two didn't hop down there."

"Sim wanted to, but I told him we'd get all grubby, and Mister Royalle would notice. So do you think he knows about it this? Should we tell him?"

"Yes, we'll tell him. I don't know why he doesn't know."

"Oh, he never comes down here. He says he hates being in anything like a cave or a basement. If he needs something, one of us gets it."

I'd brought my flashlight. "Well, I'll have a look."

She looked alarmed. "Are you really going down in there?"

"You stand by in case we yell."

"But how will you get out?"

"It slopes down, see? Be right back."

From what I remembered from the map, this tunnel didn't connect to any other tunnel, but came out somewhere on the side of the building where Petey's grandfather had drawn the circle his father thought indicated a tree. Sure enough, the tunnel led a short way and then curved to the right. In the curve, Camden and I found a rolled up sleeping bag, a kerosene lantern, and a backpack.

"These items look far too modern to be from the Civil War," I said. "I think somebody has found themselves a nice little hiding place."

"Alycia."

"That would be my guess. We oughta hang around Royalle's tonight and find out."

We followed the tunnel a little further where it sloped up. I pushed on what looked like another stone cover and was rewarded with a shower of dirt and grass. Coughing and spluttering, I pushed the cover aside and poked my head up into the small grassy area inches away from the parking lot. I took a few breaths of fresh air and went back down, replacing the cover overhead.

"The circle on Petey's father's map didn't represent a tree. It represented the outside entrance to the tunnel, a fact that Petey's grandfather either forgot to mention, or didn't want Petey's father to know. Somehow I can't imagine Carlton Royalle as a mischievous boy playing around in tunnels."

We went back to the basement entrance.

J.C. and Sim helped us out. "Are you okay?" J.C. asked.

"Yep." I brushed the dirt and dust from my clothes. "Okay, it's official. We now know how the thief got in." And I had a damn good clue who the thief might be.

Sim slid the cover over the hole. "Where does the tunnel go?"

"It comes out in the parking lot."

I could tell he wanted to explore it. "What do we do now?"

"We'll go explain things to Mister Royalle."

Petey was with a customer, and when he'd finished, I handed him the ring. "J.C. found this in the basement, but she was afraid you'd think she stole it."

"I'd never think that." He examined the ring. "Yes, this is one we were missing. Good work, J.C."

"She and Sim found something else in the basement. There's a short passageway that leads out to the parking lot."

"From the basement? But how? It has a stone floor."

"Someone carved out a hole."

"Good heavens!"

"Years ago. I think your grandfather knew about it, but not your dad."

"I never knew that. I don't ever go in the basement. I'm not good with small enclosed places."

"It'll be a simple matter to close it up. Have someone cement over the cover, and I'll show you where the other entrance is, so you can have it filled in, too."

"You really shouldn't do that," J.C. said. "It's part of history."

Petey disagreed. "Something has to be done about it. I don't want any more robbers coming up through the ground."

"I can fix a lock on it," Sim said. "And if we keep boxes on top, no one can get in."

I wondered how Alycia had managed to lift the cover. "How heavy were the boxes on top?"

"It was just boxes of extra wrapping paper and gift bags," J.C. said.

So a tall, strong woman could've shoved that aside. "You might want something heavier."

Chapter Eighteen

"Thy Rebuke Hath Broken His Heart"

I called the hospital and was told Brooke could have visitors. She was hooked up to several complicated-looking machines, but she was awake and glad to have company. We could stay only ten minutes, so I got right to the point.

"Who shot you, Brooke?"

She was trying to keep her eyes open. "I didn't see anyone. I came out to my car, and that's the last thing I remember. If I were you, I'd put my money on Chance Baseford."

Camden put his hand on hers. "You're going to be all right."

"Thank you."

"We're still expecting you for Christmas."

She swallowed hard. "I hope I can be there."

"If not, we'll come celebrate here."

"Thanks, Cam."

Maybe it was almost dying, or Camden's kindness, or just plain weariness that made her say, "I lied to you, David, about the Avenger. I did hire someone."

"I know. Tor of Comic World. Great choice, by the way."

"Damn," she said. "You're good. And I lied about having information about Jared Hunter."

"What didn't you lie about, Brooke?"

She closed her eyes. "Wanting a stupid Parkie award."

I wanted to ask her more questions, but the nurse shooed us out

◇◇◇

When we got home, Mom met us at the front door. She addressed me, eyes blazing.

"When did you plan to tell me Grady called?"

Uh-oh. "Now."

Camden edged past her. "I'll just go on in."

She pulled me into the foyer. "How many times has he called?"

"One."

"You'd better not be lying to me, young man."

"Mom, I promise. He called earlier today, and you haven't been home for me to tell you that."

"Well, he called again and wondered why I hadn't gotten his message."

"Great. Now he's checking up on you."

Her eyes narrowed. "You've got to get over this."

Maybe I didn't want to get over it. "He's just so damn mushy! Even his name's mush. Grady. What kind of name is that?"

"And Henry is a studlier name?"

"He's everything Dad wasn't."

"Nonsense! Your father could be quite gentle and romantic."

"I never saw that side of him."

"Well, just because you never saw it doesn't mean it wasn't there."

"So, you're telling me when no one's looking, Grady turns into raw meat-eating commando?"

"David, for heaven's sake." She turned away from me.

"I'm sorry." What was the trouble here? "I—I miss Dad."

She turned back and put her arm around me. "Of course you do. I do, too. Would you please get it through your thick head Grady isn't a substitute for your father? He's just a good friend of mine."

I wasn't through sulking. "He said come visit us in Florida. What's with the 'us' crap?"

"We live in the same building, you big dope. Naturally, you might run into him."

"Just so I don't run into him coming out of your bedroom."

"That's not going to happen. We're much too careful."

"Mom!"

She laughed. "Honestly, Davey. Do we have to go through the sex talk again?"

"No, no, please, no."

She gave me a hug. Her tone softened. "In case you want to know, the children's cemetery is very well-kept. The arrangements Kary and I bought look lovely."

"I don't want to know, but thanks, anyway."

"I think it would help you if you went down there and saw how nice it is."

"There's no need for that, Mom."

She looked into my eyes. "The holidays are the hardest times. Believe me, I know."

As far as Lindsey's death was concerned, every day was a hard time. "There's no reason for me to go visit her grave."

"It might give you some comfort."

Why couldn't she understand there would be no comfort— ever. "It's a big rock with writing on it. She's not there. What kind of comfort is that?"

Mom gave me another hug. "Well, it helps me. You know I can't get to your father's grave that often."

Dad's buried in the churchyard of First Lutheran in Elbert Falls, Minnesota, where he'd gone to church all his life. I didn't really want to hear about that, either. "Okay, well, I'm glad you're comforted."

She wasn't about to give up. "Have you thought about grief counseling? Doesn't your church have a group?"

"Even if they did, I wouldn't unburden my soul to a bunch of strangers."

"Then talk to me, Davey. That's one reason I wanted to spend this Christmas with you."

I was afraid of something like that. "I appreciate the effort."

"It's no effort. Lindsey was your only child and my only grandchild. We need to talk about her, even if it's just a little something."

Emotion throbbed in my throat. "No."

"Maybe share a few happy memories? Don't you talk about her to anyone?"

"No."

"Not even Cam? I find it very helpful to have one good friend to confide in."

Like Grady? I almost said. "Camden knows how I feel. We don't have to talk about it."

"Honestly, you men! It's all well and good to be big and tough, but sometimes you have to let go, or you'll explode."

"I'm not going to explode." Even though I really felt like exploding. "But I'm going to get angry if you don't change the subject."

"All right. But you haven't heard the last of this."

"How was your trip to Charlotte? Did you get cursed?"

"Oh, the exhibits were fabulous! Ellin got some wonderful footage for her show. Let me show you what I bought."

This was the perfect distraction. "Can you go anywhere and not buy something?"

"I wish I could've found one of those musical pocket watches for you. Where did Cam go? I don't want him to see his present."

"He'll know, anyway."

"Will he really?"

"It's kind of difficult to surprise him."

She rummaged in one of the many plastic bags stacked on the sofa. "Ellin said he needed some decent shirts, so we each got him one."

"He definitely won't be surprised about that. Where's Kary?"

"She said something about going out with some friends."

I almost said, "Friends in Spandex?" and realized this would've sounded peculiar. "Did she say when she'd be back?"

"No, and speaking of shirts, what have you done to yours? Have you and Cam been playing in the mud?"

I didn't want her to know I'd been down in another tunnel. "I helped move some boxes in Petey's basement."

"Well, you're a mess. What else have you done today?"

"Visited Brooke in the hospital. Somebody took a shot at her."

"Good Lord! Does this have to do with the murder case?"

"Camden says it's the same man."

"Is she going to be all right? Can she have visitors?"

"Yes to both questions, but she's had all the company she can have for today. I'll take you by tomorrow."

"Don't you think it's time to leave this to the police?"

"They're on the case, too, Mom. Don't worry."

"It's my job to worry." She paused her search in the plastic bags. "Have you thought about what I said?"

"About what?"

"About talking to someone."

Good grief, was she still on this? "I'm thinking about it."

"Good. You'll feel better. I know you will."

I would only feel better if I had my daughter back. But since that wasn't going to happen, I'd get along the best way I could, and that included agreeing with my mother.

"Yes, ma'am."

And then I had to run over to Lily's.

She met me on her porch. "Oh, David, Kary's had the most wonderful idea! The SHS is going on patrol."

Keltar the Incredibly Gifted and Destiny's Arrow came out, followed by a young woman in a tight-fitting gray leotard and tights with gleaming stars across her collarbone and surrounding the eye holes of her mask.

Keltar beamed. "Randall! Meet the newest member of our group: Wonder Star!"

The young woman smiled and put her hands on her hips. "The brightest crime fighter in the heavens!"

It was Kary.

Chapter Nineteen

"The People That Walked in Darkness"

I didn't know where to begin. She turned around. "What do you think? Virtue Vixen's left the group, so they had an opening."

She looked amazing, but I could hardly focus. "Where did you get that outfit?"

"It's one of the Vixen's old costumes. She was originally going to be Wonder Star."

Calm, calm. Keep calm. "Okay. And now what?"

"We're going on patrol, of course. If the Avenger's a rogue superhero, then who better to track him down than real superheroes, or at least, people who take this seriously."

"I didn't know you were even interested in superheroes."

"Maybe it's time I tried something new."

"Could I talk to you for just a second?" I wanted to grab her and carry her home, but I settled for a gentle tug on her arm. We went out into Lily's front yard. "Brooke's been shot."

"Shot? My God, is she going to be okay? Did she see who did it?"

"She said for me to put my money on Baseford, but we all know he wouldn't do anything so crass."

"But someone attacked her in broad daylight. Doesn't that mean the killer is getting desperate?"

"And careless."

"But why go after Brooke? Did she know Jared?"

"I don't know what the connection is. But Camden felt it, so it's the same person."

"Well, we're not giving up, are we? All the more reason for the SHS to get out there. We might learn something useful."

While it was thrilling to hear her say "we," as if we were a crime-solving couple, there was still this little matter of Wonder Star and her faithful companions. "I don't think Jordan will appreciate people dressed in costumes and masks roaming the city."

"That's why we'll make sure he doesn't see us."

"And I might have mentioned that Brooke was shot, as you said, in broad daylight."

"That's why we're going to patrol at night. What time is it?"

Her sudden question threw me. "What? Uh, almost five."

She called to Lily and the others standing on the porch. "It's my turn to make supper tonight. I'll meet you around seven. How's that?"

Keltar gave her an elaborate salute. "See you then."

As we walked back to our house, Kary peeled off her mask and shook back her hair. "You know your mother is concerned about you."

"Concerned about me? You're the one planning to—wait a minute. Did she put you up to this?"

"Of course not."

"First the leopard blouse and then a starry leotard? I sense a pattern here."

"All right, maybe she is responsible. She encouraged me to break out of my rut. You know all I've done for months is play the piano and go to school."

"But a superhero? That's way out of a rut. That's beyond any rut I've ever heard of."

"David, for goodness sake, lighten up. She told me how mopey you get around Christmas. She wants you to break out, too. I don't suppose you could talk to her about Lindsey?"

I had no doubts that Mom had put her up to this, as well. I allowed myself to sink into that beautiful warm sympathetic gaze for about two seconds. Then I pulled back. "No."

Kary gave me a long measuring stare, as if deciding whether or not to push any further. "All right. Is there anything else I should know about the case?"

I was grateful for the change of subject. "The kids that work at Royalle's found the entrance to another tunnel in the basement of the store. I don't think the police know about this one. Camden and I checked it out. We think the thief may be using it as a hideout. And we think Alycia is the thief."

"What can the SHS do to help?"

Stay away! I wanted to say. "If you happen to be near Royalle's, you might see her. Then you could call me."

"Sounds good. Now, if I want to be ready for my nightly patrol, I'd better get started on supper."

I knew I couldn't possibly talk to Mom about Lindsey. During supper, I managed to distract myself with Kary's tuna casserole. It's one of the few things she can make, and it's the perfect antidote for grief. I was so busy hunting for the edible bits I could ignore all the significant and sympathetic looks from her and from Mom. Camden did his part by asking many questions about the Egyptian exhibit, and Fred, grumbling at his end of the table was good for a few digressions, but after a while, the conversation came back to Brooke and my increasingly dangerous case. I didn't mention that Camden and I planned to go back to the tunnels tonight to confront a possible killer.

"You said the police were also on this case, Davey. Do they know everything you know?"

"Yes, of course." Everything they needed to know right now, that is. "Jordan and I share information all the time." Ha, ha.

Mom did not look convinced. "I think you should leave matters to them. What kind of Christmas would it be if you or Cam get shot? I'd be very annoyed."

"So would I," Kary said. She had changed out of her costume before she started supper and looked thankfully normal in a tee shirt and jeans.

"Camden, do you see either of us being shot?"

"Nope."

"Don't let them fool you, Sophia." Kary scraped up the last forkful of her casserole. "Cam rarely sees his own future."

"Well, then, all the more reason to leave this whole thing alone."

"Mom, I promise I'll call Jordan tomorrow."

"And?"

"And see what he has to say."

This was not good enough. "And tell him you're off the case."

"I can't do that. I have a client. Boyd Taylor's counting on me to prove he's innocent."

There was a dismissive "Huh!" from Fred.

"Fred, contrary to your warped view of the universe, I have solved some crimes."

"David." Mom put her hand on my arm. "When you decided you'd be a detective, I'll admit I was worried, but nearly all your cases have been finding missing people, or lost objects, or making sure these useless fathers pay child support. We're talking about murder here."

I'd kind of glossed over the details of my last case, which had involved murder, too. "I think we have a more serious problem here."

"What?"

"Has Kary told you about her latest venture?"

Kary gave me a defiant look. "Wonder Star, brightest crime fighter in the heavens, thank you very much."

Camden almost choked on his tea.

Mom turned to Kary in admiration. "Oh, that sounds exciting! Do you have a snazzy costume?"

"It's beautiful, all shiny gray with gold and silver stars."

"Is there a cape?"

"No, but I believe I have a Wand of Power. I'll show you before I go out."

Camden managed to catch his breath. "Go out?"

"I'm meeting the SHS at seven. We're going to patrol the city and find the Avenger."

He gave me a wide-eyed stare. "This is new."

Kary reached for the crackers. "Yes, isn't it? And who knows? The Avenger may have seen something that will lead us to Jared's killer. I'll bet the police haven't thought of that."

"That's a great idea," Mom said. "But be careful."

"Oh, I will. Someone would have to be crazy to attack a whole league of superheroes."

Camden's voice was calmer than I expected. "Kary, you realize these people are not real superheroes. They don't have any special powers."

"They believe they can do something. That can be powerful. And besides, it looks like fun. It's better than sitting in the library, wouldn't you say so, David?"

What could I say? Kary looked fierce and Mom looked pleased. The only sane reply was, "I'm not going to argue with Wonder Star."

◇◇◇

Royalle's was closed for the night. I parked the Fury where we had a good view of the store. While we waited to see if anyone would show up, I tried not to think of Kary, Keltar, and the others, leaping from the tops of Parkland's buildings and falling in multicolored heaps to the sidewalks.

"She'll be okay," Camden said. "She's with a group of people who aren't known for their athletic prowess."

"'Prowess.' Damn. Where'd you come up with that one?"

"I read it in a comic book."

"You know this is all my mother's fault."

"She'll be okay, I promise."

I scanned the parking lot for any movement. "If this is Alycia's hideout, she might already be in the tunnel."

"I still can't believe Alycia's the thief," Camden said.

"Well, she's not a very good one. She didn't take much. Maybe it's the thrill. Maybe the museum break in whetted her appetite."

"'Whetted.'"

"I'm telling you, you're falling far behind in vocabulary challenge."

Camden turned his head as if someone had called his name. "She's here."

I squinted at the side of Royalle's. A familiar tall shadow detached itself from the wall and crouched over the outside entrance to the tunnel.

Having experienced her strength, I knew I didn't want to confront her in the narrow confines of the tunnel. "Come on."

We had crossed the parking lot and were almost to her when she stood up, startled.

"Alycia, wait," Camden said. "We just want to talk to you."

She leaned forward slightly, as if to get a better look. "Cam?"

"What's going on?"

"I can't talk to you out here."

"Come back to the house with us, then. You don't have to hide in that tunnel."

"Yes, I do," she said. "You have no idea."

"Then tell me. I want to help you."

She took a long pause.

Camden reached out and took her hand, but she jerked her hand away. "Damn it, Cam. Don't do that."

Too late. He'd already seen what he needed to see. "You've been in Royalle's. And Carlene's record store, and Trilby's Antiques."

"So maybe I was looking for something."

"You were taking something."

"You can't prove that."

"Then tell me why you're hiding out here. You were attacked in the park. Is that why you're so frightened?"

Her mouth fell open. While she searched for an answer, I said, "My car's up the street."

She agreed to come with us to the car. Camden got in the back seat with her. I noticed she was trembling. "All right, look, everything fell apart. When I was researching some history, I read about this tunnel system. I told Jared and Bert about it, and we thought it would be fun to explore. Bert said there was a map like that in the museum and he knew how to get it."

"Bert Galvin, right? Ralph's son?"

"Yeah, Ralph had something to do with the museum, which is how Bert knew how to get in. We thought all the alarms were off, but Jared got caught. The police didn't see me."

"So you and Bert got away with the map."

"This was all Bert's idea. Then he ended up in some mental hospital."

"Did you take the map?"

"Yes. I told Bert I'd give it to Jared. Then when Jared and I hooked up again, I told him we oughta try using the map, but he didn't want to."

"That's why you called him a coward."

"Yeah, I might have given him a hard time."

"Where's the map now?"

"I stuck it in Jared's comics. I figured he might change his mind."

"Did you show the map to Tor at Comic World?"

"No."

I already knew that Tor found the map and decided to use it for himself, the little weasel. "But you'd had plenty of time to study the map. You remembered how conveniently the tunnels connected to all the stores. You didn't mind using it to help yourself."

She ran her hand through her short curls. "All right, so maybe I did take a few things. Just enough to get by. See, Jared and Bert and I kinda liked seeing what we could get away with." She appealed to Camden. "It was only a few things. I'm going to pay it all back, Cam, I swear."

This time when he took her hand, she didn't pull away. "I still don't understand why you thought you had to steal in the first place."

"Because I'm broke! The basketball scholarship money only lasted a few years, and then I—" She couldn't meet his eyes. "I didn't have anything to fall back on. I wasn't the world's best student, you know. I only took a few things. I didn't hurt anyone. And I have to admit I got a kick out of it. So did Jared, until he got caught."

"I know why he didn't say anything about you, but why did he protect Bert?"

I'd been wondering the same thing.

"Look, somehow, Jared got off easy. When we got back together, he said Ralph Galvin decided to be lenient, and I wouldn't have to ever worry about money again."

"Did he have some grand money making scheme? He worked at a garage. He wasn't making that much, was he? How did he pay for all your jewelry?"

"Wait a minute." I turned so I was facing Alycia. "Was Ralph paying for Jared's silence?" Her own silence gave me my answer. "Camden, I think I know what happened. Jared asked for a raise. Isn't that right, Alycia? For some reason, Ralph was paying Jared not to mention his son, but Jared got a little too greedy, and Ralph didn't like that."

"Look, Bert's just a kid. Jared let him hang out with us. He didn't want anything to happen to him, so he protected him. We were family."

The family Jared never had.

Alycia glanced up the street as if she'd heard someone coming. "All I know is, Jared said he knew why Bert had been sent to a mental hospital and that he was going to take care of things, and now I'm scared to stay here any longer. First Jared's murdered, and then somebody tried to strangle me."

"Do you remember anything about your attacker?" I asked. "Height? Weight? Did he say anything? Did you grab a piece of clothing? See a piece of jewelry, like a ring or watch?"

"I was fighting for my life. I didn't stop to see if he had on a Rolex." She frowned a moment and then said, "He smelled funny."

"Funny?"

"Yeah, like he'd used some weird cologne." She tried to smile. "Cam, honey, you aren't going to rat on me, are you?"

"If you turn yourself in and return what you stole, it'll go a lot easier on you."

Her smile faded. "I can't do that."

"But you can't keep doing this."

"I'm not going to keep doing this, believe me. I'd planned another little job, but I'm too freaked out to stay here."

"Speaking of little jobs," I said, "do you still have the items you stole from Royalle's?"

She wouldn't meet my eyes. "I sold them off first thing. I didn't take a lot. I figured he'd have insurance, anyway."

"How did you know about the tunnel under Royalle's? It doesn't connect to the others across the street."

"I did a lot of research on the Underground Railroad. The people traveled ten, sometimes twenty miles at a time. They had to have what they called stations or depots along the way, places to rest. I remember my great-grandmother telling me there used to be a farm here with a big barn used as a station. I figured there might be a tunnel around. I got lucky and found it. The only time I've ever been lucky." Her voice trembled. "Except when I met Jared. He was real good to me. And to Bert."

"Come to the house," Camden said.

"Can you guarantee my safety? I don't think so." She opened the car door. "I'm leaving town. I'm getting out before I end up like Jared."

"Alycia—"

"Cam, don't even think about following me."

"At least call me if you change your mind."

She paused. "I won't, but thanks." She ran off into the night.

For a moment I thought Camden was going to follow her. Then he sat back in the car. "What do we do now?"

"If she meant what she said, she'll leave town and be safe. That's all you can hope for. You can't make her stop her life of crime."

"She doesn't have to do that."

"Well, you heard her. Basketball just doesn't pay like it used to." I started the car. "At least she gave me some good information. First thing tomorrow, I'm talking to Ralph."

"She said her attacker smelled funny. What could she have meant by that?"

"You held her hand. You tell me."

"She was too frightened for me to get any clear pictures. What are you going to tell Petey?"

"That we caught the thief, and she won't bother his store again." I started the car. "Now let's go find Wonder Star."

"Do you really want her to see you're checking up on her?"

"What if Ellin was running around town in a spangly leotard and a mask? How would you feel about—stop laughing, damn it."

I wanted Camden to zero in on Kary's position, but he said he couldn't. He was probably lying, but later, I was glad I hadn't spied on her. Around eleven o'clock she came home tired but happy. She said she'd spent an exhilarating night. They didn't find the Avenger, but she enjoyed spending time with the SHS.

"They're a delightful group of people. Different, but delightful. And thanks for not coming after me, David. I expected to see you any minute."

"Not me. I wouldn't want to spoil your fun. Were you able to avoid the police?"

"Oh, here's the best part. We stopped at the Pack 'n' Snack near Waverly Street so Last Nerve could get an energy drink, and Jordan came by! He didn't even recognize me! He asked us what we were doing, and Free Form said we were keeping the streets safe for democracy. You should have seen Jordan's face."

Actually, I would've liked to have seen Jordan's face. "I can imagine."

"Anyway, he warned us off, told us to go home and grow up. It was hilarious."

"You missed out on those wild teenage years, didn't you?"

She paused. "You know, I think that must be why I'm enjoying this so much."

I knew then that one night as Wonder Star wasn't going to be enough.

◇◇◇

The next morning, Mom and Kary went to see Brooke. Camden spent another restless night worrying about Alycia, he said, so after he had his Pop-Tarts, he sacked out on the sofa. I went by the *Herald*. Unfortunately, Ralph Galvin was out of town for a business meeting, so my next stop was Winthrop, Inc., where there was a reward waiting for me, or so I thought.

E. Walter sneered like an elf who'd bitten into a rotten mushroom. "Obviously, you haven't seen today's paper." He snapped it open and held it up for me to read.

"Avenger Foils Robbery."

I took the paper and read all about the Avenger's latest daring escapade. This article had been written by another *Herald* reporter. "Last night, the Parkland Avenger saved an elderly woman from a robber at the Parkland National Bank's Tenth Street ATM. Mildred Foster, 72, of 126 Elm Street, said she'd stopped at the ATM around ten o'clock when a large man approached her and demanded her money. A second man dressed in yellow tights and a red and yellow cape leaped from the roof, startling the robber, who ran off. Foster said the masked man then disappeared. 'It must have been the Parkland Avenger,' she told police. 'Thank goodness he was in the neighborhood.'"

Tor's mid-life crisis had yet to be resolved.

E. Walter slapped the paper down on his desk. "Don't come back until you have the cold hard truth. And don't think you can con me out of the reward. I'm not somebody you can push around."

Actually, I could've used him for a koosh ball, but I apologized. "Seems like the Avenger's doing some good, though."

"The man's a menace. People can't take the law into their own hands. I'm determined to make the city a better place, but you don't see me acting out some juvenile fantasy, or trying to do what policemen are paid to do." He took the paper and folded it tight, so he wouldn't have to see the offensive headline. "You said you'd identified the Avenger. Don't tell me there's more than one."

"The one I caught told me he was going to stop."

"A menace and a liar."

"I'll discuss it with him."

E. Walter calmed down a little. "I appreciate your efforts, Mister Randall. You seem to be the only one besides myself who takes this matter seriously."

"I'm trying to solve a crime, but what's your reason? I think there's more to this than wanting to make the city a better place."

I wasn't sure he'd answer me. He screwed up his tiny features and made some humphing sounds. "All this superhero stuff is crap. There's no flying super man with secret powers to swoop down and rescue you. There's no secret formula, no secret words to change you into an invincible human. You get bitten by a radioactive spider, you die. You get an overdose of radiation, you die. Nobody's going to protect you from life. When I found out I had cancer, did some amazing Chemo Man point his magic finger at my lungs and destroy the deadly cells? Even all my wealth couldn't save me. It couldn't save Lorraine."

"Lorraine?"

"My wife. You may have seen her picture in the hallway. She was a beautiful woman, gracious and loving. She knew the name of every employee, the names of their spouses and children. She set up one of the very first day-care centers in Parkland here at the company. She was the one who urged me to contribute to Parkland's many charitable organizations. No magical person in a cape came swooping down to rescue her. Thank God she didn't suffer long."

"Your secretary said you were a survivor."

"Yes, but the quality of my life has been severely damaged. Life without Lorraine is joyless. There are so many things I can't do, and quite frankly, I resent some idiot leaping from the rooftops when I can't walk up a flight of stairs without stopping for breath."

The guy looked like a walking peanut, but I liked his honesty. "Have you been swamped by calls from people wanting the reward?"

"Yes. My secretary turned away another whole crowd of impostors this morning. The only promising lead was a call from a young woman who works for the *Herald*. Didn't you say you had a contact there?"

"Must be the same woman. Did she give her name?"

He searched his desk. "I wrote it down. Here we are. Brooke Verner. But I believe I just read something about a Ms. Verner being the victim of a drive-by shooting yesterday. Do you think that is somehow connected to the Avenger?"

"I'll let you know."

"You most certainly will." He gave me one of his fierce little terrier glares. "I don't imagine a young man such as yourself has had much misfortune in your life. It changes you. You either let it drag you down, or you begin to look for ways to make things right. I've chosen the latter. Whether you help me or not, I will make this right."

I don't know what made me say it. As I'd made so plain to Mom, I never talk about Lindsey, not unless I want to feel like a knife is twisting my insides. But something about Winthrop's pain and loss rang deep and true when he talked about life being joyless and making the choice to let sorrow rule you. "I lost my daughter in a car crash. She was eight years old. Was there anything I could've done to prevent that crash? That's something I'll wonder the rest of my life."

His scowly little features didn't change. "Don't let it consume you. Get out there and do something. Don't let her life have been for nothing. Lorraine would've wanted me to go on, to take care of business. That's what you do: take care of business."

I almost saluted. "Yes, sir."

"Now get out. I have work to do and so do you. Go find this stupid Avenger and get him off the streets."

Chapter Twenty

"Then Shall Be Brought To Pass"

Tor was straightening a stack of motorcycle magazines and paused to give me a glare. "It wasn't me."

"You're sure."

"Didn't I tell you I was through with that? Must be some copy cat."

"Do you have an alibi for last night, say, around ten?"

"Yes, I do, smartass. I was with Wendy."

"No way."

"After she got through laughing, she wanted to hear all about my nights as the Avenger, and she ended up thinking it was pretty damn cool."

There's no figuring women. "Congratulations."

"We went back to her place, and I flipped through her collection, if you know what I mean. Stayed all night. You can check with her."

Checking with Wendy was definitely something I wanted to do. I wanted to do anything to keep from thinking what Winthrop had said.

Tor finished straightening the magazines and went behind the counter. He pulled out one of his sketchbooks and turned to an empty page.

"Chronicling your adventures?" I asked.

He took a photo from a stack. "Wendy asked me to draw one of her friends as a superhero for a Christmas present." His pencil skimmed over the paper. "You were leaving, weren't you?"

I grinned. "Far be it from me to disturb the Avenger."

Brooke was awake when I went in to see her. She gave me a wan smile.

"Thanks for coming by."

"How are you feeling?"

"Better. It's going to make a great story."

I sat down in one of the vinyl chairs. "Speaking of great stories, what's the scoop on your shooter? Anything new?"

"No. I could say it was the Parkland Avenger, but that's over."

"You haven't seen the paper today, either? The Avenger was out and about last night. Saved a little old lady's life savings."

Her smile faded. "Wait a minute. I didn't see Tor yesterday, and you said you knew about him, so I figured he was through."

"He is. This is someone else."

She looked upset. "A real Avenger, and I'm missing all the action."

"I think maybe there's been a real Avenger all along, the one doing it right."

"What are you talking about?"

"The other night, when you came in late. Camden and I were watching a movie, remember? You looked surprised to see us up."

"I remember, but what does that have to do with anything?"

"That was one of the nights the Avenger actually foiled a robbery, something you never told Tor to do. In fact, I don't think he was even out on the streets that night, but you were, trying to find out who the hell was protecting Parkland and if he'd give you an interview."

She started to protest, and then shut her mouth.

"What kind of deal did you have with Tor?"

"I paid him to show up at certain times, certain places. I'd alert the police and write the story. Or sometimes, he just told me what he did. He had a lot of imagination. I guess that comes from working in a comic store all your life."

"At some time, were you planning to turn him in and collect the reward?"

"I was going to split the reward with Tor."

"Did he know this?"

"Of course."

The little weasel.

Brooke yawned. "I was certain Mister Winthrop would give Tor a lecture, Tor would agree to reform, and then we'd divide the cash. He gets five thousand, I get a Parkie, and Winthrop gets the satisfaction of ridding Parkland of the Avenger."

"At some point, did it ever occur to you that you were scamming a sick man out of his money?"

"I never thought anyone would offer a reward like that. Besides, I was going to return my half."

Did I believe this? "That's all very tidy. It still doesn't explain why someone took a shot at you, or why the Avenger's still at large."

"I guess that's where you come in." She closed her eyes. "Actually, this is where you go out. I'm really very tired."

I got up. "Okay, but I'll be back. I don't think you've told me the whole story."

Brooke was drifting off into a medicated haze. "Found something. Not by keen reporting skills. By accident. First, I thought it was Baseford. After all, he's got the tabloid background. He could easily make up stories. But it isn't Baseford. Damn, I wish it were."

"What are you talking about?"

"All those stories in 'Your Turn.' All made up. Not Baseford, though. Damn."

"Someone is making up all the stories in 'Your Turn'? Someone at the *Herald*?"

She nodded. "Same person. Sugar Baby."

Since I was practically leaning over her at this point, I thought she was giving me a compliment. Then it registered. "Brooke, are you saying the same reporter who broke the Sugar Baby story is writing 'Your Turn'?"

"It's Galvin," she said. "And there's something else, Randall. I saw a letter on his desk, but I didn't get the chance to read all of it. It was from his son, pleading to come home. And he said, 'I promise I won't tell about the museum funds.' What could he be talking about?"

If she was this close to uncovering a scandal, no wonder someone took a shot at her. "I don't know," I said, "but I'll find out."

The nurse stepped in and told me it was time to leave. I went back to the Fury, called the museum, and asked to speak to the curator.

"My name's David Randall," I said. "I'm a private investigator, and I'm working on a case that has connections to the robbery that happened a year ago. You told me about the robbery last Friday, but I'd like to ask a few more questions. Was the museum having any financial trouble then?"

"No, sir," he answered. "We had a successful fund raising season. It was our bicentennial."

"Who was in charge of that?"

"One of our board members, Ralph Galvin."

"Is he still on the board?"

"No, he resigned last year."

"After the robbery?"

"I believe so. Board members can stay as long as they like. It's not a paid position."

"So he was a volunteer?"

"Yes, sir. We couldn't do without our volunteers. The library board's the same way, and the arts council."

"When did you announce the results of your fund raiser?"

"Just a minute. I can give you the exact date." I heard the clicking of computer keys. "August 14 a year ago. And since Mr. Galvin is editor of the *Herald*, we got excellent coverage in the newspaper. Why don't I send you a copy of last August's museum newsletter via email? It would have all the details."

"That would be very helpful, thanks."

"May I ask how this is pertinent to the robbery, Mr. Randall?"

"I'm still working on that," I said.

◇◇◇

I went back to 302 Grace. Camden was awake and asked if I wanted some lunch.

"Be there in a minute. I'm waiting on an email."

While I waited, I went to the *Herald's* website and searched through the archives until I found the August 14 article about the museum's successful fund raiser. The final tally for the fund raiser had been four hundred and fifty-five thousand dollars, a nice chunk of change. The bicentennial funds were designated for three areas: building and grounds, administration and staff, and acquisitions. Most of the money was going to purchase items for the museum, including art work, sculptures, and some letters written by Charles Park.

"Parkland's Museum of History celebrated its bicentennial by raising over four hundred thousand dollars," the article read. "The museum wishes to thank all its faithful supporters as well as new contributors who made this fund raiser successful. The museum plans to use some of the funds to buy a set of letters written by Parkland's founder and first mayor, Charles Park, from a private collector. The letters will complete Parkland's collection of historic memorabilia."

My phone rang. It was the museum curator. "Mr. Randall, my apologies, but I can't seem to locate that particular newsletter. It seems to have been deleted from our files."

Deleted? That sounded interesting. "I have the *Herald's* account," I said. "Four hundred and fifty five thousand dollars."

"That is correct."

"Two hundred thousand for building and grounds, one hundred and twenty-five thousand for administration and staff, and the rest for acquisitions, including some letters written by Charles Park."

"Oh, we were thrilled to get them. We'd been looking for the last set for years. In fact, Ralph Galvin handled that. He knew the collector and was able to get us the best possible deal."

"How much did you pay for them?"

"One hundred and fifty thousand dollars."

"That seems a little pricey. Who was the collector?"

More clicking of computer keys. "Well, this is odd," the curator said. "I was sure we had a record of all our purchases, but this one seems to be missing. I do remember his name, though. Thomas Hampton. Odd sort of fellow, though. Insisted on being paid in cash. I told Galvin we'd have to do that in three installments. Unfortunately, Hampton passed away not long after the sale. Galvin took the rest of the money to his family."

I wrote this down. "Thanks. You wouldn't happen to have a hard copy of your newsletter, would you?"

"I'm sorry, but we've gone paperless in an effort to help the environment. A few may have been printed for some of our older members, but I don't have any here. It sounds as if you have all your information, though."

Oh, I had all my information, all right. I thanked him and hung up. I searched for Thomas Hampton and found him in Fairlawn, Virginia. I also found out he was indeed dead, and he'd died on August 16, the victim of a hit and run accident. He was survived by a daughter, so I found her number and gave her a call. I explained I who I was and that I was curious about the value of the letters written by Charles Park.

"Oh, those old things," she said. "I'm so glad he got rid of them. I wish he'd gotten rid of everything in his house. It's taken me almost a whole year to go through it all."

"He sold them to the Parkland Museum of History in North Carolina, right?"

"Yes, he said some fellow came by asking about them, so he sold them. Dad was happy they went to the museum."

"Do you remember what he got for them?"

"Oh, my, yes, I remember, because he couldn't believe those old things were worth so much money. He got fifty thousand dollars."

"Fifty thousand?"

"I know. It's crazy. But that's what the fellow from the museum said they were worth. And he paid him in cash, so we were really happy about that."

"Is that how your father wanted to be paid?"

"Not especially. It was a surprise. He was delighted, though. He said a check could bounce. Dad didn't get much chance to enjoy the money, though."

She didn't say, "Later on, that nice fellow returned with the rest of the money we were actually entitled to."

"Did he sign any sort of receipt?" I asked.

"I'm sure he did."

"Would you happen to have a copy of it?"

"No, as I said, I've finally cleaned out his house."

"I was very sorry to hear about your father's death. My sympathies."

"Thanks," she said. "They never did catch the person that hit him."

I was beginning to think I knew who that was. I thanked the woman and sat back in my chair. I turned these new facts over in my mind. Ralph was in charge of fund raising and handled an important and expensive transaction, paying the collector in cash. Then the collector had a convenient accident before he found out what those letters were really worth. The museum was broken into, but nothing was stolen. What if Ralph sent Bert in to delete any record of the purchase of the Park letters? There should have been two more receipts for the rest of the money. What if Ralph forged Hampton's signature on these? No, wait. Hampton was killed on the sixteenth, two days after the fund raiser. Another family member would've signed, an even easier signature to create.

I went into the kitchen to get a Coke out of the fridge. Camden was slicing ham, and I got him caught up.

"Learned something interesting from Brooke. She caught a glimpse of a letter on Galvin's desk, a letter from his son begging to come home and promising not to tell about the museum funds. Brooke says Galvin saw her leave his office, and if this letter implicates him in some sort of crime, he may have wanted to silence her."

He put the slices on a plate. "So now we need to find Bert."

"And if Bert's in an institution, he may not remember anything."

"What kind of museum funds?"

I told him what I'd found out from the curator and my theory about Ralph's involvement.

"But how could he get away with that?" He reached for the plastic wrap and covered the dish. "Didn't someone at the museum check?"

"Apparently not."

"How are you going to find out? If he faked a signature on the receipts, those have been probably been destroyed."

"Maybe there's something in the August newsletter. The curator said they printed a few. I guess I'll have to track them down."

"From a year ago? You'll have to find a hoarder."

I snapped my fingers. "The library."

"I wouldn't ask Kary if I were you."

"I wouldn't dream of bothering Wonder Star with something so trivial. I'll ask Mandy." I called the library and asked if Mandy could find the History museum newsletter for August. She said she'd be glad to look.

Camden put the ham on the counter and took out the cheese. I sat down on one of the stools at the counter. "What's Mom up to?"

"She's talking to the neighbors."

"Which ones?"

"All of them. She's getting the Grace Street scoop."

"Seeing who's next for a makeover."

Camden put the cheese on the cutting board. "I've been thinking about Ellie."

"You're going to drop her like a rock and run for cover?"

He pointed the knife at me. "No. I'm going to figure out a way to make this work."

"You've decided to become the star of the PSN."

"Maybe if I agree to come by the studio every now and then, that will appease her."

"'Appease.' Nice. So you stop off, give a little free psychic advice, and then you disappear into the night, like, I don't know, a Mad Shadow?"

"It's a work in progress."

"Toss me a piece of cheese." He cut off a chunk and lobbed it over to me. "You know Ellin will take every opportunity to exploit your talent."

"Maybe not. Maybe we can come to some sort of agreement."

"Like a peace plan. That's working so well for the Middle East."

He finished slicing the cheese and reached for the bread. "You realize you're going to have to make sacrifices for Kary."

"I already have. No more smoking, drinking, drugs, single swinging, lap dances, fast cars—the list is endless."

"Something a bit closer to home."

Adoption: Is It Right For You? was still on the counter. I gave the book a wary glance. "Not any time soon, I hope."

"No," Camden said, "but eventually."

I shrugged, trying to be casual when everything inside me was backing up at the idea of another child. "Maybe I'll be ready then," I said. But I didn't think I'd ever be ready.

Chapter Twenty-One

"Thou Art Gone Up On High"

By the time I gave Camden a ride to chorale rehearsal, I still hadn't heard from Mandy. He yawned all the way to the church.

"Are you perhaps becoming bored with Handel?"

He rubbed his eyes. "My nap didn't help."

"More nightmares?"

"I don't remember, thank goodness."

When I dropped Camden off at the church, Jordan met me in the parking lot in his patrol car and gestured for me to roll down my window.

"Thanks for catching the Avenger, Randall. Now I can sleep at night."

"Go easy on the sarcasm. There's a limited supply."

"Oh, there's plenty of sarcasm. Plenty of irony, too. While the fellas and I are having a celebration at the Crow Bar, our resident superhero rescues a little old lady."

"Well, what are you doing chugging beer when you should be out patrolling the streets?"

"Occasionally, we're off-duty. Anyway, I wanted to tell you, great job, keep up the good work, and when were you going to tell me about exploring the tunnel?"

He was only mildly annoyed, so I felt safe enough to explain. "Camden and I checked it out."

"You're not the only one who talks to Mandy, you know, or Carlene." He paused to light a cigarette. "I left Peterson on guard. Got a few more officers on the street, just in case the Avenger returns." His eyes are naturally narrow, but he managed to slit them further down. "Is he planning to return?"

"I don't know, honest."

"Yeah, but I think there's a lot more you do know that you're not telling."

"Look, so what if this nut goes around doing good deeds? Isn't that one less criminal for you to deal with?"

"We don't look at it that way."

Tor had said something about Bert being in a sanitarium, and so had Alycia. "Any idea where Bert Galvin is?"

"Last I heard he was in some fancy hospital up north, drying out. Why? You think he had something to do with Hunter's death?"

"I'm just curious."

"The museum determined nothing had been stolen, so Hunter served his time, and we never could pin anything on Bert Galvin. End of story. Except Ralph Galvin still likes to ride our asses, and now he's got Brooke Verner in the driver's seat."

"Not anymore."

"Apparently the girl's made an enemy. Oh, and by the way, Randall. What's with the Halloween party? This is Christmas."

"Halloween party?"

"Yeah, that group of nitwits walking around at night all dressed up in tin foil and spangles. They say they're some sort of special neighborhood watch. My men and I have stopped them three times now."

"For being drunk and disorderly?"

"For being out and goofy."

"That's the SHS."

"Stupid Human Shitheads?"

"Superhero Society. I'm surprised you haven't availed yourself of their services before."

"Do they know anything about the Avenger?"

"No, and they're just as pissed as you are."

"I doubt that. I think I said amateurs always get in the way." This statement was accompanied by a significant look.

"I'm a highly skilled professional."

"See what I mean about sarcasm? Plenty to go around." His radio crackled with a voice instructing all available units to the convenience store on Emerald and Fourth. "I'd better check this out. The Avenger must require a Slurpee to keep up his super strength." He started the car. "Tell your band of merry men to stay out of police business. I especially don't want any of them down near Royalle's tonight."

"What's happening tonight?"

"We're going to stake out the area and with luck catch the burglar. I'd better not see you down there, either." He drove off with an unnecessary squeal of tires.

I went inside the church and chose a pew near the back. I didn't feel like talking to anyone. The chorale sang about the people that walked in darkness seeing a great light. I could use a great light right about now to show me what was going on.

I didn't get a great light, but I got the next best thing. Mandy called.

"I found copies of the museum newsletter, and there's one for August. But the library closes at eight."

I looked at my watch. Seven fifteen. "I'll be right there."

Mandy was in the very back of the reference room at a row of ancient filing cabinets. She handed me the August issue of the museum newsletter. "I was lucky to find this. We're in the process of changing all this material to other formats. I'm not sure why we kept the museum newsletters when we have them on line. I guess it still worries me not to have something I can hold in my hand."

"I'm glad you feel that way," I said, "because this may help solve my case."

I looked through the newsletter and found the list of future acquisitions and what each one was going to cost the museum.

Charles Park's letters were listed at one hundred and fifty thousand dollars. This wasn't something Ralph wanted the Hampton family to know. The museum would assume he paid Hampton the full amount, hell, the curator considered it a bargain. But Ralph needed to make sure no one would question him.

The night of the break-in, this was what Bert was supposed to do. Delete any record of the transaction. Delete the August newspaper, the receipts, and possibly destroy any paper copies of the newsletter that might be lying around. Maybe stealing the map was just a way to involve Jared and Alycia, so if they got caught, the police and the museum would be diverted from the real crime.

"Mandy, can I keep this?"

"Yes. Let me know if it cracks the case."

I could tell she enjoyed saying "cracks the case."

By the time I got back to the church, the chorale was singing something else, something about unto us a child is born. I thought of 302 Grace with its lights and candy canes and stars sparkling from the windows, and then I couldn't keep from thinking about Lindsey and the happy Christmases I had with her and Barbara. Barbara had an elaborate wooden candle-holder from Germany called a pyramid that turned by itself, so the lighting of the candle always thrilled Lindsey. Barbara always made a special Christmas breakfast of pancakes shaped like Christmas trees. Lindsey loved those. And I couldn't help remember Lindsey shaking me awake at five in the morning, almost incoherent with excitement, or the way she flew down the stairs and stopped, overwhelmed, by the sight of the Barbie dolls and all their little clothes, or the pink bicycle, or the little stove that cooked real pies. She would stand, hands clasped, as if afraid if she moved, the spectacle would disappear. Barbara always scolded me for buying too much, but I couldn't help it. I wanted Lindsey to have everything. I had to believe that in her brief little life, she'd been happy.

I sure as hell didn't want to think about that any more.

Now the chorale swung into a cheery refrain about the shadow of death. Camden glanced my way. I made a face to express my opinion.

After stopping off in the park to hear a few rounds of the "Alternative Messiah," we went home. Camden went upstairs to bed. I went to my office to ponder. I spread my copy of the map on my desk, and I gave it another look. I'd been concentrating on the underground passageways. What if there was something a little higher? When the thief robbed the antique store, he came in through a trap door in the ceiling. Using my finger, I traced the route from the trap door to another passage in the roof. Here was the way in. Next to Trilby's Antiques was a building marked "Haymore Building, 1925." This was one of the abandoned buildings further down the block. Jordan and his men would search all the empty buildings.

Uh-ho. According to this map, there was a secret attic room in the Haymore Building, accessible by a wall panel and pull-down stairs. Jordan said Mandy had shown him the map. Did he have his own copy? Would he see this, or would the robber have an easy shot at the policemen from this sniper's perch?

Someone had murdered Jared and shot Brooke, and I knew that person hadn't been Tor. I rolled up the map and hurried out to the Fury. I didn't know where Jordan was hiding, but I remembered he assigned an officer to guard the entrance to the tunnel. Officer Peterson, one of the younger members of the force, was standing behind the trash cans in the alley. He turned quickly. I held up both hands as I approached him.

"Take it easy, Peterson. It's David Randall, a friend of Jordan's. I need to know where he is."

Peterson relaxed. "You're not supposed to be here, sir. It could be dangerous."

"Jordan needs to see this map."

Peterson wasn't easily convinced. "How do I know you're not the man we're looking for?"

"Call Jordan and ask him."

It took a few minutes, but Peterson managed to get his radio to work. Jordan's voice was as rough as the static surrounding it.

"Tell him to get his butt across the street."

Jordan waited in another alley beside Royalle's. He scowled, arms folded. "Didn't I tell you to keep away? What is so damned important? We're trying to have a stakeout here."

"This." I unrolled the map and showed him the room above the Haymore Building. "If your man's in there, he could pick you guys off one by one."

As we both looked up at the Haymore Building, somebody jumped from the roof of Trilby's Antiques.

"What the hell?" Jordan took out his bullhorn. "You on the roof! This is the police! Freeze!"

The slim figure, all in red and yellow, crouched on the rooftop.

Damn it, Tor. What are you trying to prove?

Then the figure turned and straightened. Hmm. Unless Tor had grown shorter and better looking since Tuesday, this was another man.

Wait a minute. First Kary and now—? This couldn't be what I was thinking.

Jordan aimed his gun at the figure. "This is your last warning! Come down!"

The figure leaped easily to the roof of the next building and disappeared. As Jordan instructed his men to give chase, I stood for a moment, undecided. Then I got back in my car, raced home, and ran up the stairs. I crashed into Camden's bedroom, expecting to find it empty, or Camden half-dressed, one foot in a yellow sock and a guilty look. He was rolled up in bed, asleep, his hair over his eyes.

I looked around, baffled. No red and yellow clothes strewn on the floor, no mask dangling from a doorknob. The window was closed. I turned on the bedside lamp and gave Camden's arm several shakes before he woke up.

"What?"

"I want to see what you have on."

He pushed himself up on one elbow. "Don't you get enough sex without having to bother me?"

"Just get up."

He pushed back the covers. He had on his usual worn white pajamas. "What the hell is all this about?"

"Oh, I had this crazy idea you might be the Parkland Avenger."

He sat up and leaned back against the pillows. He sighed theatrically. "It was only a matter of time before you discovered my secret identity."

"We had a sighting. The guy looked about your size."

"Well, I must be pretty damn fast."

"With your super alien DNA, anything's possible." Now that I thought about it, there was no way Camden could've gotten downtown and back, unless he had an accomplice who knew how to drive. "I'd better have another word with Tor—only this guy didn't look like him, at all. There must be a whole flock of Avengers."

He pushed his hair out of his eyes. "Any theories on why I would be likely to join them?"

"Sublimating your feelings in regard to your inability to prevent Jared's murder?"

I'm not sure what he would have said in reply, because at that moment, Mom came to the bedroom door, tying the sash of her—good lord—leopard patterned robe. "What are you boys up to? It's almost midnight."

I said, "Were we too loud?" and Camden said, "Sorry to wake you."

She came in. "Sounds like a serious conversation. Is everything all right?"

"Fine," I said. "I needed to discuss the Avenger case."

"This late at night? Are you sure you weren't having another nightmare, Cam? You two come downstairs and let me make some hot chocolate."

We trooped down stairs to the kitchen and sat at the counter while Mom bustled about with the milk and chocolate syrup.

Camden yawned and rubbed his eyes, but I was wide-awake. I had to rethink the case of the multiple Avengers. This Avenger tonight had been Camden's size, which is to say, about five seven, a hundred and thirty pounds, the size of your average teenager. Some kid on a spree? Fraternity stunt? Super Teens Gang initiation?

Mom stirred the milk as it heated. "Now what's so important about this case that it can't wait until morning?"

"I had some information I wanted to share with Camden."

"Next time, save it."

"Yes, ma'am."

"Cam needs his sleep, and so do you."

"Sometimes I stay up late working on a case."

"It's a silly case, anyway. As soon as this person gets tired of playing dress-up, he'll stop." She poured the syrup in and stirred some more. "You know I went by the hospital to see Brooke today. She agrees with me."

Oh, man. More interfering. "Did she tell you who the Avenger was?"

"No, but it's time for this nonsense to stop." She poured the milk into mugs and set the mugs on the counter.

I took a drink. "How was Brooke feeling?"

"Much better. She hopes to be with us for Christmas—which reminds me. I need to get her a gift. What do you think she'd like?"

"A Parkie award."

"Can you buy one somewhere?"

"Just kidding. If she's going to keep on writing dangerous exposes, she'll need a bullet-proof vest."

Mom poured the last of the milk into her cup. "I still think all this Avenger stuff is a hoax."

"Well, maybe somebody doesn't like that." The only person with his panties in a wad was Chance Baseford, and he'd never do anything as common as a drive-by shooting.

"What about all those unhappy people in 'Your Turn'?" Mom asked. "Maybe one of them decided enough was enough."

"That reminds me." I got up and went to the pile of newspapers we keep by the door with our recyclables. I dug through the pile until I found several copies of the "Your Turn" insert. "I wanted to have a look at these."

Camden set his mug down. "Have you uncovered a clue?"

"I'm not sure." I brought the papers to the counter and looked through all the complaints: not enough school buses and dogs running loose and high taxes and low morals. It was all crap, but it sold newspapers. I remembered Ralph Galvin saying he wasn't worried about another Sugar Baby story. Well, of course not. According to Brooke, he'd written that one.

Mom and Camden were waiting patiently for me to come out of my stupor.

"So what's the deal with 'Your Turn'?" Camden asked.

"I think it's possible some or all of these stories are made up."

"Even if they are, that's not really a crime, is it?"

Mom looked skeptical. "Why would the newspaper people write that stuff? It sounds more like something a bored college kid would do."

Some college boy playing a prank. Where had I heard that? The ladies of Hair's Looking At You had said something like that, too, but they were talking about the Avenger, not "Your Turn." And hadn't I had the same thought tonight when I saw the Avenger leaping from the roof? I knew a college boy who thought superheroes were cool. I'd have to ask Sim Johnson where he was tonight.

I dumped the papers back in the recycle box. "I don't know, Mom. I solve one thing and more mysteries pop up."

Chapter Twenty-Two

"Then Shall the Eyes of the Blind Be Open'd"

The next morning, Royalle's was crowded, as usual, but I pulled Sim aside. "Want to help me with my investigation?"

"You bet!"

"Where were you last night?"

His eyes bulged. "Me?"

"Yes."

"I was home watching TV."

"By yourself?"

"Mom was there. What's this all about? You suspect me of something?"

"The Avenger was out and about last night."

Oddly enough, Sim relaxed. "Oh, yeah? What'd he do?"

"Jumped around on the top of a building."

"Didn't solve a crime?"

"Nope."

Now Sim's expression was smug. He glanced around the store. I couldn't figure out why. "Nothing, huh? Well, you can check with my mom. I was home all night."

"Okay, thanks."

He sauntered back to his place behind the counter, but the swagger wasn't for my benefit. J.C. had come from the back of the store, holding a gift-wrapped box. Sim gave her a superior look. I gave her a closer look.

J.C., all in black, presented a very slim figure—almost boyish, one might say. I thought of the jokes she and Sim played and how competitive they were. I thought of her gym bag with the same team logo as Emmajean's. When she went to wrap another gift, I followed her to the back counter.

"Hear about the Avenger last night? Saved a baby."

She pulled a sheet of silver foil paper from the big roll. "Oh?"

"It was great. By the way, I told Sim, so I'll tell you: your secret's safe with me."

"What secret?"

"I know Sim's the Avenger. It's okay. He's doing a terrific job."

The paper ripped sideways off the roll. "Sim's the—" she stopped. "Oh, really? And he saved a truckload of babies, you say?" She threw away the torn paper and pulled off another piece.

"I wouldn't have believed it if I hadn't seen it with my own eyes. It was amazing the way he leaped from building to building, eluding the cops."

She kept her attention on folding the paper around the box. She bit her lower lip. "How did you know it was Sim?"

"Something about the way he turned his head, his shoulders. I'm a professional, you know. I'm trained to notice these things."

Now her lips were firmly pressed together. She chose a ribbon from the ribbon box and jerked it into shape.

I'd wound her up enough. "I know you have a lot of work to do. I'll get out of your way."

Back out in the store, I checked with Petey to see when the kids took a break. "You don't mind if I hang around, do you? I'm thinking of getting a bracelet for my mother."

"Always glad to have you here," he said.

After about twenty minutes, it was break time. I wandered to the back and listened in. Sure enough, the kids were at it.

J.C.'s voice was a furious whisper. "It was my turn! What do you mean by going out?"

Sim's voice was low and equally annoyed. "I didn't! You can ask my mom! I was home watching TV all night!"

"Then why did Mister Randall say he saw you? What was the deal with the baby?"

"I don't know what you're talking about. I didn't go out. And he said the Avenger jumped around. He didn't say anything about a baby."

"I know you, Sim Johnson. You're trying to get ahead of me. I've stopped three crimes, and you've stopped only two."

"No, I've stopped three, and you've stopped two."

"I saved that lady's money!"

"Yeah, well, I kept that thief from cleaning out the store."

"Shhh! Keep your voice down."

There was an odd silence, and I wondered if they'd choked each other. I stepped in. Sim and J.C. had continued their argument via text, faces intent, fingers jabbing at their cell phones. I watched for a while, amused, as they texted and glared. I imagined the conversation was along the lines of "UR a Jerk!" and "UR2!"

The two teenagers noticed me and froze. J.C. was the first to catch on.

"You knew it was me all along."

"No, but thanks for clearing that up."

Sim rolled his eyes and gave her a punch on the arm. "Dope."

"You're the dope!"

I held up my hands. "Okay, okay. Truce. Give me the details, and I'll make it easy on you."

"It was my idea," Sim said.

J.C. looked scandalized. "It was not!"

"Just tell me."

She scowled, put her phone in her pocket, and crossed her arms. "After the first Avenger came out, we thought we could do better. *I* thought we could do better. Sim's not the only one who reads comics."

"We're both good athletes." Sim gave her a glare. "And it was *my* idea."

Before J.C. could protest, I said, "Argue about that later. What do you mean, the first Avenger?"

They both snickered. "That bow-legged guy," Sim said. "We saw him running up the alley about a week ago when we were leaving work. Then we read in the paper he'd dented somebody's car. Well, you know how I feel about superheroes. They shouldn't be the laughingstock of a city. So, J.C. and I decided to do it right."

"The night Royalle's was robbed, I stopped the crime," J.C. said. "If it hadn't been for me, the thief would've gotten everything."

"How did you happen to be on the scene?"

She stared at me as if I'd stepped on her cape. "I was on patrol, of course."

"Pardon me."

Sim took up the saga. "Then the clumsy Avenger gets in the way of the police car. All our hard work for nothing. We had to go out again."

"This time, I kept the thief from cleaning out Carlene's," J.C. said. "You did a nice job of misdirection, Sim, I'll give you that."

I was ahead of them. Every successful superhero outing had been Sim or J.C. The idiot events had starred Tor as the Avenger.

Sim took a piece of ribbon and wound it nervously around his finger. "How did you guess it was us, Mister Randall?"

"Well, let's see. Two competitive kids, one on the gymnastics team, another one a skier."

He stared. "How'd you know I was a skier?"

"When I met you in the record store, you mentioned you were on a ski trip when the robbery at Royalle's happened."

"J.C. was supposed to wait before going out."

"Why should I?" she said. "It was my idea."

Time to set these two straight. "No, it was Brooke Verner's idea. You just improved upon it."

J.C. was still peeved. "If I hadn't been out that night, you think anything would've been left in the store the next morning?"

"The thief only needed a couple of things."

I got two sets of round-eyed stares. Sim stopped playing with the ribbon. "You know who the thief is, too?"

"I know just about everything."

He watched my face and decided to believe me. "We're in big trouble, aren't we?"

"I don't know. From what I can tell, you've been helpful, but the police aren't happy with citizens climbing buildings at night. You're going to have to give up your little hobby."

J.C. sighed. "Well, it was fun while it lasted, although it made me nervous last night when the police started yelling."

"Next time, they'll be shooting, J.C. I don't want you or Sim in the middle of that."

She glanced at the clock. "Break's over. What are you going to do, Mister Randall?"

"I'm going to buy a bracelet for my mother, and you're going to wrap it in the nice silver paper."

She and Sim looked grateful. "Okay," she said.

Sim knew there was more. "Okay for now, you mean."

"You two have to promise me you won't go playing Avenger again. The thief's given up her life of crime, so you won't be needed any more."

J.C. was interested. "The thief's a woman?"

"And no longer in the picture. Promise, or I'll tell Petey."

This got them. "Don't tell Mister Royalle," Sim said. "He's a great guy, but he'll think something like this is nuts. He'll fire us."

I looked at J.C. "Promise?"

"Cross my heart."

"Come help me pick out something nice for Mom."

She and Sim returned to work, considerably subdued. I picked out a bracelet for Mom, and on second thought, picked out one for Kary, too. J.C. wrapped them, I paid and left. My next stop was the hospital. I had a lot of news for Brooke. Not one, not two, but three Avengers had kept Parkland in thrall. I'd have to remember to tell Camden I'd actually used the word "thrall" in a coherent sentence.

◇◇◇

"Three Avengers?" Brooke shook her head in disbelief. "A great story, and here I am, stuck in bed. I wish you could tell me who the other two are."

I pulled up a chair and sat down. "It doesn't matter. They've retired. Besides, I think there's a bigger story. I talked to the museum curator. Ralph Galvin was in charge of fund raising for the museum's bicentennial, and a few dollars went astray."

She took a deep breath. "I didn't know about that, but I had my suspicions about Ralph Galvin being the author of all those stupid 'Your Turn' stories. I really respected him, David, but I recognized his style right away. When you work on a newspaper, you get to know how people write, certain phrases they use, even the way they indent their paragraphs. At first, I thought it was a joke, or maybe he was trying to get things going, but then, he was writing all kinds of inflammatory stuff, like that letter about the school teacher. I don't know if you remember that. She was teaching a book some people didn't like. Galvin almost got the woman fired."

"Is he that worried about circulation?"

"No, I think it's a power thing. He's afraid Baseford or one of the other really good writers is going to take over."

"So you confronted him about it?"

"I asked him what was going on with 'Your Turn,' that it seemed to have taken a turn for the worst, excuse the pun. He said it was none of my business, to keep writing about the Avenger. When I said I was tired of lying, he said he'd be glad to fire me and let someone else do the lying."

"Wait a minute. He knew your Avenger stuff was all made up?"

"Yes." She gripped the sheet with her free hand. "When I first saw that letter from his son, I thought it was another 'Your Turn' article." Her voice wobbled. "I can't believe he'd want me dead. Maybe he was just trying to scare me."

I picked up the phone. "So we're going to return the favor." Brooke watched, puzzled, as I punched in the number for "Your Turn," but as I talked, she slowly began to smile. "Um, yes, I want to say that I think it's an absolute shame that the editor of the *Herald* is making up all these awful stories to go in 'Your Turn' to sell papers. Everybody knows none of that stuff is true, and he ought to be taken to court, that's what I say. We have enough real crime in town. And speaking of real crime, why doesn't somebody ask that editor what he knows about the museum funds being embezzled? Seems to me he knows more than he's letting on. If he's got an explanation, it had better be a good one. It's your turn, bud." I hung up and grinned at Brooke. "Think that'll get his attention?"

"That's perfect."

"You try one."

I punched in the number and handed her the phone. She cleared her throat and spoke in a feathery drawl. "Yes, this is about the rumor that Mister Galvin down at the paper had something to do with the museum robbery. I can't believe a newspaperman would stoop so low, not at such a fine publication as the *Herald*. If this rumor is true, then I urge all the citizens of Parkland to demand Mister Galvin's resignation and turn the paper over to someone with integrity, like Mister Chance Baseford, who writes all those lovely reviews. That's all I have to say." She hung up, almost bursting with laughter. "Oh, my. Why didn't I think of this? David, we have to do more."

"I've got all day." As abruptly as she'd laughed, more tears welled in her eyes. I handed her a tissue. "Take it easy. We'll get him."

"It's not that." She wiped her eyes. "Why are you doing this for me?"

"Maybe I was wrong about you."

She sniffed and got control. "Thanks."

"I still think you're pushy and obnoxious, but that's no reason we can't work together to nail this guy."

She wiped her nose. Her eyes gleamed with tears and with her old humor. She handed me the phone. "Your turn."

Chapter Twenty-Three

"He Was Cut Off Out of the Land of the Living"

We spent most of the morning disguising our voices and calling in to complain about Galvin. At one point, we enlisted the nurse to make a call, and the Candy Striper who brought some flowers from one of Brooke's girlfriends joined in the game with a pitiful little-girl voice wanting to know if everything in the paper was fake.

By this time, I thought Brooke needed to rest, but she said, "One more call. We need to make sure he reads them all." She took the phone and punched in a different number. "Sara? Brooke Verner. I'm much better, thank you. Could you do me a favor? I know Galvin's going to be really busy today getting out the special holiday issue. Would you make sure he gets a copy of today's 'Your Turn' calls? I know he would appreciate that." She paused. "Would you? Thanks." She hung up and closed her eyes. "Time to put this story to bed."

"I need to ask you one more thing, Brooke."

"Okay."

Camden kept saying the same man was responsible. He'd been in tune with Jared's stabbing and Alycia's close call, and he'd reacted strongly when Brooke was shot, so the same person was sending all the evil thoughts his way. "Can you recall Galvin's reaction to Jared Hunter's murder?"

"Oh, he was thrilled. Big news. Mystery attacker still at large."
She yawned hugely. "Lord, I'm tired."

"I'll stop by the *Herald* and see the results of our handiwork.
I'll give you a full report."

"Thanks again, Randall. I hope we provoked him into making
a move. Just don't get shot."

To be on the safe side, I called Jordan and asked if Officer
Peterson could come to the hospital and sit for a while outside
Brooke's room.

◇◇◇

Chance Baseford poked his large head out of his office as I went
by. "Have you heard the latest? Seems the Avenger's not the only
hoax around here."

"What's going on?"

Baseford looked gleeful. "The whole place is in an uproar.
The girls in the front office thought they'd be helpful and leave
a copy of today's 'Your Turn' calls on Galvin's desk. Every single
one is about Galvin! The calls all claim he writes 'Your Turn,'
and get this, had something to do with funds being embezzled
from the museum."

"Really?"

Baseford rubbed his hands. "Oh, this is rich. He's always
going on and on about truth in reporting. He's dug a nice little
hole for himself. You may be looking at the next editor of the
Herald here, Randall."

"Where is Galvin?"

"Locked in his office, I'm sure."

Galvin wasn't in his office. I looked on his desk, hoping to
see the letter from Bert, but his desk was clean. I stood in the
doorway for a moment, feeling I should recognize something,
but it wouldn't come to me, so I left. His assistant editor was
in the conference room with several other editors, checking on
the layout for the next issue.

"Anybody seen Galvin?"

The assistant editor looked up. "He left a short while ago.
Said he had some meeting to cover."

"You mean he had his ass to cover," another man said.

My plan seemed to be working. "You guys talking about 'Your Turn'?"

The assistant grimaced. "Seems the word is out. When we asked Galvin about it, he just left. Doesn't look good."

I was really glad I'd left a policeman at the hospital. "Any idea where he went?"

A third man shrugged. "Charged out. Looked kinda gray, though."

"If this 'Your Turn' thing true, it's going to be one hell of a story," another man said. "We'd better leave a couple of columns on the front page."

"Make sure that by-line says Brooke Verner," I said.

I went back to Galvin's office. The minute I stepped inside, I knew what I'd been missing. It wasn't something I could see. It was a smell that took me back to Jared's garage. That sweetness hadn't been air freshener.

Peppermint.

◇◇◇

Camden was helping a customer decide between two shiny blouses, but looked up when I entered the boutique.

"I'd pick the blue," I told the woman. "Could you excuse us, please?" I pulled Camden aside.

"We need to find Ralph Galvin. You remember that odd smell in Jared's garage? I thought it was auto air freshener, but it was leftover peppermint. Alycia remembers a smell from her attacker, which I'll bet money was peppermint, too. Galvin chews it all the time."

Camden stared at me. "Galvin killed Jared? Why?"

"Because when Jared, Alycia, and Galvin's son Bert broke into the museum, they found Ralph already there. I think Ralph set them up. He told Bert about the map when he really needed a break in to cover up his own activities. If money's missing, then Ralph can claim the thieves stole it. Alycia leaves town before he can get to her, so Ralph makes sure Jared goes to jail, but on a reduced sentence so it looks like Ralph's a good guy, and then he locks his son up in an out of state hospital. He thought he was safe. When Jared got out of jail, he must have found out the truth, called Ralph, maybe threatened to blackmail him. Didn't Alycia say Jared told her their money troubles were over? I'll bet he was going to expose Ralph unless Ralph paid up. Ralph had to do something."

"But to stab him like that—"

"Makes for exciting headlines, and you gotta admit Galvin's good at making up his own news."

The customer held up the blue blouse. "Excuse me. I'd like to get this."

"Yes, ma'am." Camden went behind the counter and rang up the blouse. "Do you need this wrapped?"

"No, thank you."

He handed the woman her change and put the blouse in a bag. "Thank you very much."

As soon as she left, I said, "Can you tell where Galvin is right now?"

"No."

Galvin could be anywhere in Parkland. That was a lot of city to cover. Then I thought of something. "How about calling in the SHS?"

Camden liked this idea. "You mean it?"

"It's perfect. Do you know the secret signal to summon them?"

He picked up the phone. "Lily will know."

"You round them up and tell them we could use their help."

"Where are you going?"

"I think I know where Galvin might be hiding."

Camden and I had blocked the tunnel under Carlene's, and Jordan and his men had sealed the one under Trilby's. But there was the other tunnel, the one under Royalle's.

It took me longer than I liked to get across town to Royalle's. I parked near the outside entrance and took my flashlight out of the car. I had to search for the tunnel entrance, but finally found it and pulled the cover aside. Dislodging more dirt and grass, I lowered myself into the tunnel. I hadn't gone far before I smelled peppermint and heard someone's heavy breathing. A kerosene lantern made looming shadows on the tunnel wall as Galvin rooted through Alycia's left over camping equipment.

"Hi, Ralph," I said.

He swerved, breathing hard. His eyes glittered in the lantern light. "What are you doing here?"

"Out for a stroll. What you got there?"

He had a duffel bag in one hand. "None of your business."

"Not planning to stay down here, are you? It's a little musty."

"What do you want, Randall?"

"How come you're not making a break for it?"

Galvin set his bag down. "Why should I make a break for anything?"

"Maybe the superhero community isn't happy with the way they're portrayed in the *Herald*."

"Do you have something to do with that large woman dressed as Robin Hood and some geek covered in aluminum foil standing across the street? Did you tell those people to harass me?"

I was happy to hear that Destiny's Arrow and Last Nerve had answered the call so quickly. "Shouldn't bother you if you have nothing to hide. And speaking of hiding, why are you down here in this hole?"

He took out a gun. "You've made a big mistake."

"No, I think you have. The Sugar Baby and 'Your Turn' stuff probably would've blown over, but murder, that's another story."

"Murder? What are you talking about?"

"Jared Hunter."

"Why would I kill Jared Hunter?"

"Because he knew you embezzled funds from the museum. You could put your son away, and you couldn't find Alycia, but you knew exactly when Jared got out of jail. What happened? Did he call you, threaten you? Or maybe he called Bert, poor Bert who's writing letters begging you to let him come home. Maybe Bert wrote letters to Jared, too."

"Shut up."

"Camden knows everything, too, and so do all of his friends in the Superhero Society, so after you kill me, you'll have to kill them, too. And don't forget Brooke. She's not dead yet. You've got your work cut out for you."

Galvin's face twisted. I really didn't think he'd try to shoot his way out, but this was a guy who'd already stabbed one person, tried to strangle another, and probably knocked an old man over with his car. Before he decided to shoot me, I threw my flashlight at the kerosene lantern. The lantern broke, splattering burning kerosene on the tunnel walls. The brief flames sent shadows jumping on the ceiling and in the light, I saw Galvin turn and run in the opposite direction toward Royalle's. I wasn't sure if he knew the way out through the jewelry store basement, but I sure as hell didn't want him anywhere near J.C. or Sim or anyone in Royalle's.

I caught him as he was scrambling up toward the tunnel entrance, and we rolled in a tangle on the ground. He kicked himself free and gave me a shove that sent me into the wall and showered us with dirt and bits of wood. I hadn't thought about the possibility of the tunnel collapsing.

Galvin must have had the same thought because he stopped. He was just a shape in the darkness, but I could hear him breathing hard.

"Ralph, there's nowhere to go, and this tunnel could come down any minute. I don't like the idea of being buried alive, no matter what a great story it would make."

The sudden burst of light made us both squint and turn toward the basement entrance. The cover had been lifted off, and a clear female voice called out:

"Evildoer, beware! No one can hide from the light of Wonder Star!"

And there she was, looking down like an angel of vengeance.

I had a split second to decide whether to be freaked out by Kary's appearance or use her well-timed diversion. I took the diversion and grabbed for Galvin's gun.

"Kary, stay back!"

Galvin's shots went wild, pinging into the walls, sending clods of dirt flying. I managed to pry the gun from his hands, but he yanked free. I tried to grab him as he ran past, but missed. The kerosene had burned out, but my flashlight was still on and had rolled to one side, so he had enough light to escape.

No, damn it! He couldn't get away now.

But once again, I underestimated the Power of Good.

Galvin looked back over his shoulder to give me a smirk and fell over something that went, "Oof!" I tackled Galvin, and we landed hard on the packed dirt of the tunnel floor. By now, I was tired of this idiot. Jared had been a friend of Camden's, and that was enough for me. I was pounding Galvin's head into the ground when someone's hands pried me off.

"Take it easy, Randall. I'd like something left to arrest."

Jordan's deep voice reached some last piece of civilization in me. I sat back, breathing hard. Flashlight beams spun around the tunnel as Camden and another policeman came running. Jordan hauled Galvin up, read him his rights, and handed him over to the policeman. I got up slowly. I straightened my clothes, and then noticed the black shape that had so conveniently played speed bump for Galvin's escape. Two eyes gleamed from behind a mask.

Jordan dusted off his uniform. "Who's this?"

"Jordan, I'd like you to meet Parkland's one and only true superhero, the Mad Shadow."

"The Mad Shadow zipped by the shopping center and gave me a ride," Camden said.

"Please tell me it was a Shadowmobile," I said.

"A Mustang GT. But it's black."

The Mad Shadow nodded. "And then I hurled myself into the darkness to heed your summons and apprehend this criminal."

"Thanks," I said.

Jordan peered closer. "Mister Shadow—or is it Ms?"

The Shadow hunched a shoulder. "I'll never tell."

"Well, the Shadow needs to come along with us and answer a few questions. Purely professional, man to man—uh, crime fighter to crime fighter."

"Anything to help the fine officers of the law."

"Now that's what I like to hear. You, too, Randall, Cam. Let's sort this out."

◇◇◇

It took a bit of sorting. Camden and I waited in Jordan's office until Jordan finished interrogating Galvin. We agreed not to say anything about the timely arrival of Wonder Star, who left as soon as the police arrived and returned to her lair like the wise superhero she was.

Jordan came in and sat down at his desk. "Well, you were right, Randall. Bert Galvin was the one who urged Jared Hunter to break into the museum. Somehow, Ralph Galvin convinced us that it was Hunter's idea, and Bert was cleared of all charges."

"All to distract you from the real crime, the embezzling of museum funds."

"That's exactly what happened."

"I think either Jared Hunter was threatening to come forward with the truth, or demanding money from Galvin, so Galvin had to kill him. Since readership at the *Herald* was down, Galvin killed him in a gruesome way to get some headlines and pinned the crime on Taylor, another of Hunter's friends. When there wasn't enough evidence to convict Taylor, Galvin had to get rid of anyone who might have known about the museum funds."

"How does Brooke Verner fit into all this?"

"Brooke found out Galvin wasn't just making up 'Your Turn' articles. He was manufacturing all kinds of stories. She was getting too close to the truth about Hunter's death, so Galvin tried to silence her, as well. He might have gotten away with it, too, but something spooked him."

Jordan gave Camden and me a narrow-eyed look. "I wonder what that might have been."

"A couple of calls to the 'Your Turn' line?"

Jordan opened a folder on his desk. "I believe the number is closer to thirty."

"So Galvin remembered about the tunnels and decided to camp out until he could leave Parkland."

"Yes." Jordan opened another folder. "All this to cover up his embezzling. Doesn't make any sense to me, but then, these killers never do."

Camden had been quiet through all this. "Make sure he doesn't kill again."

"Oh, trust me. He's going under the jail. Gonna make a hell of a story for the *Herald*." Jordan sat back in his chair. "Okay, your work here is done. Go home."

I looked around for my speed bump. "You're going to let the Mad Shadow go, I hope?"

"Yeah, it was right helpful."

"It? You didn't find out the Shadow's real name or gender?"

Jordan gave me a look full of satisfaction. "I'll never tell."

Camden didn't say much on the ride home. When we pulled into the driveway and parked, I said, "Must be a relief to have this sorted out."

Camden looked off into whatever black depths he looks into. "He really enjoyed killing. He thought about it all the time. But the worst thing is he never cared for his son. You see where I'm going with this."

"You don't know if your father cares for you or not. There could be a legitimate reason why he hasn't contacted you. Let me find him. Of course, it'll cost you extra because I'll have to rent a space ship."

"No. I think I've had enough of the father-son dynamic for a while."

"Okay. Whenever you're ready."

"The only thing I'm ready for is Christmas."

Chapter Twenty-Four

"Glad Tidings of Good Things"

The morning of Christmas Eve, I woke to the smell of pancakes. Downstairs I found Mom and Kary in the kitchen. Mom spooned batter into a pan while Kary used a cookie cutter to cut the cooked pancakes into the shape of Christmas trees. She had powdered sugar on her nose. When Mom wasn't looking, I gently wiped the sugar off. I'd thanked her before for her diversion, but I thanked her again.

"My pleasure," she said.

Mom gave me a kiss on the cheek. "Good morning. How many pancakes would you like?"

"Start me off with five."

Kary arranged five trees on a plate and handed the plate to me. "There you go. The syrup's on the table."

Fred, unfortunately, was already at the table, mangling his pancakes. "Morning, Fred."

He made a noise that probably meant, "Back off."

No problem. I wasn't going to sit near him. I set my plate down at the far end of the table and returned to the kitchen for coffee. "Camden up yet?"

"I looked in on him a while ago," Mom said. "He was sleeping so well, I didn't bother him. It's about time he had some decent rest."

"Well, the killer's been caught, so that should take care of any nightmares."

They brought their pancakes to the table and we all sat down. Mom reached for the syrup. She didn't seem too pleased. "Kary told me about the two of you wrestling down in that tunnel."

"We were all down in the tunnel, Mom. Camden, Jordan, the Mad Shadow. It was Old Home Week."

"What were you thinking?"

"You have your wild fashion choices. I wrestle bad guys in tunnels. It's all about having fun."

She looked as if she was going to launch into a lecture. Then she said, "Fair enough. But your fun is much more dangerous than mine."

"Not when I have Wonder Star to watch my back."

"Well, that's true. Maybe the two of you have more in common than I thought. Still, that was a crazy thing to do. Galvin did all those awful things just to cover up his own robbery at the museum."

Jordan had found out something else about Galvin's son. "Jordan says Bert's in a mental institution in Richmond. He's tried to commit suicide several times. All he wanted was to come home. That was the reason for Camden's crying spell. He was in tune with Bert that day."

"The poor boy! Will he have to stay there?"

"Jordan's got somebody working on that. And he's already confirmed what I suspected about forged receipts."

Mom poured syrup on her pancakes. "What about the stolen jewelry?"

"Alycia sold it, but Petey's insured. And he's very happy the thief wasn't one of his employees."

"Then everything's solved."

"Pretty much. Syrup, please."

Kary passed me the syrup. "Brooke called to say she can come spend Christmas Eve with us if someone could pick her up."

"I'll be glad to do that." I soaked up more syrup. "Anybody heard from Ellin?"

They shook their heads. "I need to have a word with that young lady," Mom said.

We spent a little time in pancake heaven, and then while Mom encouraged Fred to have another stack, I helped Kary mix another batch of batter. She seemed a bit distracted.

"Are you all right?"

She reached for the spatula. "Ralph Galvin purposely kept his son in a mental institution and then went on a killing spree. That is so twisted." She poured batter into the pan and watched as bubbles formed. "I hope our next case isn't this bad."

Our next case. That sounded good, but I had my concerns. "So Wonder Star is still planning to keep the heavens safe?"

"I really enjoyed being Wonder Star, but I might try something new next time."

Not exactly what I wanted to hear. "Tell you what. I'll do all the leg work like Archie, and you can stay here and ponder everything like Nero Wolfe."

She raised the spatula in a warning manner. "I've read Rex Stout and I'm not sure I like the comparison. I'll be Archie, and *you* can stay home and ponder."

"How about if we try the Nick and Nora thing and be the crime fighting married couple? We could even have a little dog."

"I'm not ready for that."

"We could name him Scooby, so I'll remember not to undervalue you."

"I would like to thank you for not interfering. I know you wanted to."

"I did."

She turned the pancakes. "So with you backing off and your mother here, this has been one of the best Christmases I can remember."

"Me, too." Different, but okay.

From upstairs, we heard Camden singing "Every Valley."

He was okay, too.

◇◇◇

That evening, we all went to the chorale's performance of the "Messiah." Every valley was exalted and every mountain and hill made low. Afterwards, we stopped by the park and enjoyed the Alternative Messiah's rendition of "And the Glory of the Lord." The glory of the Lord was revealed, or I should say, re-vee-led, thanks to Buddy's earnest plunking and Evelene's wild hammering. It was a true measure of my acceptance of Mom's new look that I didn't flinch when I saw her eyeing Evelene's nose ring.

At home, Kary played carols on the piano while we made the Christmas Eve feast. Brooke assured me she felt well enough to come over for a few hours, and her doctor had given her the okay, so I picked her up at the hospital and brought her to 302 Grace. Before dinner, we took some time to remember Jared. Camden said a few words about his friend, and Kary said a prayer, saying she was certain that Jared was now with his heavenly Father and the family he always longed for.

We waited a while, thinking Ellin would show up. When she didn't, we went ahead with dinner. Mom had outdone herself with roast chicken, sweet potato casserole, green peas with dumplings, and fresh biscuits. We ate so much we decided to save the coconut cake and pecan pie until after we opened presents.

Fred sat over in one corner, scowling at his new sweater and NASA calendar, while the rest of us sat around the tree. I put on a Santa hat and passed out the gifts. Kary had wrapped up a gift certificate to Carlene's and the New Black Eagle Jazz Band's latest CD for me. As I expected, the leopard pattern was well represented. Camden had found a leopard pocketbook at Tamara's, which was expensive enough, even with his discount, to be from the both of us to Mom. Mom had some earrings for Kary, and Kary had a scarf for her. Both of them were delighted with their bracelets from Royalle's, although Mom gave me a look as if questioning my decision to give Kary such an expensive gift.

"Petey gave me a good deal," I said. "I couldn't pass it up."

Kary put her bracelet on and admired it from all angles. "I love it. Look at all the little stars."

"For the best crime fighter in the heavens."

This earned me a kiss from Kary and another look from Mom.

Mom had gotten Camden a light blue shirt and a silky blue tie with a diamond pattern. He thanked her and then opened his UFO book. "This is great, Kary, thanks."

"You don't have that one, do you?" Kary asked.

"No, I don't."

I couldn't leave it alone. "See anyone you know?"

He balled up the wrapping paper and threw it at me. I retaliated, and then everyone joined in the battle. Brooke watched, bemused, as Camden and Kary used the sofa as a barrier against the onslaught of paper balls and wadded tissue Mom and I laid down from behind the tree. Cindy went into an orgy of delight trying to catch the paper. Her antics landed her upside down under the tree, tangling her claws in the Christmas tree skirt. She shook herself free and streaked for the kitchen, trailing tissue paper and ribbons.

Mom called a truce. "Brooke hasn't opened her special gift."

We came back to our seats. Brooke brushed pieces of ribbon out of her hair. She unwrapped the box and grimaced at her Parkie. "Thanks a lot. You get the guys at Spencer's Gifts to make this up?"

"Read what it says."

She turned the award around. "'For Excellence in Investigative Reporting'?" She gave the Parkie a closer look. "This—this is a real one! But the Avenger was a hoax—most of it."

"The award isn't for the Avenger. It's for exposing Ralph Galvin's 'Your Turn' scam. Without your help, I never would've figured it all out."

She kept turning it around in her hands, examining it from all angles. "A real one."

"Your new editor agreed you deserved it."

"Chance Baseford okayed this? Now I know I'm dreaming."

Mom reached under the tree. "Here's one more box for you, Davey."

The box was long and thin. I thought I knew what was in it. "A Christmas tie. I need one." I tore off the bow and unwrapped the gold paper. "Or a gift certificate to Ned's House of Porn."

"I don't think so, dear."

The long, thin box had been a disguise for something small wrapped in green tissue paper. When I felt the smooth round object, I knew what it was and felt oddly relieved. "Dad's watch."

She beamed. "Let's hear it."

I held it in my hand for a while. I remembered how it would be warm from his hand and smelling faintly of tobacco. I remembered the steady ticking and the satisfying click of the latch. Up popped the lid. "Twelfth Street Rag" burst out in happy, jingly sound. I couldn't say anything.

Mom was bursting with pride. "Cam found it. I called your cousin Victoria and let her talk to Cam. As soon as he took the phone, he knew where it was. Your Uncle Louie had let Victoria's son play with it, and it was behind the bookcase in their old den. No one had been down there in years. Neal says to tell you he's sorry. He doesn't even remember playing with it."

"That's okay." I closed the lid. "I'm really glad to have it. Thanks."

Mom kissed my cheek. "Merry Christmas." Then she had to kiss Camden and Kary and Brooke and even Fred. In the midst of all this goodwill toward men, the doorbell rang.

Camden got up. "It's for me." He went to the door and opened it. There stood Ellin, all in emerald green, her earrings like gold stars. She smiled and handed him a large package wrapped in blue. "Merry Christmas."

He tossed the package aside. "I've got something for you, too." He caught her in his arms, and gave her a long kiss.

We were all leaning around so we could see. When they finished, we applauded and called, "Encore!"

Camden went to the tree and found her gift. "First she has to open her present."

I didn't think Ellin could blush, but her cheeks turned the same becoming shade of pink as the new lace nightgown. "This is beautiful, Cam, thank you."

"You have to come over more often," he said. "We have to find some way to make this work."

"I'd like that," she said.

The phone rang, causing Camden to look up. "It's for you, Randall."

"The Avenger calling to thank me for clearing his name."

Camden had a curious expression. "No. It's something quite special."

Special? I picked up the phone and heard E. Walter Winthrop's peeved tone.

"Mister Randall, excuse me for interrupting you at home this evening, but I need to know a few things."

"Yes, sir?"

"Your daughter's full name?"

I had to swallow hard before speaking. "Lindsey Marie Randall."

"And something she liked to do?"

"She loved to dance. What's all this about?"

"Excellent." I heard papers shuffle. "Mister Randall, I wish to establish the Lindsey Marie Randall Memorial Scholarship for underprivileged children, specifically those who wish to further their education in the arts. May I have your permission to do so?"

Now I couldn't speak at all. Camden took the phone. I hadn't even noticed he was there.

"Mister Winthrop, Mister Randall accepts your most generous and thoughtful offer."

"Good," I heard the reedy voice say. "I'll call him next week with all the details. Good night."

Camden hung up the phone. "Merry Christmas, Randall."

He went back to Ellin. I went back to the island. Kary had given Cindy a ribbon to play with so she could gather up the rest of the ribbons and paper in a garbage bag. Mom was in the kitchen, stirring up batter for another batch of cookies.

"Who in the world was that calling on Christmas Eve, Davey?"

I sat down at the counter. I knew if I didn't hold on to something, I would float away.

"Mom," I said, "I'm going to tell you all about it."

To receive a free catalog of Poisoned Pen Press titles, please contact us in one of the following ways:

Phone: 1-800-421-3976
Facsimile: 1-480-949-1707
Email: info@poisonedpenpress.com
Website: www.poisonedpenpress.com

Poisoned Pen Press
6962 E. First Ave. Ste 103
Scottsdale, AZ 85251